Drawing a Blank

Drawing a Blank
Portrait of a Smokin' Serial Killer

R.K. Finch

iUniverse, Inc.
New York   Bloomington

Drawing a Blank
Portrait of a Smokin' Serial Killer

Cover design and photo manipulation by R.K. Finch
Cover model, Renée Salewski
Photographer, Shambala

iUniverse books may be ordered through booksellers or by contacting:

iUniverse
1663 Liberty Drive
Bloomington, IN 47403
www.iuniverse.com
1-800-Authors (1-800-288-4677)

ISBN: 978-1-4502-6288-0 (sc)
ISBN: 978-1-4502-6290-3 (dj)
ISBN: 978-1-4502-6289-7 (ebk)

Printed in the United States of America
iUniverse rev. date: 10/18/2010

To Jason, for all of his love and support. To Renée, for agreeing to put a face to no name. And most of all, to the Internet industry, for producing such a large quantity of the dirty bastards that inspired this novel.

PART 1

1.

The elephants are going mad.

All across Africa they have been killing human beings, killing other animals, in an increasingly violent way for the past ten or so years. Running into towns spearing humans on their tusks. Raping and killing rhinoceros. Murdering each other.

Being the sensitive creatures they are, with their long, long memories, elephant society is very highly developed. They carry out rituals and mourn their dead, revisiting the bones of their ancestors and caressing them with their trunks for years afterwards in a similar way to how they wrap their trunks around each other in greeting. Young elephants are raised in a complex group made up of the females in their communities. Young males are kept in line during their formative years by elder bulls. They have an extensive communication system, visual signals and patterns of subsonic vibrations, which further bond them to each other.

But years of poaching and habitat loss have caused the herds to dwindle. The support systems are no longer there; the young are often raising themselves. They realize what all large mammals have known for some time – they are dying out, they will not survive for too much longer. Kept in parks and ranges, controlled by others, their very society is breaking down.

And they're mad as hell about it.

2.

I am on my way to a lawyer's office I have never been to before, to pick up something left to me by a man I was involved with who recently died and remembered me in his will. I am not expecting anything. I'm not terribly concerned, either, whether or not he is living or dead, which in itself is a lenient statement, and perhaps because of that I should feel as though I should not receive whatever it is he left me. But I don't feel that way; I feel largely indifferent at most.

I am in a good mood, actually, as I walk down King Street in a flattering, short business outfit, showing a lot of leg, flexed and tawny, swaying to the rhythm incited by my 3-inch Louis Vuitton heels. Men are doing double takes, women are regarding me with envy and I am suffering the same tingly thrill I used to get when I was thirteen and walking down Lexington Avenue in Kitchener. This is the shit I live for. Everything else I do is just to get me in a place where I feel like this. Hot. It's so much better than Happy.

I put out my cigarette with a sensual twist of my ankle and go in the building indicated by the address on the letter I received from the lawyer. I estimate it will only be a short meeting, under an hour, but I pat my purse to ensure I've slipped in a supply of nicotine gum, just in case. I never go more than thirty minutes between cigarettes. People always comment on how good I smell despite such a nasty habit. I can't really say why the smell doesn't stick to me. Maybe it's because I'm a hygienic person.

I re-emerge from the lawyer's office one hour later, spit out my gum and light a cigarette. If I were a normal person, I'd be shaking at the very least, maybe even heading north on the subway and taking a jaunt over to the Bloor Street viaduct, where I could hurl myself off of the suicide bridge. Paul has left me everything. His big glass penthouse, his car, seats on the boards of his four companies and millions of dollars in cash and investments. Everything.

There was also a very touching letter to me, long, about how his relationship with me had been the most important and long-lasting of any in his life, that I'd taught him so much, shown him so much, had been, in fact, the only woman he'd ever loved. He was sorry for all of the pain he had caused me over the years and was overjoyed that I had contacted him again early that year. And so on. You know the story.

I take the note and toss it into a recycling bin as I put out my smoke and head into the subway. I should have brought the car so I could chain-smoke. Damn.

3.

Lately I have had the very strong urge to go away. Somewhere far. Disappear.

I've never traveled anywhere, except this very strange and pointless trip early in my career. During that trip I realized my first and possibly only real, strong fear: I'm afraid to fly. Terrified. A goopy pool of tears, tears that feel nothing but are present nonetheless, protesting the entire journey. Embarrassing. So I don't make travel plans. I'm not going anywhere. The past few years, I've barely even left the city. I don't want to go anywhere, either. Except maybe to the great outdoors, where I have also only visited most rarely. Somewhere quiet.

When I was in my early twenties, the company I worked for, Silacorp, sent me to China. It didn't make any sense from the outset. First of all, at the time, I was but a mere peon, a graphic designer, knowing nothing of the dark side of business. My Ottawa boss, Steve Alexander, king of our office but in the grand scheme of the company little more than a pencil-pushing manager himself, called me into his opulent suite one day. I had been lobbying him for a well-deserved raise for some time and had been ignored; when he called me into his suite that day I assumed it was to either reject my inquiry, or to hold it over my head and offer it only in exchange for a nice long blow job, as he had been known to do to other women in the office, women who far too often agreed to this blackmail. In my case, however, Steve had another trick up his sleeve, which was to spend a half an hour telling me how talented and indispensible I was, how far I was going to go in the company, how wealthy and respected and admired I was going to be.

I knew he was full of shit; I knew I wasn't any more talented or qualified at the time to be anything more than I was. In fact, I was pretty sure that if it weren't for the sudden onset of the Internet revolution and the lack of skilled workers in the industry, I would not even be where I was then. But I was barely out of University, sure I was going to make a mark on this world, convinced I was going to lead a different life than that which had seemed obvious to me in my teenage years and turned out to be much more accurate than the fantasies Steve imbued into my impressionable corporate mind. Steve Alexander was good at one thing: convincing people to do what he wanted, and as much as I had observed that particular trait in him I had always felt that I was above it. In this, my first and only experience in allowing someone to stroke my ego into a veritable erection that left my mind swimming with ecstatic visions of material release, Steve was again successful. Despite everything that was about to follow, I believe this is the moment that my homicidal hymen was punctured. Though Steve proved to do worse things to better people, when I think back on it now I believe this is why he ended up suffering the fate he did.

Steve said they had to send me to China to help the men in our office over there put Chinese characters into HTML pages. I didn't know how, but I looked it up, figured it out and accepted the offer, wondering only vaguely why they would send me in person to do something I could email in a very small file.

A free trip to China when you don't even know you're terrified of flying is a really great deal, so I didn't say anything. A free trip to China when you're ten miles high on the ego-trip hammered into your head about your imminent executive success can push almost everything else out of your mind.

So I went.

4.

I landed in Hong Kong after a harrowing 14-hour flight and realized the limo that was supposed to have come to pick me up and deliver me to the Empire Hotel in Kowloon wasn't there. After wandering aimlessly and mutely around an airport so big you can see it from space, I found a car service to the hotel and took that. Luckily the car service was free. Silacorp had asked me to put all my expenses on my credit card and file them when I returned to Ottawa, but in a fit of genius I told them I did not have a credit card and that they would have to give me cash for the trip and otherwise pay for the hotel and anything else beforehand. After much wrangling, they agreed to give me $1000, most of which I had converted to Renminbi and a smattering of U.S. denominations; the rest was safely tucked away in my purse as traveller's cheques, and that was all I had. Any other expenses were dependent on arrangements made by Steve's assistant before the trip.

I arrived at the hotel to find the bill for my room had not been processed. I wheedled and argued with the clerk, but to no avail. I told them how I would be stranded in Hong Kong if they did not let me have the room, which was clearly booked for me, but for which the faxed credit card payment, from our CEO himself, John Esteban, was in my opinion intentionally unsigned. Xu Tan, a dashing man about five years older than me who managed our Hong Kong office and showed up at the counter beside me right around the time I realized I was getting nowhere, ended up paying for my room out of his own pocket. Relieved that I was not going to end up sleeping on the streets, I suggested to Xu Tan that he show me around town and we party our asses off. After seeing a great deal of the city core, alive with people and energy, we ended up in this bizarre sort of club that I could not call a karaoke bar, but where karaoke was available in small, mostly private rooms. I did a striptease for Xu Tan and another business associate and let them both lick my nipples before laughing at them and keeping them from anything else. Usually I'd finish the job, but I worked with these people and had my career to think of. Nipple-licking tends to get a man hot for you, but doesn't take him so far he's angry when you turn him away. Second base is only halfway home, either direction.

Turned out the company had not done the necessary paperwork for my temporary work visa either, causing another day's delay in Hong Kong before I could go to my real destination in Beijing, and costing Xu Tan another night's hotel bill, for which I freely admit I paid him back in kind. John Esteban, who I was positive would have returned

my many messages and cleared up the payment fiasco at the Empire
within the 36 hours I was in Hong Kong, was still AWOL. I finally got
my visa and left for Beijing; this time flying was an even less pleasant
experience. The airplane was to my mind clearly purchased from the
U.S. circa 1960, judging from the upholstery. The pilot, drunk or inept,
flew the plane in a disconcerting swaying motion that made me feel
as though we were on the cusp of a tailspin every two to five minutes.
The "entertainment" consisted of what looked like state-sanctioned
tourism videos, which made me feel as though if I could understand the
language I would be in danger of being indoctrinated into a cult. When
we landed at the Beijing airport, it was in the middle of the tarmac,
where we were ushered into the back of a large truck with a caged
wagon hitched to it and ferried to the terminal. I went to the terminal
entrance to look for the limo I was already sure would not be there, and
it wasn't. Instead I was accosted by what seemed to be a taxi driver, who
had been following me for some time and knew I was stranded. He took
my bags and put them in his car, giving me no choice but to call for
help or go with him. The doors were closed and locked before I noticed
he didn't have a meter. An hour's drive and many fantasies about being
sold to a harem later and we arrived at the Traders Hotel where I was
booked. He *only* charged me $500 cash for the ride, too, and figuring
it could have been worse and glad that I had had the wherewithal to
demand Silacorp provide me with the cash needed, I did not protest,
though a deep-seeded rage towards Steve Alexander for sending me on
this trip to begin with had begun to grow.

It took quite some time to hunt down what name this hotel room was
under, but eventually they figured it out. I finally settled in and called the
room extension I had been given to meet up with my associates, Sheng
and Lu Zhong. They descended upon me as though upon a saviour.

"You're here to save the project, to do the presentation in Tianjin,"
Lu Zhong told me. "Thank goodness!" Sheng exclaimed, because
they had no idea what was going on and time was running short; the
presentation was the day after next.

I told them they must have made some mistake, I was there merely to write some code for them, code I was prepared to write, but I realized quickly that they thought I was there to build the entire demonstration module. And knowing HTML, which is a fancy way of saying making the clicks work on a web page, in no way qualifies me as a programmer, which would be writing the sort of code that makes your payment work when you buy something.

To be fair, I went to the "office", really a double suite in the same hotel I was staying in, where Sheng and Lu Zhong also seemed to be living in the bedrooms, and checked out what they had. It wasn't much. It was a non-functioning demo of a previous project my company had done for another client. I thought maybe I could fake something purely in HTML if I guided the demo, but I had never made a presentation. I honestly didn't even know what the project was for; I was told something about it being an online accounting product or something. It was 1997 and e-Commerce, or buying and selling things on the Internet, was starting to take off, but it was still new, really new.

As was I. I didn't know what to do. I spent a few hours trying to do what I could, but there was too much work, the only computer I had to work on was a laptop, the only graphics program I had at my disposal was Corel PhotoPaint, a far cry from my preferred Photoshop, and it didn't matter anyway, because I didn't have a mouse, only the stupid little inaccurate nub between the "g" and the "h" on my keyboard that wouldn't obey my commands. As it neared the middle of the night and I was quickly succumbing to jet lag and utter confusion, I decided I needed to contact my company back in Canada. Chain-smoking and drinking freely from the mini-bar, I spent the next four hours on the telephone and online.

No one answered my calls, even though it was the middle of a business day there. No one answered my emails. Just like my experience the day before – was it only a day? – John Esteban and the executives in Jacksonville, Florida, the very men whose credit cards were funding my trip, would not return my calls. It slowly dawned on me that I was being used, but for what I could not fathom. I realized they had knowingly sent me to China after knowingly telling the men there I would do the demo and the presentation. But I didn't understand why. Furthermore, that afternoon Sheng and Lu Zhong told me they had never been paid. It was November and the "office" had opened in August, and besides that the room was taken care of and they could stay there for free, everything else they did, including the equipment they were working on, had been purchased on their own dime. When I asked them incredulously why they would work that hard for a company who might never pay them, they told me it was better than most of their alternatives in communist China. I suddenly remembered a man back at my office in Ottawa who wasn't able to get reimbursed for a business-expense for over three months, and I wondered what was going on with my company and how it might pertain to me being on a suicide mission in Beijing. For the umpteenth time on this trip, I was glad I had demanded cash.

I called the airline and discovered I could not change my ticket without the permission of one of the people in Jacksonville who was refusing to call or email me back.

Finally, fed up, I sent an email to Steve Alexander, John Esteban and every other executive in my company, in every office in every country we were in, telling them I was resigning, that I was also taking my vacation immediately and that as of this moment they were holding me hostage in a foreign country and I would proceed with this understanding in my attempt to get home. I told them I was leaving the hotel in one hour to go the embassy and contact the media. Funny enough, someone, Steve's leather-tanned, bleached-blonde assistant, whose official job was to get my bosses' clothes dry-cleaned and arrange for sandwich delivery during boardroom meetings and whose unofficial job was to keep Steve sexually satisfied, called me within five minutes, after several hours of being completely ignored. I was assured that I would be booked on a flight the next morning at eleven o'clock, local time; there had apparently been some change in the project which had confused people on both sides and resulted in me being where I was.

and being a real human girl. The movie D.A.R.Y.L. came out when I was a kid and I started to wonder if maybe I wasn't a humanoid slipped into my family unbeknownst to them to be monitored by the government for some secret military project. Not until I was a teenager and came across the word "sociopath" did I think there was another explanation. So, there are others like me. And most of them are "evil". Interesting.

I devoured everything I could read on serial killers when I was a teen. While finding my place in this world, I'd tried my hand at being preppy, banger and Goth, to no avail. Some sort of earth-muffinness seemed to suit me when I was younger, but soon enough I traded it in for designer business chic. It faded into the general populace more easily. I never really wanted to stand out.

Serial killers, I came to the conclusion, had, for the most part, too many issues. Oh wah, my mommy locked me in a box while she screwed strangers for money so now I kill women who look like mommy. Oh wah, my penis was never big enough and some girl laughed at me when I was fourteen and now I only have sex with dead women who resemble that girl. Over and over again til kingdom come. Mommy – penis. Or, penis – Daddy. I understand the obsession but the subject matter, ugh, it's boring. That's what comes of yet another field of work entirely dominated by men, in a society whose best attempt at defining a female serial killer is Aileen Wuornos. The real female serial killers, of which I'm sure there are many, have failed to be caught, because women plan better, we think better and we know better.

I don't have personal hang-ups like other serial killers have had. Why should I? My upbringing was comfortable, and short of the rather disgruntling experience of discovering I was probably a sociopath, self-aware and alone with it, I didn't really have any problems. I went to schools in Kitchener during the eighties, meaning I had the opportunity to have large groups of friends without ever having to be close to any individual, so I never raised any suspicions and was seen as a fun, popular girl, if a little mysterious and perhaps somewhat slutty. I always have loved sex. Sex with one or more men, as often as possible. I was discreet and most of my escapades were left unknown by most people, though rumours did tend to float around from time to time. I knew I was a trophy to these boys, in much the same way many of their types would one day become trophies to me.

We moved to a small city, or large town, east of Toronto when I was sixteen and the girls I befriended there weren't much more intuitive or interested in anything that didn't suit their immediate need to consume and acquire material things. We all hung out with football players, making it even less necessary to have a soul. Ah, that pool of boys did me right and good many times over those last couple of years of high school.

I thought, perhaps, some day I would wake up and discover I had a conscience.

What happened instead was that I developed an obsession. Not an obsession over punishing someone for something they said to me or people whose boobs were bigger than mine or anything, but an obsession over justice in general. Anything I saw that was unfair by definition churned around in my head like a crooked picture until I was compelled to straighten it. People called me passionate, altruistic, kind, but they were dead wrong. I was merely obsessed.

Whether you're obsessed with cutting out the hearts of virgins and holding them in your hand, obsessed with keeping your doors locked, or obsessed with a song, it's all the same thing. Sometimes the obsession lasts for months, years, forever, but very often it just turns itself off. You listened to that song one too many times and the next time you think about it you strongly want to play something else. It's gotten old. It's boring. People often say serial killers will never stop, will never be satisfied, and if they stopped killing it means they're either incarcerated or they're dead, but often, they simply get bored of it, like the way a kid grows out of a childhood toy. People who don't believe an individual can harness three or four sides of a complicated personality over the course of a lifetime are more boring than a dead obsession.

11.

I like how I look in wigs; I like how I look smoking cigarettes in them. I like the way a wig, some colour contacts and a little makeup can transform me into an entirely different person. I often go to clubs this way. I also like to wear gloves. Long gloves that go all the way up my arm. I love armbands and belly-bracelets and silver garters. I love anything that lightly binds me. Wigs have this similar effect.

One night about a year after the Silacorp debacle I was at a club in Ottawa called the Bullpen. It was supposed to be an "older" crowd, ranging from about 22-35. I was wearing a blonde wig. Silver makeup. Black vinyl strapless mini-dress. Looked like a kid from the NYC glam party-scene in the eighties. I was slightly buzzing on vodka and feeling the effects still from a line of coke some chick had offered me in the bathroom a half hour earlier. Dancing on the floor with a group of people, I suddenly felt some breath on my neck.

"You're magnificent," a deep voice purred in my ear. I turned around and saw who it was. It was time. It was my old boss, Steve Alexander. My old married boss. My old married boss who had demanded blow jobs for paycheques from some of my weaker female counterparts, destroying families and lives, only to get away scot-free with a sizeable settlement package and an intact reputation. My old married boss who had sent me on that hellish journey to China to only result in trying to destroy me for not destroying the Tianjin project. And I immediately realized he had no idea who I was.

"Really," I looked him deeply in the eyes. "You're okay yourself." I blew smoke over his shoulder; you could still smoke in bars in those days. I wasn't sure what I was planning but I was enjoying going with the flow. I felt hot.

Steve introduced himself as we drew closer and closer together, not actually touching but grinding nonetheless to the music. "Don't touch," I cautioned, making him stay an inch away from my skin. "Wouldn't want to ruin the surprise. Do you have somewhere we can go?"

"Yes, I live alone, let's go," he said, turning to head towards the coat check. Lives alone. He hadn't even asked me my name yet. I followed him out the door, a thrilling sensation running through me. We walked half a block to his car, a sleek black BMW, naturally, boring, and drove the short distance to his house, a mansion in the Glebe. Walking inside, I took a mental inventory.

Wife – still clearly living there but out for the night.

Silacorp – still too recent to be discounted as having an effect on Steve.

Myself – wearing a wig and high gloves, haven't touched the man, haven't touched anything. No prints, no DNA, no evidence.

"Would you like a drink?" Steve asked me as we walked through his gorgeous living room, glass furniture all around. He headed over to a small dry-bar in the corner.

"Why don't you let me get you something? Don't you have anything more interesting than scotch and brandy?" I asked. "How about some liqueurs. Blue Curaçao? Ever had a drink called the Genie? It makes it so when you cum the vibrations are amplified ten times over and extended by minutes... care to try?"

Audibly licking his lips, Steve smiled at me, his precocious bar-slut and said, "No, I've never had a Genie. Why don't you make me one? I think there might be a bottle of Blue Curaçao in the kitchen, corner cupboard near the sink."

"Good, you sit back and relax now." I walked across the room and through a door into the kitchen. Steve was out of sight. I got to work. First I looked in the cupboard he had directed me to confirm he really did have Blue Curaçao, noticing he also had vodka, gin and scotch. I looked under the sink and saw what I had hoped to find: a bottle of Drano. I poured some into a small tumbler I found in the cupboard. *Ha*, I thought to myself, *it actually does look like a drink. A disgusting one only a frat boy would drink.* I went back to the cupboard and took down a tall water glass, filling it about a quarter full with water. I put an ice cube in each glass, picked them up and walked back to the living room, curious about what would come next.

"Here you go," I said in a seductive voice as I walked towards him. "I'm just having a shot or two of vodka before I have a Genie, to give me an extra edge. Tell me what you think of my creation." I handed him the glass as he stood to receive it.

Steve held the glass out to me. "Here's to amplified orgasms." He tossed the entire contents of the glass down his throat.

Immediately he looked up at me, gasping. Reaching out, he started walking towards me. I backed away with a smirk on my face. He tripped over the leg of the glass coffee table beside him and teetered for a moment before crashing through it face first. A shard of glass punctured his throat and blood began spurting out in a comical arc. I felt as close as I ever had to bursting out laughing as he lay twitching there on the floor amongst the ruins of his table. Taking care to avoid the blood, I walked over to him, took his hand, wrapped it around my water glass and placed the glass on a little table across the room.

Suddenly the scene looked familiar to me. Smiling to myself, I uttered the words "*Corn Nuts*" before turning and walking out the door. I lit a cigarette, walked a block down to the canal, found a dark corner, took off my wig, turned my jacket inside out, fluffed up my hair, walked a few blocks, chain-smoking, and flagged a cab. When I got home I threw the wig and clothes I was wearing into the incinerator. The shoes I dropped into a bin for Value Village a week later.

It was ruled a suicide. No investigation. That was my first.

12.

Gable, my dog, was a gift from my parents three years ago at Christmas. He was a tiny little puppy and I'm certain was given to me because my mother always agonized that I spent so much time alone, working, running around the city unprotected. I tried to tell her I liked being alone, that I didn't need any companionship, from dog or human, but she naturally never believed me, never even suspecting her daughter's true nature. If she felt better about me having a dog, then in her mind I would feel better.

Mother was an exceptionally emotive person and she strove to be the best mom in the world. Blonde and perky and young, her mothering mentor was Elise Keaton from the television show *Family Ties*, though her children were nothing like the Keaton's and her husband, my father, was nothing like Michael Gross. My father was a judge, appointed after many years as a lawyer, and sat on the bench in the courthouse in Kitchener, deciding the fate of many criminals and innocent people alike. He mostly made the right decision, but sometimes did not, which he freely admitted. Sometimes his hands were tied. Sometimes the law demonstrated that it was not evolved enough to deliver real and true justice.

It was through watching both my parents, but mostly my father, that I was able to construct the justice-oriented framework that I used to guide me through my life in the absence of my own morality. Through conversation and a lot of reading, I was better-versed in the law than many lawyers, and as such could easily remind myself what it was that the collective history of western civilization thought was right and wrong when I found myself in a pinch.

What became the conundrum of my life, the one that led to me finally becoming who I now am, was that I early on became aware that there were still too many holes in the law, in our civilized structure of justice, to really see itself play out properly. There were so many abuses that people could unleash upon each other, so many vague insinuations, so many things that could not be proven, even beyond a reasonable doubt, that as such those who treated each other badly from what would be described as a moral or ethical point of view were rarely punished. I decided that it was my duty, with my unique ability to distance myself from the doubts and emotions that plagued other people, to bridge that gap. Where there was no law, but in my mind a crime, I would become judge, jury and executioner.

Soon after I got Gable, as he grew with enormous speed from furry, chubby puppy to aristocrat, I wondered if my parents had not given me this dog because they believed something was wrong with me – more wrong than not getting married and having kids – and wanted someone to watch me and keep in check.

I was aware early on that Gable could see right through me. His big, brown eyes would look at me sternly, telling me he could see into my black soul, warn me that ultimately I would never get away with what I thought I would, that I would be caught, that insanity would devour me and I would see the end of my existence with electricity being pumped into my skull and beyond.

It's not that I could hear his voice, but it's not that I couldn't, either. At first I didn't like it at all, but could see no useful reason to kill an animal, and didn't want to give him away in case he was forced to live out his life in a shelter or with some person or persons who treated him cruelly for no reason. He was, after all, a good dog, even if he did keep me on edge and make me aware of things I wouldn't have otherwise been aware of, not only about myself, but about the world around me.

On top of it, having Gable was often a good excuse to not travel for work, to not have to visit my family, to not have to engage in many of the activities I found boring or uncomfortable or useless. He unwittingly gave me more time to do the things I wanted to do. As I think of this right now, I turn and look at him appraisingly.

I do what I can, he says with a wink.

13.

I hate the anti-smoking campaign for many reasons.

First of all, living in downtown Toronto, I strongly believe that cigarette smoke is the least of what I inhale that is carcinogenic and harmful to my health. A few years ago NOW magazine put out a report that there were something like 290 known carcinogens in the air in Toronto that aren't even counted in statistical facts released about the state of our air. When I was in school I spoke to people from South America who loved Toronto because the air is "so clean", claiming that the smog in Venezuela is so severe it comes out of all your mucous membranes. A friend of mine who traveled around Europe told me she blew black crap out of her nose the whole time she was in London. Half the countries in the Middle East have no programs in place to prevent pollution, not of air, earth, or water. When the plane took off from Beijing I turned around to get an aerial view of the city and was unable to see anything because the city was immediately eclipsed by an opaque layer of murky yellow-brown smog. In Nova Scotia they get warnings to stay out of the "acid fog", sister-toxin to "acid rain", traveling across the ocean towards them from Europe.

Febreze and its legion are the products of the devil incarnate. Besides the air outside, the millions of gas-guzzling SUVs on the road, the pollution from industry, garbage, lack of nature, the average person in this city is further encouraged to poison themselves from inside their homes. Spray *Febreze* everywhere! On your clothes, carpet, furniture, car, closets… everywhere and as often as possible. Also, please buy a Glade scent-story or dispenser that gives you the options of a scented mist being distributed every 9, 18, or 36 minutes. Since no one really got the message about Teflon in the 80s when it was announced it had carcinogenic qualities, we've decided to take microscopic samples of it and add it to your bathroom sprays. Hell, make it aerosol. Don't get me started on the "anti-bacterial" product revolution. In Kleenex, soap: everywhere, creating superbugs at the speed of light. Please, inhale these tiny molecules; nothing will hurt you, ever, nothing except nasty cigarettes.

After all, we're certainly accustomed to ingesting carcinogenic products. Half the medications prescribed to us for the plethora of "syndromes" hounding everyone in spades these days have side effects, often in small print and interesting wording, including cancer. Or how about the pill, decreasing your risk of the highly curable cervical cancer but raising the risk of the aggressive killer ovarian cancer or breast cancer? Or Gardasil, the "cancer vaccine" that really is an HPV vaccine and can increase your risk of cancer if already infected; no plans yet to thoroughly test people before applying the vaccination to the whole child-bearing female population.

Then, if you haven't had enough yet, please, eat some of our fresh meat. Meat from animals forced into cannibalism, full of anti-biotics and god knows what else, whose only measure of health before it is slaughtered and fed to your family is whether or not it can walk without falling down. Animals never allowed to have a life, standing in a stall, awaiting the proverbial cleaver. There is as much science connecting stomach, colon and other cancers to meat consumption as there is connecting smoking to lung cancer, but there's no campaign, no all-encompassing legislation-altering campaign, against meat.

I suspect all of you come into more contact with the aforementioned products in a day, week, month, or year, than you come in contact with cigarette smokers, unless you are one. Oh yeah, you were free and clear of an untimely death until you went to that small-town Swiss Chalet with a smoking section! Ninety minutes in that establishment and you are condemned. If only Febreze could kill cancer the way it indiscriminately kills so many microbial organisms we depend on for our survival.

There is a reason cigarette smokers are targeted. Some of it has to do with truth but most of it has to do with a basic human tendency to need to feel superior to others and wield power over them, and another basic human tendency to be greedy and want to cash in on a fear-induced campaign.

Anyone who ever smoked is a liar if they tell you it had no effect on their health, that's for sure. And almost everyone has heard stories about both the old man dying with a cigarette in one hand and a scotch in the other on his 98th birthday after smoking since he was eight years old, and the kid who died of terminal lung cancer at twenty-four after smoking only five years. So that, without any science whatsoever and just a modicum of instinct, is what we know: smoking definitely affects your health for the worse, killing some people early on and leaving others to live as though they'd never smoked at all, and no one knows who fits which profile. With science we know little more.

What we do know is this: The people who stand to make profit off of selling cigarettes now stand to make profit off of selling nicotine-related quit-smoking products, like the patch, nicotine gum, the inhaler, the lozenge and so on. These people are no idiots; they could see their empire crumbling long before we could due to the lawsuits they settled out of court that we were not privy to knowing about. They bought into the nicotine business and said, "Hey, we have absolutely no problem profiting from smokers and ex-smokers alike." Ever asked someone just how long they were addicted to nicotine after quitting smoking?

Almost ten years ago, when the first stirrings of what is now a very successful anti-smoking campaign were just being heard, I started to become extremely paranoid of cancer. No other disease. Not death. Just cancer. My own body declaring mutiny. Unsettling though it was, it was actually a comfort to know that in this particular case, I was not alone.

In order to understand better the intricacies of this enveloping paranoia, I volunteered for a short period of time in the palliative care ward of Ottawa General. I came in three times a week for two hours at a time and visited with people who had little or no time left. Most of the people, though not all, who end up in the palliative care ward of a hospital a) have cancer, b) are not wealthy, c) don't have the support systems most of us take for granted and d) do not feel as though the medical establishment did everything it could. They often felt as if their needs were ignored. They felt as though they were being treated as a number or a case study. Their requests to treat their whole health, their nutritional, psychological, spiritual and physical health, were not met if those requests fell outside a very loose definition of open-mindedness afforded by the hospital (a Christian chapel with options to other religious advisors, allopathic nutritionist, pharmacological psychiatrist and options for massage), which they usually did. Because these extracurricular treatments are offered only with the understanding all allopathic treatments are being adhered to; you can see a nutritionist, but you're still getting chemo, you're still getting radiation, you're still getting surgery. If you start to refuse these treatments because you want to explore other options, less invasive, less devastating, you are quite literally threatened with total abandonment by the medical establishment. Oh, you have every right to take ownership over your disease and you have the right to medical treatment, but if you're not going to do it our way, don't come back.

Well, most of these people a) have cancer, b) are not wealthy and c) don't have the support systems most of us take for granted. They can't take the chance of being left out to dry by the hospitals as well. This constant, improvable blackmail almost always works. Especially when the person fighting actually or perceivably alone for their rights is under the effects of a whole lot of medication. Pay no mind, that person is talking crazy; everyone knows that homeopaths are capable of little else than a comforting placebo...

Dying of cancer, actually *dying* of cancer, long after the hopes are dashed and the treatments have been explored and there is no hope left, which is when I came upon these people, isn't actually that bad. Down with the establishment, but keep the morphine. Dope me up so I'm giddy and seeing visions and sleeping restfully and feeling little more pain than a drug-free person with severe fibromyalgia and you know, it's not the thing I still feel causing my heart to race when I think of the disease.

The smoking, yes, I can name my cancer. The smoking has been so good to me, my life is so irrelevant, I care so little, this is not an issue. Though, another excellent reason why I hate the anti-smoking campaign is because though I supposedly have the free will to purchase and smoke my cigarettes I am subjected to looking at tumours and the gums of cadavers so people who never smoked can feel smugly that I was "informed". I have never known a smoker who didn't know about lung cancer. Remember what I was saying about Nine Inch Nails and all the Tipper Gores out there misunderstanding the point?

No, the scariest thing about cancer is that it means that no matter what, at some point, for a great length, a greater length than it needs to be, I will be at the mercy of the Canadian health care system, degrading by the moment; just lost ten points while I wrote this.

14.

This is the short version of the history of the Internet Business Revolution:

Once upon a time in the 1990s a group of smart young American men decided they could make money off of programmatical advances made on the Internet, a tool long-used by the Government, Universities and Geeks, to share information online. When, amidst scoffing and catcalls by arrogant members of the business establishment, they proved they could indeed make a profit and share their knowledge at a profit to others who wished to make a profit with them, what we know today as the World Wide Web was born. The language the Internet spoke at the very beginning was HTML, or Hyper-Text-Markup-Language. Just call it HTML for all it matters. It's basically just English.

Soon, people everywhere were flocking to be a part of the Internet Revolution. There were more jobs than there were qualified people to work at them. The Internet learned how to integrate real programming languages into its HTML pages, working in the background on robust computers and transmitting information to the pages over a server. Ads were taken out in newspapers imploring waiters and factory workers to give up their jobs and go back to school for a very short and very expensive program that would guarantee their financial success immediately upon graduation in such fields as e-commerce, e-learning, inside sales, programming, animation and so on. Where just a few months before people were not considered qualified to be a programmer with fewer than four years of study, the Internet had somehow provided a method by which we could, for the same cost as a four year program, be just as qualified in just ten months.

Within a year or two, the market was flooded. There were simply too many people apparently qualified and too few jobs available to employ them. Many companies, like Silacorp, had been lost to the woes of bad planning or the collapse of the Japanese stock market in 1997-98, and at the beginning it had been easy to tell the short-term colleges from the real colleges and universities. But far too soon, the lines began to blur. People were getting "Computer Science degrees" in less than a year. Even more people lied on their resumes. Foreign countries were starting to hire their own qualified staff and the need for Canadian and American Internet companies began to dwindle at the same time the competition began to grow.

Only second to the oil and military industries, 9/11 was a godsend to the Internet industry. Stocks fell. Companies went under. Salaries took a plunge, by more than half in some cases. Within a year these people who were graduating from programs that still promised them they'd be millionaires in the next year were lucky to be hired at minimum wage. And everyone had something to blame it on.

Now years later, we big shits at the top have recovered, but I know for a fact that you kids at the bottom haven't seen much change, except for the worse, because I read the monthly reports.

The Internet has done to business what *A Current Affair* did to regular news. With a lot of flash and wool-pulling and bullshit, it captured the attention of wider audiences than truth and sensibility did. People would rather tune in to a news program and learn only sub-par information while ignoring the very pressing matters affecting everyone in the world, than tune into a boring, non-flashy alternative. Rather than trying, and possibly succeeding, in convincing people of the gravity of what they were missing, the news programs changed their format to be better able compete with entertainment-related news programs like *A Current Affair, Entertainment Tonight, Star!* and the dozens of others that popped up around them.

The result is a news and entertainment industry that spends millions of dollars on needless complementary programming, like brand design, motion screens, slates, instructional graphics, special segment introductions, interstitials, etc. Most of the time all of these things cost so much money simply because the technology and the means to understanding it are beyond the reach of more conventional television programmers. Because we like to control other people and are infinitely greedy, we take advantage of the ignorance of these newbies and bleed them dry for something that could be done in-house for a fraction of the cost with the acquisition of one truly talented and productive employee.

Sometime just before Y2K, the Internet had a baby and that baby's name was New Media. New Media was like the kid you have in order to extend and take over your empire while you're free to vacation in Fiji and make executive decisions on only the most important issues. New Media had many new talents, like being able to make web sites that acted like all those annoying new additions needed by television stations in their endless effort to out-flash each other. They called this Flash. And if New Media could make web sites that did this, why stop there? Why not move over to the CD and DVD world, video transcoding and streaming (showing videos on the internet) and video games, video and audio communication, infringing on new territory, unwelcome, blurring the lines even more. And by god, the most genius thing of all, New Media could make banner ads, store vast amounts of personal data and sell it to the highest bidder, spawning two new sub-industries, Online Advertising and Data Mining.

Oh, babies having babies…

15.

There's a sort of blackness hanging over me. It's always been there, since my earliest days. It pervades all of my memories of that time just as it pervaded my few dreams and nightmares during that time. It shares symptoms with many types of disorders and syndromes named by modern psychiatric practitioners, but it's none of those things, if those things even do really exist in a tangible way to be experienced by so many individuals. When I was a child it was one of many reasons I believed something was inherently wrong with me, but no amount of attention or treatment has helped. I used to have a sense of doom that was nearly crippling. Whether or not it is started by or starts my paranoia is a mystery, but the two are rarely seen apart from each other.

Ah yes, the sense of doom. Funny, it's one of those "symptoms" of "syndromes" that head-doctors ask, as though feeling a sense of doom is indicative of mental illness. I ask you, if you're living on a planet that is rapidly declining due to activities you yourself are party to, in a world dominated by injustice and selfishness and unreasonableness, where idiocy trumps wisdom, where sociopaths can live amongst you without detection, where atrocity after atrocity outnumber good deeds, in a city where you work long hours for too little money to survive on, in a market that takes weeks to even months to hire and even then only on contract to save money, where people whine and bitch and act as though they are entitled to someone wiping their very ass for them, where the wealthy and successful, including myself, take far too little time to recognize the gap between our pointless success and the suffering of others, where we're warned every day about the demise of our civilization, *would it be at all strange to feel a sense of doom?* How is it possible that identifying and reacting to reality could be a symptom of a mental illness and denying it a symptom of sanity?

This is the thing; they're wrong. I can tell you this in a way no one else might be able to, because I do not possess many of the other emotions that disturb all the rest of you suffering from these mental illnesses. I do not cry. I do not get so depressed I can't get out of bed. I do not scream or wail or fight. I don't feel sorry for myself, or anyone else. I don't feel compassion or guilt; therefore I'm not affected by the actions or reactions, opinions or morals, of others. But I do see reality. And if you see it too, you would be perfectly sane to notice it is accompanied by a sense of doom.

I used to have a grey cardigan with a zipper and big pockets back when I was maybe six or seven years old. It was my favourite sweater. I loved it. Every night before bed I would lay it over the back of my desk chair beside my bed, put out my favourite loafers beneath and go to sleep. The cardigan and the loafers were so that I could quickly go outside when the fire I knew was going to consume my house and my family finally happened. I didn't know when, but we lived in a house, houses burn and so there must be a fire someday at our house. If not, I was certain I would need that cardigan and those loafers when an air raid siren went off alerting us of a nuclear strike, or if a tornado made its way through the valley behind our house. Anything could happen, really, and you couldn't be more prepared.

But then I started having these dreams.

In every single one of the cardigan-dreams, it went something like this. My family was visiting someone else for dinner. There was a fire. Everyone got out safely. I noticed I had left my grey cardigan inside. Someone (a different person in each dream) would go back in to get it for me. They would die. I would mourn my cardigan.

I used to go through a fair amount of anguish when I was young, wondering why I kept killing members of my family and caring only for the cardigan, wondering why I would do that in the next dream when I'd already learned from the previous one. I had no problems with anyone in my family, except one sister, and had no reason to not want to be with them anymore. In this first experience in facing my own personality my six-year-old brain decided the fault lay with the cardigan. Into a box it went and into a dark little crevice in our crawlspace, never to be seen again.

What happens to me, in my inability to process some emotions properly, is that it gets transferred to physical sensation. If I am what most people refer to as happy, I feel it in my body more than in my mind. If people refer to feeling as though their heart is breaking, I literally feel as though my physical heart is breaking while left unencumbered by emotion. If I feel stressed out or anxious, rather than have racing thoughts or urges to cry or yell or collapse, my body literally feels stressed out, it becomes wracked with pain, and if I didn't know better, I'd think I had early onset of a degenerative muscle disease like ALS. I am in pain all the time, from head and face pain due to the nerves around my occipital bone, to back pain caused by tensing my shoulders to my ears all the time and hunching over a computer, to abdominal pain, which used to be the bane of my existence but in recent years has become more like background noise.

As a very young kid, right around the cardigan years, I began experiencing frequent, long-lasting "stomachaches", which would begin with a tightness in my stomach proper and over the next eight or so hours engulf my entire abdomen, until I could do nothing but lie on my bed rocking back and forth in agony. At some point I would induce vomiting to try and relieve some of the tension, which always backfired and left me in a state of perpetual vomiting, at which time my parents would take me to the emergency room where after several more hours of waiting, I would be shot up with Gravol or Demerol and released.

These stomachaches would hit at random times with seemingly random causes, but they were always preceded or proceeded by the blackness. Most often I would be awoken by the pain sometime in the middle of the night, but it could start halfway through a hike with my friends, while sitting in class, while relaxed or stressed. I could never really pinpoint *where* it hurt so doctors rarely touched an actual painful spot. For a long time they thought I had an ulcer; my doctor was particularly pleased to possibly be the physician of the youngest case of ulcer in Canada at the time, but it turned out that wasn't the case. My appendix also remains intact. Ultrasounds have revealed nothing. And at some point around the age of ten, I learned I could largely control the pain with my mind for short periods of time, indicating to me it was not a disease or obstruction.

Sometime in my early twenties I stopped eating meat for a while and for the most part the abdominal part of my chronic pain stopped, at least insofar as it incapacitated me. When I finally started eating meat again, it seemed to have solved itself. It still hurts 90% of the time but I can live through it. Which is good because I need all the strength I can get to get through the rest of this constant, roaming, non-stop, break-free, body pain. Right now it's in my back, mid and lower, spreading around my sides. Earlier (and still but not as apparent at the moment) it was my neck. When I woke up this morning it all conspired to trick me into thinking it was my lungs, which it may very well be, but I have bigger troubles right now, because my hip is screaming in a way it hasn't in several years.

Around ten years ago, I used to go to the doctor a lot, because as I became an adult it occurred to me that no one would be in this amount of pain if something weren't wrong with them. I had been raised to think of a doctor as some sort of magical, wise creature who had my best interest at heart and who knew everything. I had been, and still am, told that pain is there for a reason, to alert you to something being wrong, and as a result I was constantly on alert. Well, doctors found nothing. Over a decade I had 3 lung x-rays, 2 ultrasounds, a couple of operations and a whole shitload of blood tests. When the physical was exhausted, the mental was explored (laughably). Being no stranger to getting high, I even took some of the drugs they offered me. Anti-depressants, tranquilizers, pain-killers and so on.

Anti-depressants were discarded almost immediately. These nifty little drugs can take a normal person and turn them into a monster. And they can take a monster and unleash within them a deadly wrath. Let me explain.

People unwittingly fall into varying degrees of two categories: Good and Bad. These categories live completely separated from any individual's hormone levels, personal experiences, genetic makeup, etc., but they do act in tandem with all of these. Cursed as we are to be the way we were made, the reasons we do Good and Bad things are due entirely to choices we make within the confines of our own makeup.

For instance, I have no scruples. I could kill you soon as look at you. If you're a certain type of person and I have a certain type of inclination, I may very well do it. The reason I don't kill most of the people I know and see is because I choose not to. The reason I choose not to could be multi-fold. In most people's case they choose not to kill people or do other Bad things because they have morals and ethics, because they have a conscience and would feel guilt, because they value the importance of human life, because they feel bound to religious and secular demands that they must not kill, because doing so would result in punishment or even death. I do share some of these reasons but not in the same way. I don't have a conscience and I won't feel guilt, but I do respect people's basic right to life and recognize that without rules we would dissolve into chaos. I am aware of the safeguards we have in place to deter and punish murderers and I have no urge to spend the rest of my life incarcerated. Killing people is generally messy and I don't like to be messy. I am obsessed with justice and I can recognize whether a murder is done to a total innocent or to a convoluted mess of someone who deserved it. Despite my inherent human shortcomings, I am, I think, a Good Person.

If I were a Bad Person, then I would be a truly uncontainable beast. I would be Ted Bundy, or John Wayne Gacy, or Paul Bernardo. I would be the children who killed their peers in all the high school shootings the past few years. I would have no impulse-control, no ability to discriminate and no vision of my own future. I would also get caught.

Well, there are plenty of Bad People out there who aren't sociopaths, who haven't crossed any lines, who don't do much except insult people for no reason and abuse their spouses and children and beat on those they see as weaker than them. And when Bad People get depressed and are given drugs that rob them of their impulse control, that distort their personality until it is flat and unfeeling, you know what you have? A Monster. Because no drug in the world *changes* a person. It only amplifies what is there already, it only skews your judgment. If you are prone to violence towards others or yourself, even if you never display that inclination, an anti-depressant will bring that quality out. If you're prone to being shallow, an anti-depressant will bring that quality out. If you're prone to being very gentle and introverted, an anti-depressant would bring that quality out.

And if you're prone to committing murder, an anti-depressant will bring that quality out.

16.

I am sitting in a meeting in the big boardroom at my office. Around the table is Frances, the CFO, Jim Dieter, the CEO, Grayson Albertson, the CTO, two assistants, the Creative Director, three senior Project Managers, an Account Manager and someone I don't recognize but think is another assistant. We have just finished a long, four-hour discussion about the end of quarter figures, a new product launch and a competitor who must be put to rest. I point out the competitor should be dealt with fairly, defeated by our excellence and not by our underhandedness, so when we acquire them and fire half their staff, it is all done in a fair way.

"More of your moral high ground!" Jim exclaims. "It's none of your concern, really. You just focus on making sure internal operations run smoothly and let us worry about acquisitions," he finished condescendingly. I wished hard that Jim hadn't also missed the boat, one of about twenty invites, myself included, who did.

"Jim, dear," I smile flatly at him. "If any operation by someone in this company involves sabotaging or spreading rumours that are untrue about a competitor, it *is* my business, it is *exactly* my business and I *will* deal with it." He knows I have the power to stop this. I decide to egg him and everyone else on for a while; might as well drag this pointless meeting out to use up the whole day. Nothing better to do. As with most things in business, we really could have taken care of all of this in about thirty minutes.

So the meeting proceeds. Food is called out for. The light outside begins to fade, letting us know for sure that summer is finally over. When we're finally wrapping things up, I ask if the three other executives wouldn't mind staying for a few more minutes.

"I'm quitting, Boys," I say emotionlessly.

They are flabbergasted, not expecting this at all. I remind them of what they already know, that I had inherited Paul's legacy and that with his money and business holdings I felt it was a conflict of interest to continue working for a competitor, and I leave out the obvious part – who the hell would want to keep working in a bullshit industry when they are suddenly quite self-sufficiently wealthy. My own high standard of living can be met with no more work; I felt no urge to continue… no, my urges these days are of the approaching winter, the open sky, the peace of isolation. I want to leave before I fall into another bout of needing to kill these useless little fucks.

I leave that day. They don't let executives work out their two weeks' notice or anything; it's just a recipe for espionage. If you quit, you are immediately the enemy. These men I have worked with for the past five years are suddenly no more than strangers, paranoid competitors regarding me with suspicion. A pain spreads across my chest as I contemplate the uselessness of such an endeavour; imagine if I had had a soul to put into this work – where would it be now in this thankless, cold world?

I decide to celebrate my emancipation from the business world by getting dolled up in a long red wig and dark black makeup, pale skin with sparkles, black contact lenses, a padded bra and a skin-tight dark blue minidress. Sleek black thigh-high stockings, spike pumps. No gitch.

I go down the block to a bar I know is often frequented by my business peers. My skin is tingling and my pussy is throbbing as I enter, wondering who, if anyone, will recognize me. I go to the bar and sit down demurely on a stool, asking the bartender for a vodka tonic. He regards me hungrily. I smirk and innocently use my tongue to rub the corner of my lips. In the mirror behind his head I can see the entire bar without ever having to turn around. Exactly where I want to be.

Within the hour I see my hopes are not to be dashed. Jim Dieter walks through the door, alone. This is a common occurrence. He glances around the bar to see if anyone he knows is there, which lucky for me they're not, and he proceeds to the bar. When he as about halfway there, I casually turn on my barstool, making sure my impressive profile is visible to him as he approaches. Like holding out cheese to a dog, he almost without knowing why starts to veer in my direction. One stool over, he glances at me and says to the bartender, "I'll have a gin and tonic," thinking that's what I'm drinking.

Turning his attention fully to me, he drawls, "How's it going?" I smile back at him and put my straw in my mouth, sipping.

We talk for a while; tonight I'm an out of work actress trying to make some connections who had heard this particular bar sometimes attracted high level television and movie executives. Jim tells me he was the CEO of a Very Successful New Media Company, with many connections in The TV and Film Industries and it was my lucky night, because getting to know him could prove to be very good for my career. I agree.

I steer the conversation towards sex as early as possible, suggesting we go back to his place. His fate, still up in the air when he arrived, was now sealed, as I reflect that this man who had worked with me closely every day for half a decade does not recognize me at this proximity, despite my slightly altered appearance. He doesn't even think I look familiar.

Jim has a fabulous apartment, not as big as Paul's but just as nice. He, too, has a rather large terrace overlooking the lake and that's where we find ourselves a half hour later, drinking Port and laughing (fake on both parts I'm sure) over mundane, useless topics I know for a fact Jim isn't even interested in. Years of condescending to me and every woman he worked with has left Jim feeling very superior indeed. He has a reputation of getting a little rough with the women he goes out with as well; he is a misogynist through and through. Used to play squash with Paul yet hasn't expressed a word about the loss of half of his executive peers in the last month, to me or anyone else that I've heard of. Funny, you get a Bad Person with a certain level of selfishness and greed and for the most part, an analysis of his actions will leave him indistinguishable from a sociopath. Jim doesn't lack the ability to care about other people like I do; he just chooses not to care. If you gave him the time or framed it properly, he would feel extreme amounts of remorse over the way he has treated people over the years, if he could be made to "understand" the effects of what he's done, as opposed to myself who is aware of all of these things and simply *cannot* care. Jim has raped the minds and bodies of so many people I cannot count; people who were good and kind and did nothing to deserve it. He has chosen to take the compassion and feeling he was so lucky to be born with and bury it.

Suddenly bored and wanting to go home, I tell Jim if he stands on the half-ledge of his terrace (the ledge is in two steps, like a seat or stairs) and drops his pants, I will suck his cock in a way he's never experienced before. Shocked and excited, he almost jumps to the step, undoing his pants as he goes. I walk over to him, gloved hand wrapping tightly around his short, thick penis and bring my mouth as close as I can without touching. "I hope you like the way I do this," I say coyly, pumping him, and he nods, eyes already half shut and that god-awful porn-star look crossing his face. I pump his cock so that it is actually pulling his body to and from me, and on the next release, I push, hard. A couple of dance steps and a look of horror later, a cry that sounded something like "Heeey!" and Jim is sailing over the edge of his balcony towards the mess of a construction zone below.

"Thank you for a lovely time, I'll let myself out," I say over the edge, the closest I ever feel to really laughing at something, body still tingling, muscles relaxing.

I've got to get out of town. Too many people missed that boat. This could potentially never end.

17.

I have one friend. Her name is Renee and I've known her since I was a little kid. She is the complete and utter opposite of me.

We grew up together in Kitchener. By the time Renee was twelve, her mother and step-father had died and she started to spend a lot of time in Toronto with her real father, moving there permanently in Grade 12 and leaving me for two difficult years by myself at Forest Heights Collegiate. I joined Renee in Toronto after high school and we still get together about once a week.

Renee is the closest thing I've ever met to a real psychic. An empath. She feels *everything* and always has. She has always been my model for a real feeling person and without her in my life, I may not have been able to learn to integrate so well into society. I used to use Renee as an indication of the opposite extreme of me; to act somewhere in between my own total detachment and her over-involvement in everything seemed to pass me off as "normal". I learned from Renee to create facial expressions that conveyed feeling, such as wincing in sorrow at the death of a bird on the playground, or looking sincere when giving someone an apology after saying something nasty to them.

As teenagers, Renee enjoyed hanging out with me, as I seemed to her to have no fear and was always able to find us a weekend adventure that was exciting. She liked talking to me and confiding in me because I never told anyone anything and she knew her secrets were safe. She enjoyed my advice because it allowed her an opportunity to escape from her over-developed sense of empathy, which she found to be both a blessing and a burden (another thing I learned from her; people tend to group things about themselves as blessings and burdens as opposed to thinking of it as just being *them*).

When we were still very young, prepubescent, Renee told me one day with surprising frankness that there was something different about me, something empty. She said she could read, if not the minds, then the hearts, of almost everyone else she met, but in my case, it was just blank. Throughout our friendship, she would repeat these sentiments from time to time. Now working as a painter in the studio she inherited from her father, she as recently as a week ago told me she had planned to paint a portrait for me for the upcoming Christmas, but every time she tried to focus on expressing the depths of my soul on canvas she drew a blank. There was nothing to say. I guess you can't draw what isn't there.

18.

Politicians, the public, shiny, self-serving, power-hungry, malignantly narcissistic ones, look as though they are wearing a full body mask and are at any moment going to rip them off and reveal the insect that lives beneath. Like Vincent D'Onofrio in his excellent characterization of the Cockroach for the movie *Men In Black*.

For anyone obsessed with the concept of justice, politicians like this are an affront. They embody a certain type of person and with that, a certain type of ideology – which is more psychological than political – that spits in the face of justice and also, for that matter, common sense. Their obvious disdain for the people of the country they represent is tangible. And the worst part, the worst, is that this sort of politician opens a door to allow others like them to be known. Others like them: blind, selfish, greedy, intolerant, dictatorial, capitalist bastards.

In the same way I admire Renee for being able to show me a functional form of a Good Person, so too did my youth show me that the world at that time was a functional model of a bunch of inherently Good People. Most people have, like me, always seemed interested in justice. They have seemed to have common sense. If you listened to the comments being called in to radio shows, or letters written into newspapers, Canadians were, with the exception of a few major topics, such as Quebec, or the U.S., extremely balanced in their approach. Our politicians have historically acted with diplomacy and well-thought out approaches to solving problems. We have always symbolized peace, education, health and forward thinking. Even the Conservative governments of our past were *progressive,* that word being the very thing dropped by our new Conservative party who wishes to keep the progressive vote.

No more. With the worldwide rise of fundamentalist republicanism and neo-conservativism came a whole army, quite literally, of people I would have never before likened to North Americans. Nasty, immature, name-calling fuckers who wouldn't even know what to do with themselves if everyone ended up agreeing with their nonsense and they had nothing left to bitch about. Bad people, people who don't really believe in justice, people who *wish* they were sociopaths so they could carry on and not be so consumed by the never-ending fire of their denied guilt. Embarrassing people, people who sound so ridiculous and hyper and red-faced in their attempt to put down everyone they see as a rival, people who are so arrogant when given a fraction of power over anything, an arrogance that grows exponentially with the power they gain. This, this thing we have right now, is a country I don't even recognize, it is one that validates everything I have ever determined in my careful reasoning of the world as Bad.

There is a toxic mixture floating around the world today that is an equal combination of Bad, Ignorant and Religious. This is what, obvious or not, fuels the neo-conservative movement: the perfect mixture of Bad, Ignorant and Religious. Rush Limbaugh has it for breakfast.

It most recently started with George W. Bush in 2000. Really. Seriously. That person was seen by who – bad ignorant religious people – as a "strong leader"? A "decisive politician"? A "good man"? This deplorable backwoods twit, who slaps his wife's ass as she walks offstage after making a speech, who has been responsible for more deaths than *the plague*, is considered even "okay"? I quite certainly do mean some offense when I ask his supporters, are you retarded? Are you retarded to think that in any way the "who cares what's left after I'm gone" attitude of the North American neo-con is "the way to go"?

Even the ones who don't think this, what these past few years begs is the question, "Why are you letting this happen?" I understand why I don't really care, but why don't you?

As an outsider, I have to tell all of you that you're not coming across looking terribly well. After the whole history of our planet that we know of to date, we haven't learned a thing – in fact, I think we've undone quite a bit we had known already. I find it hard to admire other humans in the least when they are in positions to do something about something that is wrong and instead they just whine and lie and contribute to it. The people who *would* help, who *would* create change, well, they've been systematically though metaphorically shackled by the others; they have no power to make change and the more they implore you to do something about it, the more you kick them in the teeth and pollute them with your SUV and complain you don't live in a gated community.

At least, in the world that I live in, a world without feeling, without emotional colour, I can still uphold justice. You could die in front of me and I would feel nothing; you could beg me for help and if I didn't want to, I could walk away guilt-free; I have absolutely no obligation to myself or anyone or anything else to do something good, period, and yet I do. And it's not easy. I rid the world of capitalists who are contributing to the destruction of their fellow man and the planet. I rid the world of Bad People.

You would too, if you didn't feel so awful about it.

19.

Tonight I am going to a hockey game. Leafs vs. the Habs. My executive peers are having a "retirement" party for me there; we have a box. I love the corporate box experience at a hockey game, always have. Love the excellent seats, the ability to really participate at the game and love the private indoor area, with a smoking area, stocked bar and option of a server. It is my favourite perk of being an executive and tonight I'm getting ready to really party.

I've been going to hockey games since I was a little kid. My dad was a fanatic. Not only NHL, but OHL as well; we had seasons tickets to the Kitchener Rangers, Junior A, and went to a game every Friday night and Sunday afternoon for more than half the year. When I was still really young, I can't even remember – maybe seven or eight years old, we went to a game, Kitchener against North Bay. We were seated in the Reds, where we always were, which were pretty good seats, just at around the centre line. The game was going normally until near the end of the second period, at which point there was a fight. I remember there being a lot of fights back then in Junior hockey. That was a big part of the reason the games were so fun.

Well, this night, the fight was started by a North Bay player and the Kitchener people *did not like it*. They heckled and yelled at the North Bay team, threw food and other items onto the ice in an attempt to give their team the upper hand in the fight. More and more players joined in and more and more fans crowded down out of their seats to watch. Finally, someone threw a full pop can and it hit a player in the head, one of the North Bay behemoths. He charged the stands and the culprit was there to meet him. They fell over the boards onto the ice and all hell broke loose.

I watched, fascinated, from my seat, about twelve rows up from all the action. When I looked around me finally I found that my father and two sisters had disappeared. One of them I could see faintly across the ice in the Yellows with her friends, but my father and other sister were nowhere to be found.

That brawl went on for almost an hour. When it was over, people were being dragged out by the police and arrested, some people were leaving in an ambulance and the auditorium and ice was covered with litter. Yet, they decided to finish the game. The old couple that sat beside us every week picked out my father in the crowd in the Green section and I ran over to find him. He said he couldn't come back to our seat because he'd been kicked out for punching someone. We watched from the Greens while they scraped the blood off the ice, swept up the garbage and brought out the Zamboni to make it as though it never was. The game continued, but the crowd, what was left of it, was subdued. I can't remember who won.

But at every game I went to after that, I somehow expected another fight to break out. I realized that day there was little difference between the events of that afternoon leading up to the brawl and any other hockey game. It became clear to me how precariously close to chaos we are at any given time, that the actions of a moment could take our very loosely functioning order and cause us to dissolve into the palpable chaos that lies beneath.

As I walk around Toronto, I look at the buildings, the layout of the city, the people who live here, the different groups who function above and below ground in this melting pot of diversity, the secrets kept by the brick and concrete, the muddy crevices, the endlessly deep shadows. I wonder how or why the terrorists have not hit us yet, with the way Canada has been acting; with the image of itself it is projecting as a close-minded, childish, capitalistic imperialist. We are barely capable of governing our own lives anymore, much less our institutions or our cultures; we're so completely inept, we've broken so many promises and no, we're not alone by far in consequence or cause in comparison to others, but we're getting there.

I walk around Toronto and I wonder what it is going to look like when that one thing does happen; the thing that made the North Bay Brawl happen, the thing that changed the face of hockey in Kitchener for years to come, the thing that will change the face of life in this city, and maybe on this planet, for hundreds more. I wonder what that thing will be. I wonder if all the regular folk will be ready for it, above it, beyond it, or just wade in and go berserk.

The buzz at my party is the recent suicide of Jim Dieter. I find I have a great deal of luck and in this case my luck was that Jim apparently had a habit of standing on the very ledge I suggested he stand on and jerking off for the viewing pleasure of the few rich condo-owning neighbours who could see him. His blood-alcohol level was well above the legal limit and the conclusion was drawn that he came home from work, drank a lot, dropped his pants, teetered and toppled over the edge while flogging himself for all to see. There is even some talk in far corners that the reason Jim was so inebriated was his sorrow and stress over my resignation, being that I had been such an integral part of our company. It was such a cut and dry case of suicide no one even checked the cameras at the building entrance to see if anyone had come home with him or left alone. I shake my head at my good fortune.

The game is fantastic. I leave the Air Canada Centre and decide to walk back to my condo, about fifteen blocks away. I teeter down the street in my high heels, drunk off of the dozen or so glasses of wine I had downed at the game and look around, remembering all my nightmares as a kid. Why hasn't someone gotten a hold of a dirty bomb yet and decimated this or some other city? There are certainly enough floating around out there. I know why, yet still I feel like a child, bludgeoned with visions of mushroom clouds and sandstorms.

The reason why no one has done this is because human beings are equipped with a conscience, a natural respect and wonder for the world that gave them life and an internal method of distraction from strong urges to commit acts of mass destruction. The emotion of compassion and its opposite, guilt, are what keep us from destroying ourselves. That thing, that very thing I have always wanted and cannot make for myself, no matter what; the one thing I have learned so hard to replace with logic and reason and choice, and do quite an excellent job of, if I do say so myself, resulting in the loss of no innocent lives, is what keeps the world from destroying itself.

People work very hard to be like me. They try to convince themselves they're not really killing individuals if a big group of them opens fire on another one, like in an army. They try to convince themselves it's not murder if they say God told them to do it, and they have further convinced themselves they'll get compensation for this in the afterlife. Not just Jihadists; there are no shortage of Americans who think they'll get a special place in heaven after slaying a few thousand Muslim extremists, either. They try to convince themselves if they erode the decision and the choice to kill enough, no one will be at fault, like the system of orders being carried down a hierarchy so the person pulling the trigger is nothing but a measly private, a new recruit, trained to do whatever his commanding officer commands. They try to convince themselves their "enemies" are not human, one side depicting the other as some sort of abomination of humanity, some sort of evil with no core and no limit, a monster, if you will. And they definitely convince themselves long enough to do severe, irreparable damage to each other and this planet. But so far, not permanent destruction; that would take the work of a sociopath. And so far, the human conscience has caught up to the idea, or human beings have caught up to a would-be perpetrator, before such a decision could be made.

Just because someone has no morals doesn't mean they're evil. They probably wouldn't make very good parents but they're not bad pet owners, if they like the type of animal they are caretakers for. They're subject to the same sorts of temptations and obsessions all people are and most of the time this does not lead them to murder. Becoming a murderer is much more complicated than that. You can be subjected to childhood trauma, you can be convinced by someone else it is for a virtuous end, you can be motivated by mental breakdown or emotional emergency, self defense, or vigilantism. If you are also a sociopath and subjected to any of the above things, it can become very, very easy to make the choice to be a murderer because the moral consequence of your action has no meaning. However, being a sociopath in no way means you're particularly smart or motivated to do any of these things. In fact, most sociopaths are so socially inept they couldn't possibly organize the manpower or make the deals needed to carry out a truly destructive act. It's only when charismatic, functional sociopaths get it into their heads they need to do something to effect change on, or completely destroy, the rest of the world, that you need to start getting frightened. Charismatic, functional sociopaths like those evil political leaders running through modern history right up to the House of Commons in Ottawa and the Reform Prime Minister in Conservative clothing, not to mention those who prop them up and convince them they're powerful… and like those wretched heads of business who destroy lives like American bombs destroy churches and schoolhouses.

Yes, the elephants are dying, folks. They're making a stand. They're becoming more aggressive; they're not going to be wiped off this planet without a fight. And it only takes one split-second to start a brawl.

20.

Renee is looking at me from the table as I approach the patio of the little coffee shop on King Street we usually meet each other at. Her eyes look tired and she is slumped over as though she is either very stressed out or hasn't been feeling well. As I draw closer I decide to err on the side of stress. I pull out a cigarette and sit down.

"Jackie-boy's back in town," she says dully after a few moments.

"Fuck you, are you serious? When?"

"I've been getting hang-up calls all week, but last night he left a message." Her voice is shaking.

"What did it say?"

"It said he needs a place to go, that he's getting his shit together but just needs a place to stay for a few days while he waits for his first paycheque and gets an apartment. Says he forgives me for everything. He still loves me." I could tell from her voice she was buying this.

Fucking psycho. "Renee, you're not going to let him stay with you, are you? Don't you remember what happened last time? Don't you think he remembers? You let him stay and you're going to end up being the ingredients for Christmas Pudding."

"I know," she said, sounding like a teenager. I was getting bored already. "I should never see him again, but it's not like it's his fault, it's not like he means it…"

Jack was Renee's Big Love. They went out through their twenties, while Jack tried to make it as a rock star, along with half the other people in this city. He was actually pretty good, but had not the dedication or wherewithal to deal with the business side of being a "successful" musician, couldn't keep a manager because of his violent personality quirks. He was a dirtbag, basically, a dirtbag with a shitload of talent. It was obvious from the start that something wasn't quite right with Jack, but it made him who he was and was part of the reason he gathered the following he did. Renee thought they were meant to be.

But as he approached twenty-five, Jack really began to change. He was losing his mind. He wasn't sexy anymore, he was dirty in a different way, a sad way, a dangerous one. He would sit in the corner on a pillow and rock back and forth for hours, listening to Tool and writing out non-existent equations madly on graph paper with a charcoal pencil, convinced he was going to work out the magic formula hidden within the music that would explain the conspiracy of the U.S. government's control of sunlight. He was drawing pictures, blood and guts, people he knew, making judgment in the worst, saddest, most useless and illogical way possible.

Renee tried to ignore it at first, attributing it to his artistic temperament. But when she went home with him to visit his family and he crawled up on the roof and wouldn't come down for two days, she really began to worry. She called me from Coburg and asked me what to do. I told her to come home. She didn't. When Jack finally came down out of sheer hunger he beat her up, as well as his own mother. He was arrested and kept overnight but neither pressed charges and he was released. The police wanted to commit him but he refused and no one would sign the papers.

Because she loved him and he was clearly in trouble, which I obviously had no patience for, she continued to keep seeing him. Beating on her became routine over the next few months. And Jack is no sociopath; he was losing his mind and committing horrible acts while caught up in another reality, but when he realized what he'd done, when he was lucid, he was overcome with guilt and was inconsolable. Renee, who I had always admired for her strength, independence and common sense, kept inviting him back and began to disgust me to such an extent I started to consider beating her to death and leaving her in a park somewhere, but in reflecting upon the information available to me in this world on what was happening to her, in learning about battered woman's syndrome, in weighing this all with the right side of justice, I decided she was acting the way normal humans act in such a situation and the fault lay with Jack.

I am acutely aware that if I kill someone, the people who love them will mourn their loss. Though I have never experienced emotional pain, I can construct a functional model of it, based on what I have seen of many different kinds of pain, how much it hurts to lose someone you love. I do not wish to cause such pain for no reason to people I have named in my life as friend or innocent, because it flies in the face of justice, it is not what people do, and for that reason and that reason alone I did not kill Jack.

Instead, what I did was sit down with Renee and have a, ahem, heart to heart. I explained to her what was happening to her, what she was becoming and that it was going to destroy her life, plain and simple, if not get her killed. I explained to her how Jack was succumbing to schizophrenia, was not going to get better without some sort of treatment and that he was dangerous to her safety. Over the course of an afternoon, upon which I nearly walked out several times due to the volume of her tears and level of drama, I convinced her there was only one thing for her to do: report Jack as a danger to himself and her and commit him to a psychiatric ward. She finally agreed it was what was best for him.

I was incredibly impressed once again with how justice and ethics can make up for lack of morals.

Neither Renee nor myself had ever committed anyone before. Turns out to not be very difficult. Disturbingly easy, in fact. We went down to the court house and asked to see a Justice of the Peace. We explained our case, with surprisingly little eye witness detail. We said on tape we thought he was dangerous. Renee had to sign a few pieces of paper. We were out of there in an hour. Unfortunately, what we didn't know was that the police were immediately dispatched to pick Jack up and throw him into the little white van, complete with men in little white coats. He was at home, entertaining five or six of his bandmates and friends when there was a knock at the door. His friend opened it and the police barged in, demanding to know which one was Jack. He identified himself and they literally dragged him out of the apartment, despite the fact that he was calm and cooperative. Of course, when he realized he was being dragged out in his cut-off jogging shorts and wife beater with no shoes and or belongings, he began to protest, at which point the men in actual white coats entered and forced him into a straitjacket. At this point they informed him he had been committed by his girlfriend. Absolutely uncalled for.

Jack was kept in the hospital for six months. Renee visited him religiously. She claimed he was just like he had been before, completely healed, and she was thrilled about it. They were talking about moving in together when he got out, getting married, having a family. After all, the only thing wrong in their relationship was his mental illness, and they were better now.

All of this prompted me to go and visit Jack one day when Renee was busy. We sat in the common room staring at each other for some time. Jack has never liked me; he knew, too, I had been the one present with Renee when she had committed him.

"Why are you here?" he finally asked me.

"I hear you're moving in with Renee when you get out of here." I was staring at him. I could see it in his eyes, like I can in the eyes of so many of my prey; he had tasted violence, he had tasted evil. In my victims, the pay-off, the get-you-off, the conscience-buster, was always greed or power, but in Jack's it was madness. He was free in his madness; in lucidity, controlled by careful doses of mind and body-altering medications, he was bound. He would go back if he could and the reward of his madness would obliterate the guilt caused by any evil acts committed along the way. Renee was still in danger.

"Yes, we love each other," he stammered, bothered by the look on my face, recalling, no doubt, precisely why he disliked me.

"I want you to do something, Jack," I said, leaning forward. He nodded and leaned closer to me. "Look in my eyes while I say this so you'll know just how serious I am."

I gave him a second to really get a good look going.

"If you feel your madness coming back to you when you're out of here and living with Renee, if you feel just one twinge, just one, and you don't leave her immediately, leave town, leave the province, leave the country, just get away and I find out about it… *I Will Kill You.* Understand? Do you believe I am serious?"

Jack continued to stare at me, as if mesmerized. Finally, he regained his focus. "Yes, I believe you," he whispered.

"Good, then. You understand. And believe me when I say I wouldn't mind the opportunity; I've been holding back where you're concerned for far too long." I kissed him on the cheek, got up and walked away, heels clicking on the hospital floors.

To his credit, Jack was true to his word, though may not have been if he hadn't seen me early on in his unraveling. He and Renee ended up living together for about five months after he got out of the hospital. One day I walked up to their house to find Jack sitting on their porch, rocking back and forth with his arms in a certain position that belied the onset of his mental disease. As I walked up the front path, he looked up and saw me, and we had a moment of silence wherein I knew he remembered my threat and rightfully believed it still to be true. The next day he was gone. He left Renee no explanation, though I told her why he'd probably left, minus my threat. She never heard from him again.

Until this week, apparently. Now she is considering allowing him back into her life. I personally don't care either way, Renee can do what she wants. My threat still stands, and to be honest I am rather looking forward to the release of knocking off Jack since my pool of executives is getting a little thin and I am trying to wean myself off the whole activity anyway. I just let her talk for a while, still about him, and tune out, pleasant expressions and interested comments on autopilot while I chain-smoke and think of other things.

21.

I have a dildo called the *G Freak Blue Jelly Dong*. It's amazing. It's got a suction cup on the end so you can attach it to all sorts of interesting surfaces, making it even more fun. Sometimes I hang it on the door of my refrigerator, at just the right height, and torture myself walking by it all day, getting hotter and hotter, knowing how simple it would be to just drop my panties and...

Lately I've been indulging in my love of exhibition. Inheriting a nearly all-glass condo can do that to a person. Instead of going out to bars all the time, picking up strangers, having orgies and increasing my risk of getting HIV or some other disgusting STD, I've instead been putting on solo performances for my dozens of close-by neighbours. Really, there's nothing better than lathering myself up in a nice hot bath and walking through my condo with all the lights on and none of the blinds down. To take my *G Freak* and settle in for a long, loud session in my tunnel-like hot-tub on the edge of my terrace with all the floodlights on. To sit in the middle of the bed, on my knees, spread eagle, sitting tall, with a pair of binoculars around my neck, acting as though I'm looking out at the view, then swing around and "finding" someone staring at me, then pretending they're making me hot, discovering the *G Freak* as though by accident tangled in the sheets and pressing its twisted tip against me while still in eye contact through my binoculars with my Peeping Tom.

It helps pass the time.

I made a pact with myself after my first murder that I would never allow myself to lose control of it. I never want to be someone who feels compelled to commit acts of murder, who has given in to such a thing. There are two sides to every addiction: the natural propensity to be attracted to the object or activity at hand and the inability to break a habit one freely chose to enter into. I get urges, for sure, but I feel as though they are healthy emotionally-replacing reactions to the injustices I see in the world, since I have no other outlet. I want to live in a world without greedy, selfish motherfuckers who are so lucky to have been born with a compass I do not possess, who are so lucky to be able to enjoy things I can never enjoy, like love, compassion, sadness, sympathy, grief – all the things that make human nature rich and worthwhile; I will not watch them thoughtlessly take all these things for granted and cast them aside for a few material pleasures that will make no mark upon their importance in history.

I also have no intention of ever being caught. So far, no one has ever suspected one of my killings to be a murder; they have all been ruled suicides. I am meticulous about not leaving behind any evidence at a crime scene, at not killing anyone wearing the same coloured wig or looking like the same person at all. I know what you're thinking, serial killers want to have people know what they've done, that they want their killings to have a legacy, to mean something, to satisfy some need. Well, first of all, fuck you, what the hell do you know about being a serial killer? And second of all, everyone will know what I've done. *That's what this book is for.* I don't need to destroy myself and spend the rest of my life in prison so that people get the point a few years earlier. No, my point will be made. I'm just not going to get messy doing it.

Messy is something I avoid at all costs in my killings as well. I guess it's like someone who smokes cocaine and considers the habit to be in control, yet who would consider themselves out of control if they were to ever snort it. It's like that with killing, too. If I push someone off of a ledge or poison them with Drano, it is part of a larger act, a philosophy, a politic; it's me expressing my identity. But if I start letting myself get too fascinated with the scene, the death itself, well, I consider that trouble. Then it's just a matter of time until you get caught. And, fun or not, it's kind of gross when the fun is over. I don't need to start wasting time cutting off limbs, cutting open torsos, removing organs, indulging in my curiosity about what they taste like, what they feel like. I don't need to keep fingers or toes as souvenirs. I don't need to get sloppy and start indulging in activities that make me accidentally leave DNA or fibres at the scene. I don't need to waste time and energy and heighten the chances of me being caught by putting myself in a situation where I have to dispose of a body or clean a large space or come up with an alibi. Eating people and slicing them to pieces is not a philosophy, it's a sickness. Just like cutting, or bulimia, or drinking.

So, when I start to feel that same feeling that comes upon me when I crave a cigarette, when I feel the urge rise to kill while recognizing there is no reason, no logic, behind it, I try to curb it by putting on a *G Freak* sex show for my neighbours.

As I said, it helps pass the time.

22.

I'm sitting on the terrace one late afternoon, soaking up some sunlight, when I suddenly realize that I miss Paul. I sit up bolt-straight; this may be the first time in my entire life where I acutely, *acutely*, feel something. What's this like, my brain is scrambling to register. I was lying there thinking about nothing in particular, when a series of images flashed through my brain, Paul and I in different conversations, sitting together here where I am living now, picking out furniture, making meals, watching television, getting ready for the theatre, waking up together... Then a rush of nauseous tingling filled my abdomen and a phantom pain, a tickle, something deeply internal, a tumour maybe, suddenly and completely filled my chest, forcing my eyes to fill with tears, my heart to race and a sound escape my lips. A ... sob.

The moment I identify it, it's gone. Like a dream that is vivid the second you wake up but slips away from your grasp before your very eyes, never to be recalled. It was like that. I can repeat the symptoms of the experience like I can repeat the symptoms of all the human experiences I have imitated over the years, but it's to no avail for I cannot conjure up the *feeling* again. I'm not sure I want to, me, who loves control, who plans and carefully executes each move I make, I don't think I want to know what it's like to be motivated by emotion. No, no, no...

I get up, run across the room to my closet, inside, picking clothes off of hangers trying to find a pair of pants and top in my frenzy to get out of these walls, away from what just happened. I get dressed and pull on the cute white tennis shoes I bought last week, grab Gable and run out the door, almost forgetting my keys. We go downstairs, I smile and wave at the doorman as he comments on me going out so casually while we dash out of the building, into the street, into reality, a reality that is cold, familiar and now suddenly confusing.

God, I wish I could leave the city. I wish I could get out. I know full well I can, but then I stop. Where would I go anyway? What would I do? How would I fill my days if I weren't in the city, stalking, hunting my prey, ridding the world of those who can't appreciate what they have? I feel I need to get away but I simply don't know where to go. I could go to Europe, take a plane ride, but what then? The world is all the same now, all one big cookie cutter town, placed again and again across the decimated landscape. People looking the same, acting the same, dressing the same, eating the same foods and living in the same sorts of buildings. Big box stores and corporate labels, plastered everywhere, advertising blotting out the stars, industry clogging the air. No, if you're on this planet, are a stranger to nature and prefer not to fly, Toronto's as good a place as any.

It's been two months since I inherited Paul's money. I kept my old house as a rental property, hired a property manager to run it, rented it out. I have really no reason to stay in the city any longer, except for Renee, who I think I should stick around for since she asked for my advice concerning Jack's return and may need it again. Meaning, I may need to get rid of him for her. The only other reason I have to stay in the city is what I already said; I have nowhere else to go and nothing else to do. What should I do next? I think it's time to plan my strategy. Politics, maybe. Perhaps I should get my law degree. I walk the streets, chain-smoking, the afternoon fading into evening, the lights coming on around me as the city changes casts and prepares for its second act of the day.

The knot that has been tightening in my stomach for the past hour has spread out slightly, caught the rhythm of a long standing pain just under my ribs and started to radiate outwards, in turn catching onto the spindly out-reaches of a common muscle which constantly hurts just behind my shoulder, causing the overall pain my body is experiencing to be too much to be ignored any further. I have to sit down.

I may as well admit the real thing on my mind. I'm not walking the streets in some angst about what I'm going to be when I grow up. I simply and honestly do not care, though my future looks blank and that does make me feel a certain anxiety. What I'm worried about is what happened on the terrace. I'm worried because of the glimpse of what I'm remembering as a bout of emotion, because of what it means. I'm worried because if it means what I think it means my world will come crumbling down around me. In my wildest nightmares I never even thought this might become a possibility.

My leg is asleep. I light a cigarette.

What will become of me if I start feeling emotions? Missing Paul is just step away from regretting he's dead, you know. Regretting Paul is dead is just step away from regretting all of them are dead. I'm a fucking ethical person, goddamn it, I make choices based on logic, and justice, and ethics, and I did not count on the possibility of having to take fucking emotions into account! I am just the sort of person where if I began to feel remorse for the murders I've committed, I'd turn myself in, just out of respect for not only the dead (I can't believe I just thought that), but out of my respect for the systems humans have created to keep their functioning members, which I would then be, in line.

I'm starting to hyperventilate a little. I do not want to experience firsthand some of the sentences I've read about, namely, "being eaten alive by guilt", which sounds pretty damn close to "rotting to death in prison", another thing I don't want to experience. No, no, if I had to contemplate the enormity of the human monster I am I would go insane, completely insane; I would go insane and be caught.

I go to light another cigarette and think better of it. Then I look down, my hands halfway finished putting the smoke back in the pack. What the hell am I doing? I almost scream. I don't think I have ever put a cigarette away in my life, much less "thought better" of it. I feel like I'm having a mental breakdown. I want to curl up on the bench I'm sitting on and try to obliterate the world. The only thing I *don't* want to do is kill. A little ball of panic has risen in my throat and I know I cannot let it win.

I am so nervous; the pain is threatening to take me down. I have to get back in control. Gritting my teeth every time I land, my muscles and organs screaming in fiery protest until they realize I don't mean to appease them, I spring into a sprint and run as fast as I can for about ten minutes until I find myself, exhausted, back in front of my building, and go back upstairs.

I pour myself a glass of Port and take three Valiums. Forty-five minutes later a four-alarm fire couldn't have roused me.

23.

It's been a week since that day, Emotion day. I've been fairly busy since then; had a few meetings with colleagues of mine who heard I'm free agent and want to discuss me working with them on a consulting basis, went to two of the four board meetings that Paul left me to, bought a new car and almost bought a sailboat. I don't know anything about sailing but the boat was really interesting, really big. I still may, this summer. I'd have to hire some sort of crew, though, and that's what I balk at.

I haven't felt a thing since that day. Not one thing. Just to be sure I went out and electrocuted some little Internet prick I met at a martini bar a night or two later, and it went off without a hitch. It was just a fluke, like shitting blood for no reason. It was a product of stress.

It may sound weird, but that experience has taught me how much I like myself the way I am. I put a lot of hard work and energy into being such a successfully functional sociopath, into being such a meticulously careful serial killer, into carefully forming the best identity someone with my challenges and talents could form in a world of humans who follow the moral codes they follow. I don't want to lose who I am anymore than anyone else. If any of you woke up one day and realized you had lost the ability to feel anything – love for your spouse, family, children, empathy for your favourite television shows, the ability to cry at weddings, the ability to mourn your dead – you'd think something was wrong with you. Well, me too – I'd feel as though I'd lost my mind if I suddenly had to start dealing with feelings I was in no way trained or equipped to deal with. All the play-acting in the world can't get you ready for that anymore than it can get you ready for amputation.

I decide to kill an hour this afternoon and go to the Mackenzie House museum down by the Canon Theatre. I love that museum; I haven't been in years but it looks and smells the way I remember it, though the staff looks younger. Volunteers. I raise my eyebrow. Maybe I should do more volunteering, I reflect, I certainly do have the time. I haven't done that since I used to visit people at the hospital. I could do anything, now, really.

I am the only one on the tour, which is hosted by a tiny, charming old woman who seems to know everything there is to know about William Lyon Mackenzie and his life. She tells me about his time running his newspaper, his failed attempt to lead a coup during a Canadian winter, the bounty on his head, the kindness shown him by people who offered him a place to stay when he was on the run, then who raised the money for him and his family to move into the little house here on Bond Street. She takes me from room to room, giving me the time and silence to admire the furnishings, most of which are not original to the house, she tells me. I stare for some time at the oil paintings of the Kings which hang on the wall on either side of the fireplace in the living room, trying to discern from their blank expressions and old-fashioned clothing how old they might have been when they posed for them, but I give up in frustration.

This museum is particularly nice, if you're into old Canadian heritage houses, because it still has functioning gas lighting fixtures, lending an extra charm to the experience and allowing fanciful people such as myself even more upon which to escape temporarily into a world so thoroughly expunged from our experience. I am also very fond of the old tradition of the full brick oven and kitchen in the basement, with the deep, full windows letting light in, with the extra insulation against the fury of the winter months, where coziness of body can imitate coziness of spirit and even I could be content.

Maybe I'll buy an old heritage house in the country somewhere. Live the rest of my life out in a fantasy world. If only I thought I could handle the upkeep, I curse that I'm such an urbanized brat…

24.

It's only going to get worse, Gable tells me. *Bit by bit, as your psyche breaks down, you're going to have more and more of those days of emotions, until it drowns you, strangles you, kills you. Then you will make a mistake, a big mistake, and you will end up in an insane asylum for the rest of your life, strapped to a bed, drugged and abused by hospital staff who not only don't give a shit about you, but know everything you've done and think you deserve to die. They will torture you until you can't take it anymore, but there will be nothing you can do about it.*

"Never!" I say out loud. "I'm not going to get caught. I've quit, I've quit killing and I'm getting out of town. I can more than control myself. If they haven't caught me thus far they're not going to catch me. No one suspects me for anything, not one murder, not even the explosion. For a cute dog you sure can be a bit of a fear monger." I pat him on the head.

Just telling it like it is, Gable responds. *You can sit there with your head up your ass all you want but someone's already onto you, you know it, you can feel it. That's why you feel the pressure to leave. That and because you know you're not in control. You just like to hear yourself talk.*

"Shut up," I say, putting out my cigarette. I get up out of the leather armchair and go upstairs where I strip down naked and take longer than I need to find my workout clothes. I put on a sports bra and pair of shorts, put on some socks and lace up my runners and go downstairs to the little gym.

First I spend a half hour on the treadmill and then I spend another half hour working out the rest of my body. Gable follows me in but I point at the door and say, "Out!" and he dutifully turns and leaves. I put on some music, *The Slip*, and work out to that. Then I go back upstairs, sweating and glistening, and strip back down, grab a towel, open the patio door, turn on all the lights and walk slowly to the other end to the hot tub. Reaching into the bar fridge beside it, I take out a chilled glass and mix myself a quick vodka tonic before sinking my body into the tub. I reach beside me and find a cigarette case, fully stocked. I take one out and light it.

Presently Gable comes out across the patio and puts his head on the side of the tub. *I'm sorry I pissed you off,* he says contritely.

"No problem, buddy."

25.

This past year the downtown core went wireless; from the Lakefront to Bloor, from Church to Spadina; you can just turn on your laptop and magically be connected to the Internet (if you have an existing wireless account). Toronto did this to remain technologically competitive to other cities which have recently done this same thing, like San Francisco and Chicago. If there was any protest to making this happen, it wasn't reported, certainly not with the fanfare and attention that the merits of this decision, of this new plan, were getting from the local media. After all, who doesn't want to be online, all the time, and for a limited time at no cost?

If you were paying attention over the past year, you would have noticed these funny, shorter-than-usual, flat-faced antennas springing up on the tops of virtually every building on every main street corner in the core, all bouncing our Internet and cell phone signals off of each other in an effort to provide us with reception at any given moment and our service providers with profit. Of course, the reality is that Rogers is still incapable of providing a signal in the middle of the day on the corner of Yonge and King Streets on a regular basis, but this is what they sell us in their advertising. Service: second to none. Indeed.

No one seems to talk much about the radiation. Only in passing really. If you try to engage someone in a serious conversation on the matter, I'm always a little surprised to see just how much fear is present, lurking just below the surface, on this scary and little-understood phenomenon. When you start thinking about it and the enormity of it hits you, it's hard to turn it off again.

Go, search on Google, all the people who have gotten brain tumors and know in their heart of hearts it was for talking for 1200 minutes a month on those gargantuan old Motorola's from the late 80's to the mid 90's. Look at all the people still experiencing this; people, sensitive enough to the radiation that they can feel it when the phone is on and pressed against their heads, getting brain tumors just above the ear on the side they hold the phone, right where the antenna comes out and the signal is being transmitted from the tower. Look at the rise of cases of testicular cancer in young men, men who inherently walk around all day long with their cell phones in their jeans' front pocket. The rise in breast cancer where women are encouraged to always have their cell phone in their breast pocket, or shoulder bag which they hold up in their armpit. Look at the people complaining of a syndrome related to these transmission towers where they experience increased and chronic body pain, muscle weakness, headaches, dizziness and being generally unwell.

You can't look. As soon as you do, you realize you're swimming in it. It's not a matter of giving up your cell phone.

Even before the wireless grid was unveiled in Toronto, you could open up your wireless enabled laptop anywhere downtown and find five or six wireless networks available for you to connect to. If you talk on a cordless phone you can often pick up other people's signals in the same neighbourhood and eavesdrop on their calls. If you look around you at any given moment nowadays, almost everyone you see will have an activated cell phone, blackberry, iPod, laptop, or video game somewhere on their person. You can't get away from it; the invisible poison rays of radiation are bouncing off and around and through you every minute of every day you spend in a first world urban setting in our modern society. The unnatural light and heat of these devices is bombarding you with additional and different radiation. The way our normal physiology unfolds is being compromised by all of this and it's showing up in the health of our people.

There is a justice issue involved in the nightmare of systematic radiation poison we are facing here in our cities. The first problem is exactly who the hardest hit victims are. They are not, as you might initially imagine, the people indulging in the activities that require the constant bombardment of radiation to begin with. If you look at a map of downtown Toronto and square off the grid, you will see who really lives within it.

On the eastern border: Church Street. Densely populated, yes, but not by a majority of Internet savvy, technology-dependent, wireless junkies. More like heroin junkies. Low-income workers, mostly living and working within the grid in our service industries. Students of programs at Ryerson, George Brown and other schools in the area. Children. The Gay-bourhood.

The north border: Bloor Street from Church to Spadina. Not so many people living in this area. The majority who are here all the time are students, homeless people and condo owners. Working in the area, corporate, retail, service and several high end and medium run hotels.

The western border: Spadina Avenue. Runs south down through Chinatown. Hundreds of thousands of immigrants, market workers, construction, students, artists and social services all operating out of this area, often never leaving the neighbourhood. Needing email access, perhaps, but not immediate wireless access 24 hours a day.

And the south border: the Lakefront. Besides the hundreds of homeless people affected, the most of the people who actually live in this area are now the ones requiring this change in city operations, this constant access to wireless networks. But there are still thousands more in this incredibly densely populated city who have no idea what they're living in.

The point is, they don't have a choice. My condo is on the border of the grid, not technically in it, but close enough I still get all the signals. I'm covered in radio waves, every night, every day. I personally do not care, I am fucked anyway, I know this, but others do care and in the society we've structured, if we are not to be hypocrites, they deserve to have the choice about whether or not they live and work in an environment that is saturating them in radiation.

I remember when cell phones first became really affordable and really accessible in Canada. It was the Christmas of 1995 and Cantel (purchased by AT&T Canada, and then by Rogers Wireless) was offering the *Amigo*, a "compact" new cell phone that came preprogrammed and cost only $20 a month. I bought one for myself and for my parents. I gave up using my home phone and because of the novelty of it, I talked on it as often as possible. We were encouraged to; that's what the companies said to do. I was already twenty at the time, and over the next few years I began to become curious when I noticed how many teenagers were getting cell phones. I had thought it was common knowledge that the radiation emitted from cell phones was closer to microwaves than radio waves and had the ability to penetrate almost four inches into an adult's skull, with unknown effects on children who are still growing; *Scientific American* had had an article on the topic back in 1999 already. I began to comment to people how unfortunate it was going to be for themselves and their children ten or twenty years later when everyone had cancer, but people laughed as though I was making a joke. I never make jokes.

So here we are again. Another piece of shit to add to the pile. One school of thought denying the dangerous effects of exposure to this type of radiation and another demonstrating them. Just like global warming. Just like all the chemicals in our food and household products. Just like with our pharmaceuticals. And we act like we're not falling apart. Like we don't need a nice, big, eye opener.

26.

This morning the headline on the front page of the Toronto Star read, "Police rule out Terrorism in Toronto Harbour Ship Explosion" with the subheading, "believe the work of one person; checking Internet 'blacklist' for suspects".

My stomach starts to flutter. This is an unfortunate turn of events. After ten years of successfully dodging any suspicion whatsoever, I know that this time I will at least be subjected to one if not more interviews with the police as they try to figure out who could have caused the ship to explode that night in August. I cannot foresee a way I would end up as a final suspect, but the fact of my inheritance alone will make them look at me more than once. Curse you Paul, you're laughing down there in hell, aren't you, you sorry, sorry, sore loser?

What is really disheartening is that the authorities immediately suspected terrorism in this situation, and *then*, upon deciding the act was committed to kill a particular group of people and send ribbons of fear through those who remained, now define it as *not* being terrorism. Of course it was terrorism! Or, does that only apply when the terrorist is brown-skinned and Islamic now? Or a member of a domestic anti-government militia?

My, we have such a narrow view of things these days.

There is a law in Toronto prohibiting buildings along the waterfront from exceeding a certain height. This is to maintain a certain look for the city, and to ensure that a lucky few don't scoop up the good views and leave the rest of the city behind a wall of metal and glass. In the 1980s, if you drove down the Gardner Expressway, you would have noticed that the condos weren't much taller than the expressway itself, and that from a good vantage point anywhere between Front Street and Bloor Street you still had a clear view of the lake.

One day, a developer bought up some land on the waterfront and decided to make a magical new, modern, crystal tower of condos that he could sell to the nouveau-riche. It soon became apparent this developer was building with no regard to the height restrictions imposed by city law, which inspired others like him to buy up more of this lucrative property and begin their own development projects. A court case sprang up to determine whether or not these condos were breaking the zoning laws and should continue being built. But the developers were smart and they were motivated by visions of dollar signs. They knew their lawyers could stop up court proceedings for years. No injunction was brought against continued construction *during* the court case because those types of injunctions are usually suggested by developers whose business interests might be bruised. So as the case dragged, the condos kept going up. More and more went up. They sold every unit. Now the building and land was not technically owned by the developer being charged. The project was complete; he had sold and profited. The court wasn't going to force hundreds of people to give up their investments and their homes and tear down a building so some jerk in a crappy rental on Bloor Street could see a sliver of lake, now were they? Of course not. So the law still stands, no condos over a certain height and far above it, the condos still stand.

Or how about the "disarmament" of nuclear nations? Seems to be going really well, doesn't it? Nukes lost, nukes sold, nukes made, nukes hidden, nukes tested, nukes *used* – that's what we get under the international guise of disarming ourselves. The average person has absolutely no idea how much radioactive waste and its effects are floating around in our atmosphere from our continued obsession with such a dangerous weapon. The U.S., passing laws condemning "terrorists" for what they've done has, as the only nation to ever be officially convicted as a terrorist state, opened Guantanamo Bay, they kill, they torture, they rape, they destroy and they impose their very faulty and barely manageable "beliefs" on others under the banner of "freedom".

Funny, Western Civilization has been the same since its inception. Its war-cries today in the case of "freeing" the civilians in Iraq and leading their country into "democracy" are no different than almost 200 years ago in 1812, where former U.S. President Thomas Jefferson referred to the conquest of defeating Canada as "a matter of marching". The Colonial American Imperialist, arrogant and selfish, thinking only of their petty ongoing disputes with the British Empire, took it upon themselves to declare war against Britain (see: declare war against Al Qaeda) and instead invade Canada (see: and instead invade Iraq). Under the caterwauling of being on a mission to "free the Loyalists from the rule of the British thumb", all the U.S. wanted to really do was not only displace a group of people they had already displaced not 30 years previous in the War of Independence, but just to gain more ground in North America. Manifest Destiny was, is and always will be the mainstay of American foreign policy and if you buy into the bullshit it's not, then they got you.

Say one thing, do another.

Fighting for freedom – it's such an arbitrary declaration. Humans grasp at the weakest things to justify their insatiable need to fight. Throughout the animal kingdom, no other species kills so randomly and for so little reason than does the human. Only when animal societies break down do we begin to see how abominable behaviour goes hand in hand with the dismantling of culture ritual. Only when they're on the brink and about to go over the edge do we see behaviours like indiscriminate destruction, killing for sport, raping of other animals. Only when balance is gone and hope is lost.

27.

The very act of being seen as evil intonates an extreme intelligence.

If you discover the village idiot has killed and dismembered a local girl, and as he is tried and convicted he, despite clearly enjoying this adventure, displays a lolling inability to comprehend what is going on around him, you would have a hard time truly thinking of that village idiot as "evil".

However, if you caught the parish priest in the same situation, and as he is tried and convicted he listens attentively to the proceedings, looking smug and laughing out loud when confronted with people's horror at what he has done, above the proceedings, seeming to know something the rest of us don't, amused, it's hard *not* to think of that person as "evil".

Basically, the way the cards are dealt, if you are stupid and psychotic you are just sick, but if you are smart and psychotic, you're pure evil.

Evil genius. Like a wily coyote.

28.

Osama Bin Laden had a crush on Whitney Houston, so much so that he was purportedly willing to "break his colour rule" and make her one of his wives. Now, when you consider that Bin Laden must therefore have watched Western entertainment shows and read Western entertainment magazines, it becomes very difficult for a reasonable person to follow the logic between his knowledge of Whitney Houston, (not to mention the crush and talk of taking out a hit on her ex-husband Bobby Brown) and wanting to destroy the evil Western infidels. Furthermore, when it comes to liking celebrities for their talent and inspiration and sympathetic life, even following the goings-on of two strung-out has-beens like Houston and Brown shows a considerable lack of taste. Bin Laden followed Western culture and found what was most to his liking, what he was attracted to, were the shameless displays of a drug-addicted, broken, beaten woman who had lost everything and was very close to complete personal annihilation. Bin Laden is beginning to sound more and more as though he should trade in his headdress for a wife-beater and settle down in a nice one-roomed trailer on the outskirts of Tornadoville, U.S.A.

It looks like maybe Whitney Houston is on the mend. She has

finally dumped that wretch of a husband, Bobby Brown, and has apparently entered rehab. She used to be the emblem of a strong, independent woman and maybe she'll find her way back there someday. I guarantee you at that point she will no longer be so attractive as a new addition to Bin Laden's apparently impressively large harem of wives.

Reminds me of all the documentaries I've watched on the plural marriages of so many fringe-Mormons in Utah. Big, fat, bearded men running these families of inbred children, with several feeble, broken, gentle, smiling wives singing the praises of their wonderful husband and his ability to manage so many people, in this his difficult burden of a role as supreme ruler of his own little kingdom. Very often this big fat bearded piece of trash also runs his own church. I marvel that there is always a group of people to follow any crackpot who stands in front of them and declares his leadership.

There is absolutely nothing in Bin Laden's vision of the world he wants to be the leader of that speaks of any rights of freedoms for anyone outside of his hierarchy of chosen few. He incites the anger and energy of others by wresting support from their near-broken spirits, manipulating the pain they're going through and urging them to battle with promises of annihilating an "enemy" to free them from their miserable lives. This is much the same rhetoric used by the U.S. in rousing support for the War on Terrorism.

The truth is, the actual sides in this war, the U.S. Administration vs. the Jihadists, are both oppressive, dictatorial governing bodies who care little about the world or the people in it outside of how it directly benefits them. These two groups are two sides of the same coin.

As *The Who* so wisely said, "Meet the new boss, same as the old boss."

29.

I was recently visiting my family and helping them clean out the basement, where they had accrued decades and generations of material possessions.

Much of it they were sorting to put in an auction and those of us who showed up to help were given permission to take whatever they fancied. I considered it a great stroke of luck that I came upon an old camera bought by my grandfather long before I was born. It was a Kodak Retina II from circa 1958 and it was beautiful. It came in the original case, with all the original accompanying documentation, and two additional, expensive-looking bayonet-mount lenses, a wide angle and a telephoto.

Today for the first time since picking it up months ago, before the explosion, I take the camera out of the case. I have no idea what to do with it. Despite my history and experience in New Media, I don't know how to use a manual camera. Digital, fine, but film? It is a beautiful piece of equipment though, and I have nothing else to do, so I decide it is time to figure out how to use it.

I go down to Henry's and sweet-talk some young boy into showing me how to use the camera. Turns out, like most things in this world that people attach ego to and talk about like it's so complicated, it is pretty easy to pick up. A half an hour later, loaded with film, I go out on the town.

Turns out, I'm not half bad. I have a good sense of space and composition. The first few rolls of film I get developed, breathlessly excited like a child, come out beautifully. The colours pop, the lines are crisp, clean; they're very attractive.

Soon enough, though, it's too cold to take pictures outside. My fingers are freezing off and I'm losing focus due to shaking so hard. I go back to Henry's and buy a tripod and one of those little balloon things you trigger the shutter with from a distance, and go off determined to spend the winter photographing indoors. I realize, too, that it doesn't take much more practice to figure out how to develop my own photos, since I have the space and the time and Henry's seems to have the book and the equipment. I load up and go home to set up my new darkroom. Black and white is fine by me. I learned in Internetland how to colorize black and white film on the computer, so I am well able to add colour if I need to.

I spend the next couple of days photographing the view from my bedroom. I take many, many pictures of the hallowed area of water where the boat sank, my trophy, and develop them without trouble in my new darkroom.

In one of the photos I swear I can see the ghostly figures of men in suits just under the surface of the water. It's about as clear as a ghost is superimposed over a photograph on an episode of Montel Williams, about as clear as the face of the Virgin mother in a Mexican tortilla shell. Still, it's troubling, it makes my skin crawl. I scan it into my computer and play with the levels a little, bringing up the starkness of the blacks and the whites, sharpening the edges, softening the grain, and I print it out at 11x17 and hang it on my living room wall, right across from where I sit whenever I entertain people at my apartment.

I am sitting and staring at this photograph when my telephone rings and my doorman informs me Renee is here to visit. I tell him to send her up. I unlock the door so she can come right in.

A quick up and down of her when she enters the apartment reveals no scars or bruises. Jack has not started beating her yet. I am almost disappointed. It's starting to form in my head that I would like him to be the last, the last before I go, maybe take my own dive off the balcony, fly away to kingdom come.

Renee actually impresses me by telling me she is simply beginning to tire of Jack and all of his problems. Exciting though they were at twenty-two, now in her thirties she finds she's not so willing to be fascinated by his boring griping. He's on his meds and still wants to be a musician, but the meds have taken the edge off of his talent, it's just flat now, nothing spectacular and nothing standing out. She knows he's not going to make it, and she can't help but be a little embarrassed now as she regards him as behaving age-inappropriately, like so many aging rockers who can't let go of their youth. She had been letting him stay with her at the studio, but she has decided to tell him he has to leave. Being the sweet girl she is, because in no way does he deserve it, she even arranges for him a place to live. Renee is positive she is making the right decision and is looking forward to moving on from Jack once and for all.

I have a feeling he isn't going to take it so easily.

30.

I don't even know where I am. I'm looking around but all I see are lights. I went out earlier this evening to a bar after taking about two grams of mushrooms. I am wearing a black wig with shoulder-length curly hair, fastened carefully, electric blue contact lenses with heavy black make-up, dark lips enhanced to almost twice their size, shiny black stockings, knee-high leather boots, black silky minidress with long gloves.

I remember at least five martinis, absolutely. Meeting two, or maybe four, big burly men my own age, all sanded and coifed and tanned to perfection, one of whom I have had business dealings with before but who of course didn't recognize me. Dancing for hours on end with my new boyfriends, drinking with them, making out with at least two of them on the corner sofa of the club we were in.

Going back to a warehouse owned by one of them. Pretty sure they're all going to die. Having a fantastic threesome (foursome?) and falling asleep in a tangle of limbs and soft skin. Okay, I know where I am now. I woke up in the middle of the night feeling horribly ill, crawled off to the bathroom and spent the next several hours throwing up and passing out on the floor, which is where I lay still. Standing up shakily, I take a robe off the back of the door and go back out, a little worried I lost my mind and killed them all under the influence after leaving so much DNA at the scene. I breathe a sigh of relief as I realize they are all still sleeping peacefully. I gather my things together as quickly as possible and quietly leave the apartment, catch a cab and going home.

The whole evening didn't go as planned. There had been a

particular person I had been hoping to run into at that bar, the CEO of a large charity who was profiting fiercely off of the good-will of others. However, he never showed up and the rest is history.

For the best, really. I'm just not sure what's been happening to me lately. Ever since the day of Emotion, I feel like I've lost a little bit of the titanium grip of control I had hitherto had over my life. It used to be that when I thought something, that's what I thought; when I decided something, the decision was made. If I set forth to be a good businessperson, I was, and if I set out to be a moral and ethical person, I was, and if thought I should give something up, I did, and if I thought I should change something, it was changed.

Lately, though, it hasn't been that way. I find one minute I'm thinking one thing and the next it's completely different. At least five times in these pages alone, and millions of times in my own head, I have said I need to stop killing. I have said it was over with the boat. I have said I won't be doing that anymore. I have suggested I just might not find it interesting anymore. And yet within these same pages I've admitted to killing, already, at least three more people. I have admitted a failed attempt to find someone who didn't show up.

And in that, I have changed my MO. It's morphing, slowly. What I don't understand is what is changing and why.

I am stepping back and regarding it logically. I used to be absolutely, completely, feeling-free. I had no passion. Everything I did was calculated. Everything I did was done to please me, and to please a structure of society I admired.

This guy, this guy I missed last night, he's not in Internetland. I've never even met him before. I read about him in the newspaper, and I know of him through some of my associates. He is a terrible person, but I do not know firsthand of the atrocities he has committed, I am convicting him of that simply by his adherence to a stereotype that has sprung up around my victims. When I think of him, and anyone like him, bile rises in my throat and I'm reminded, though not thoroughly, of that day I missed Paul. I am angry but not in an emotionless sort of way; I am angry in a way that I don't want to be angry and I want it gone, whether by ridding the world of this man, or making nice with him. These subtle changes in my personality are disturbing, to say the least.

Again, I feel the urge to go, to disappear.

31.

I have often wondered what it would be like to live in a society that actually prepared people for death. It would change everything, right down to how our buildings look, I think. It would change the way people think, act and treat each other. It would change the way business is done. It would even change how I function, because "death" would not have the same vision or experience or consequence as it does now.

What if we were taught to actually accept our deaths? In this culture, to accept your death one moment before a doctor tells you there is absolutely nothing else that can be done is tantamount to suicide. We don't *accept* death, we fight death, we beat death, we conquer death – these are the stories we tell ourselves.

The medical establishment has gained enormous ground during the course of my lifetime alone. If Terry Fox, who ran right past my family's car one day somewhere near Thunder Bay with an amputated leg to raise awareness about cancer but died before getting across Canada, had been diagnosed today, it is likely he not only would not have died, he probably also would have been able to keep his leg. We can cut people open and replace parts with other parts and take incredibly detailed moving pictures of the insides of our bodies and diagnose rare illnesses and much of the time, cure the patient of their ailments or at the very least, lessen the suffering.

Science is a fascinating area. If we continue looking, humans will eventually completely decode the human genome, we will successfully clone other people, we will be able to cheat death in many interesting other ways. We will figure the whole thing out if you give us enough time and enough access to information. *We split the goddamn atom!* Which is precisely my point.

People seem to ignore the very large, very fuzzy line about where science for science stops and science for rule starts. Let me explain. That's fucking great, great!, that we can split the atom and use that to kill shitloads of people. Excellent. It's great we can cut people open and we can fix them by sewing them up and taking stuff out and replacing things with other things, animal or mechanical. Wonderful news. From the point of view of science, these are great accomplishments. If we could graft the head of a pigeon onto the body of a tarantula, that would also, from a scientific point of a view, be a great accomplishment.

In the case of the pigeon and the tarantula, it is easy to say "just because we can doesn't mean we have to" and a large group of people could have a very reasonable conversation about the good and bad points of being able to scientifically manufacture such a thing. Is the animal(s) in pain? Has its life been shortened? What will its role in nature be and how will that affect other animals in its environment? Is it ethical that we should do so? It's easy to have a conversation about the pros and cons of a scientific act when it is science for science's sake; but add in the money/power factor and this conversation becomes a lot more difficult to have. In the field of medicine these days, it's damn near impossible.

As soon as possible, which usually translates into one's mid-to-late twenties, we are encouraged to take serious concern for our health. Especially lately, with cases of cancer, obesity, diabetes and other diseases making daily headlines. Especially lately, where in every commercial break on television, before movies, during the news, in the newspaper, magazines, on the bus shelters, we're being constantly informed of drugs and conditions and diseases we should ask our doctors about. Especially now, after years of the War on Terror have slowly worn down everyone's nerves, where no one with an outward consciousness is able to ignore the very sorry state the world is in.

We go for physicals. We tout the benefits of "catching things in the early stages". We do what the doctors and the advertisements tell us; that they agree with each other, those doctors and advertisements, makes it all the easier. We worry. If you go on the Internet and look up any ailment, you will find hundreds and hundreds of people posting symptoms and experiences, looking to each other for support, terrified out of their minds, walking scared, trapped. I never look on the Internet for symptom relief. On the Internet, all roads lead to cancer.

In *this* society, if you are chasing phantom pains, being diagnosed and treated, paying great and constant attention to the state of your health, you are supported by the medical establishment. The more interesting your case is, the more they are interested in you. In this society if you are preoccupied with health concerns, you will always have a home here. We are trained from a very young age to fear the diseases out there that can get us, so a great deal more of us than you'd think have this on their minds a majority of the time.

And then, finally, wonder of wonders, something does go wrong. No one knows who will be stricken with what and when. But at some point you get to enter the system. Go to your doctor with symptom A. Get tested. Two weeks later, irregular results are returned, so you are sent to a specialist. If your doctor is very well connected, you get into a specialist in days, but if they're not, or if you're like so many who depend on clinics, it could take months. Go to specialist. Get tested. A week or two later, results are returned. Something is Wrong. You Need Treatment. Surgery and some drug therapy. Surgery is scheduled for one to six weeks later. Recovery is estimated at a week or so but in reality you don't really feel yourself for more like three or four months. Half a year has passed since you first went to your doctor, and this is a very, very good scenario. In reality it would be closer to a year, at least.

Let's say that's where it ends. You had a benign lump, or a curable infection. But if you're like most of the people I've observed in my careful analysis of human behaviour, you've been affected by this experience. Henceforth you are more aware of your body than those who have not had this experience. You and your naturally hyper-sensitive hypochondriac brethren, unfortunately make up the majority of our society today, because almost everyone over twenty-five has had some sort of medical scare, no matter how short-lived or safe, and no one in our medical establishment is going to make you feel very good about it. The worse you feel about it the more the *mental* health establishment benefits, and pharmaceuticals everywhere in between. We watch television shows that support this structure. *ER, House, Grey's Anatomy,* to name a few on this season, make medicine into this sort of holy game, where they routinely cure people who would likely not be cured in real life, where they just "cut out the cancer", where people get multiple unnecessary CTs and MRIs as the doctors delight in the challenge of diagnosis. This is how things work.

So, in the time between the illnesses, in the time before your demise, before the "fight" you're preparing for begins, humans all seem to live in a purgatorial state of worry and denial. Five, ten, twenty, fifty years, and worming around in the back of your mind is the knowledge, the memory, the vision, of what you will go through when your time comes and a lot of cosmic wheeling and dealing to ensure it doesn't come to that.

And then, the fight. You have… cancer. With a five year mortality rate. You "decide" to fight. You get the chemo, you get the radiation, you take the drugs, you do everything the doctors tell you to. They cut you open and remove the cancer. You're sick, you're frail, you're completely consumed by your illness and your treatment and your life effectively grinds to a halt while you fight to ensure it never grinds to a halt ever again. But… you die anyway. The cancer had a five year mortality rate, after all. Maybe it was just your time. Maybe there was some negligence from the doctors. Maybe your medical staff didn't advise you to treat the spiritual or environmental causes of your disease. Maybe you didn't "want" it enough. Who knows? All I know is that in the majority of people I've visited with this disease, this was their story.

Fight to the death. It's a mantra repeated around here far too often. The religious claim is that they have accepted death in that they have manufactured great stories about what they will meet when they pass through that final doorway, but of course no one does or ever has known for sure. They're all only theories and to believe in one wholeheartedly to the exception of any other idea is to be a fool. Believing you will go to heaven does not make you anymore prepared for death than believing you will go nowhere. It's just another tool of denial. It in no way changes how you act and think and feel within your *life*, and therefore about the face of death itself.

So what if we did live in a society where we were prepared for death? What if the five years described above were spent enjoying life? These are the questions I have for people, as I would neither be particularly upset about my own disease to begin with and have no problem facing death, it's certain aspects of *life* I am short on succeeding at. What if they never found out they had the cancer at all? In the first year of diagnosis and treatment I just described, that person already knew something was wrong with them and putting a face on that didn't change what they already knew, though it did satisfy the greedy minds of Medicine.

What if, after that first scare, the twenty years leading up to the eventual disease did not include a preoccupation with their health, consciously or subconsciously? What if it was so absent conversations didn't stop abruptly when someone mentions a disease such as cancer; what if it didn't show itself in how defensive people get because of their own experiences? What if people didn't "fight fight fight" til their death and just accepted it early on?

It wouldn't be the ultimate end, then. It would not be something to fear. It would not cause me to see it as the one best way to express myself. I would find the thing that was the ultimate end, the real death, the real punishment, like torture, was the spectre of death and nothing else; if people only realized that if they could cheat the fear of death they could cheat their attachment to the human body period, wouldn't become exactly the sort of people they've spent eternity acting the opposite of, they would not in fact lose their life much sooner than their bodies will actually perish.

I think though, if society cleaned up its act, if we learned to accept death and not spend more than half our lives trying to avoid it, a great number of people would be out of a job. A whole lot more people might be dead. Many may never have been born. The planet might not be burgeoning and burning and rotting. And I might have been whole.

32.

For the past ten years I have had a rule that once a month I will be kind to a stranger – really kind too, not just dropping a quarter in a cup but sitting down and listening to someone for a while. I actually quite dread this exercise, but I figure it helps keep me "in shape" so to speak, when it comes to acting normal. I figure someone like me, if they weren't like me, would probably do this on a regular basis without even thinking about it; they would have passion for it, a drive to be kind, they would experience it with all those emotions that make it easier to listen, to empathize. I approach it more like a teenager (almost all of whom, in my opinion, are temporary sociopaths), like a task I have to do and don't want to do and do only with the least actual interaction possible. I'm not out to change the world, just out to make sure I'm as healthy as I can be in it.

I don't perform this task by standing up and saying, "I'm going out now, to be kind to someone for a slightly extended period of time" and then go hunting. More like, if I come across someone and do a quick check and realize I haven't been kind in a month or so, I will take the time to do that, fifteen minutes in my increasingly less and less busy days.

I decide to go for lunch at one of my favourite low-end restaurants, Squirly's, who serves the most delicious butternut squash soup I have ever tasted, and I go to sit in the back area of the restaurant, the area you used to be able to smoke in, which you still can smoke in a little on a cold day if you open the back door and don't let anyone see you. I sit in the corner near the door and almost don't notice a girl lying one of the red leopard-print couches at a table across the room. I even recognize her: she used to live across the street from me when I had my townhouse and I would talk to her once in a while. She is, if I recall, a designer in my own industry. Right now she looks like maybe she is crying.

"Honey, are you okay?" I ask, approaching her. I can't remember her name. She looks up; she *has* been crying. She recognizes me and tries to smile.

"Oh hey! How are you? I haven't seen you in a long time!" she replies.

"Yes, I moved out of the neighbourhood, just had to come back for my favourite soup," I tell her. We chat for a couple of more seconds and then she asks if I want to join her. Since we are the only two people in this room and we know each other, it seems pretty stupid to not sit together.

The girl, whose name I recall suddenly was Hannah, starts to tell me what her problems are. As per my monthly rule, I attentively listen to her.

Hannah tells me about her disillusionment with the industry right now. She has been freelancing for most of the past ten years; she has an excellent portfolio, having done the creative for campaigns such as VW and Telus, and has the most diverse set of skills I've ever seen, especially at the senior level. Whenever she has a contract, she is highly acclaimed and winning awards and considered an excellent asset. Her contracts typically last three to six months, with much downtime in between.

It was the downtime that was upsetting her right now. Hannah tells me that before 9/11 she was able to land a new job within about a week of finishing an old one. This, despite that the industry was already beginning to go into a bit of a recession; it was just organized. If she saw a job posting on Workopolis or Media Job Search Canada's web sites and she was qualified for it, she knew that she would know whether or not she was hired for a job within a week or two, because the people hiring managed their own responsibilities well.

9/11 had a bigger effect on people's workmanship than it did on business itself, Hannah says. It gave people an industry that was all about working as little as possible for as long as possible, and allowed them to drag out very simple and important tasks for great lengths of time. It has snowballed until people now thoroughly believe it. I know exactly what she is talking about. I have had contractors bill me four to six hours a week just for them to check emails. I've had people routinely tell me a task that should take an hour of focused, steady work couldn't possibly be completed in less than a week. It's ridiculous what we have convinced ourselves we are, or rather are not, capable of.

Hannah's experience in job-hunting, which she has been doing approximately three times a year for close to a decade, is that what once took several days has gone from taking several weeks to several months. Today she is crying because she's finally letting go of the hopes at getting a job that she went to the interview for a month and a half ago, that she had initially applied to over three months before that, a job they had told her they had been "hiring" for for over six months. And this place was one of the three big television stations in Toronto, so one would assume they had their shit together.

It had gotten to the point that Hannah began to suspect she'd done something wrong; her portfolio or resume must not be up to par, she must have seriously offended someone along the way and gotten blacklisted. But then she comes across one of the few organized people still existing out there and has it reconfirmed that she is not lacking in skill or experience, but that the industry itself has slowed to a crawl in getting anything done. When she's working she witnesses this firsthand; at her last contract they were "desperate" for Project Managers (one of the simplest positions to staff in Internetland since they are mostly useless and do next to nothing) and by the time her *six month* contract was finished, they *still* hadn't hired anyone.

"How is this possible?" she asks me, her eyes filling with tears again. I try to ensure there is a suitably sympathetic expression on my face. "How can they expect you to be able to survive for months and months while they hum and haw and fuck around and can't even be bothered to do their shit properly? Why would anyone even *want* to work for someone like that? They prove to you before you even get an interview that they don't respect anyone but themselves. They expect you to jump when they snap their fingers. And what happens? I'll tell you what happens! They wait so long they lose all the good talent and they end up hiring some retarded, inept twit who's related to one of the executives and works for sub-par wages, and the whole industry continues to degrade! The more experience I have, the harder it is to find a job these days! This industry is being run by children!" She starts to sob again. "How is anyone supposed to survive?"

I try to say something comforting, like I've heard Renee do so many times. I also agree with her. I tell her how it was the same in my company, the one I just left; it was just a daily reminder of how pointless and useless the whole thing is. She seems grateful someone agrees with her.

I start drifting off a little; Hannah's story is reminding me of more injustices in the industry I had noticed but not had on my own list. I've rarely been out of work and have never worked in the Human Resources development, so the inability of those departments to do their jobs right goes largely over my head; I read reports and assumed the delays were inevitable, as I have never analyzed the numbers myself. I start wishing I had not yet resigned because this sort of behaviour was deplorable and the people allowing this happen, the people heralding these abysmal activities, should be punished, should be held accountable. I actually get Hannah to tell me the name of the person in charge of the hiring process at the television station she's been waiting on, and consider making myself available to him some evening in the near future.

We chat a while longer, I receive and eat my soup and we finally split up and go in our own directions with no plans to meet up ever again. I feel my good deed for the month has been accomplished and

I can concentrate on more pressing matters. I run a few errands, stop and buy an excellent sexy skirt and long piece of silk I plan to throw over a glass table to add some colour to the living room and I head back to my building on foot.

Outside the door to my lobby, I put out my cigarette and start pushing the revolving door, watching the concierge speaking with a man at the counter. He looks… official. I start to wish I hadn't come home yet; I can feel the paranoia surge inside me. I'm sure it's nobody. It's nothing.

I get in the lobby and start walking across the thick Arabian carpet towards the elevator. The concierge calls out to me and I turn around. He beckons me over and introduces me to the man, a Detective Gerald Beech. I smile at him as I would anyone I was receiving at the office.

He tells me he is investigating the explosion on the lake and is questioning anyone who was invited or who had any suspicious connection to any of the people killed. He tells me I'm an interesting person on both counts, because I narrowly missed being on that boat and because I inherited all of Paul's money and worldly possessions.

He asks me if I wouldn't mind if we went upstairs and talked for a few minutes so he could ask me some questions.

What can I do but agree.

PART 2

1.

I met Paul Schmidt at the first company I ever worked for in Toronto, where I was hired as a Project Manager and he was already working as a Web Programmer. It was about six months after 9/11 and I was experiencing a little bit of what Hannah told me about regarding finding a job. Just before my money ran out altogether, I got this Project Manager gig.

In Internetland, Project Manager has some funny connotations. It could mean a variety of things, and does, but there are an essential group of tasks that allow me to describe this role at a high level. If you work for a progressive, established company, being a Project Manager could be a successful and satisfying endeavour for a talented young Internetlandian. But more often than not, success as a Project Manager is based on gender; based on gender in a sick, deniable way that the new Big Boys will not admit to.

There is another role in Internetland which takes even further advantage of the "lesser sex", as the Big Boys clearly think of us, very close to being a Project Manager, but in the case of a woman, interchangeably called a Project Coordinator.

A Project Manager manages a project, which could be in itself many things. Once a client is signed on and has worked out what they want from your company, the Project Manager writes up the paperwork, plans the budget, creates the schedules and makes it so the designers and programmers deliver the project back on time and on budget. PMs don't have all the power in the world, they can't usually hire or fire someone, but they can make that happen; they also usually manage the client relationship (unless there is another functional role of Account Manager in there, which only occurs in some companies), acting as a conduit between the technically savvy and the technically ignorant. So, if you are a programmer or designer, the first person above you in hierarchy will be your Project Manager.

A Project Coordinator, on the other hand, is really just a glorified secretary. She (and in Internetland, it is almost always a she – the only two "he's" I've ever come across in this role have been incredibly gay or exceptionally inept) is the one who does all the *nasty* paperwork, all the irritating project tasks, like putting nice pieces of coloured paper on top of files, or cutting out labels, or updating endless rows of GANTT charts. She makes sure everyone has what they need supply-wise and that they understand the tasks set out before them. She is not considered to be a "boss" of any of the designers or developers; she is recognized as an "assistant" and is treated thusly.

At this job, where I met Paul, I was hired as a Project Manager. The ad I responded to was called Project Manager. In the interview and on my contract my position was referred to as Project Manager. But the reason they hired a rather attractive and youthful female to do the job was because they were *thinking* of the role as a Project Coordinator. In my case, it was a grievous error. I had been through this wringer before; my management skills were at a far higher level than they had any idea of – I was trained to manage departments of hundreds working on multi-million dollar projects, not the silly little one-off print jobs this department handled.

The head designer at this company sealed my fate by way of his attitude towards me. From the start he treated me like his own personal assistant. My role was to direct his work, to discipline him, to manage his projects, but he ignored my direction and instead consistently asked me to do things like get him coffee or pick up his papers from the printer when clients were around, undermining my authority and keeping me from doing my job properly. Everyone there saw this. People were embarrassed for me.

That was how I really got to know Paul. He asked me if I wanted to go for lunch one day and told me he had noticed what was going on and had seen it before. We spoke about the work we were doing there, mostly promotional design for print, but some integration into New Media, which was what Paul did.

Over the next few weeks, Paul and I began to hang out exclusively at work. We met for coffee in the morning, went to lunch and usually had drinks together after hours. He was an interesting man, big, soft looking, yet strong. He moved as though in slow motion, giving him the aura of being exceptionally gentle, but in reality he was a crass, judgmental, cutting sort of person if he didn't like what you were doing. He had no filter when it came to honesty. He spoke to people in ways that would be the demise of most, would cause most to lose respect, or be disciplined, or lose their jobs, but something about the combination of his attitude and his big, sweet, strong, white-man-ness just made people obey him and think he was very powerful. Paul had all the earmarks of a future leader in some capacity.

He also had all the earmarks of a closet misogynist. Beneath his gentle chivalry lay a deep-rooted belief that women were an inferior species, amusing and necessary but never to be considered equal in intellect, humour, or worth to a man. He was a knock-off of a previous generation of men who would have had grand dinner parties and retired to the smoking room in his velvet smoking jacket with his male counterparts after a meal to discuss politics and business and puff on a pipe while the women kept themselves busy making sure the men had everything they needed and gossiping about inane topics over their needlepoint.

Misogynists are interesting creatures from the point of view of a sociopath who is always looking for another sociopath to identify with. Misogynists are basically sociopaths when pertaining to women; they don't acknowledge or respect a woman's right to anything, although they may pretend to, and therefore they conduct themselves around women with only their own interests in mind, free of conscience. Racists are the same way. There is little difference between a misogynist's base attitude towards women and Israel's attitude toward Palestinians, or Iran's attitude toward Israelis.

So Paul was a heart-breaker. He had never had a relationship with one woman for longer than three months in his entire life, and was always "dating" a series of women to keep one from ever getting serious.

Something about the combination of his appearance and attitude made him extremely sexy, so he had no trouble getting what he wanted. After not too long, it became apparent he wanted me.

We had sex one night in the bathroom at the bar we had gone to after work, starting a sort of covert affair whereupon we met whenever we could without raising suspicion in the workplace. We did not spend time alone together outside of work, except for bars and other social events. Neither of us had any interest in a relationship, me especially. But I couldn't resist him. He was so hot for me. I would see him and he would tell me how he had jerked off already four or five times that day just so he could retain control while I was around, and even that didn't help him, and I really had no choice other than to rid the boy of his angst. After all.

My first experience with Paul lasted about eight months, the entire time I was working at that company, until I unwittingly removed a barrier in his career and he stepped all over my face in his scramble to position himself for it.

2.

I am sweating hard, having just spent the past half hour on the treadmill, and plan to go to the hot tub for a dip before getting dressed and going to my kickboxing class. I am very much enjoying the workout room that Paul (with my help) had put in the condo; it lets me work out whenever I want without having to bother with the gym anymore. While I was still an executive going to the gym was a pretty necessary part of my job, not only to look good, but also to fit in with my supposed peers; it was a great way to both keep an eye on fellow colleagues and do some of the networking and relationship building that was so necessary to my success in the company and the industry.

I have a great body. I am tall and shapely and super-strong. I am one of those women who are lucky enough to not get too much bulk when

I work out; therefore my arms are cut muscle and sinew, like Courtney Cox or Angelina Jolie. My stomach is also rock-solid, enough definition to be seriously attractive but not crossing the line to gross. Same goes for my ass and legs. I weigh in at my healthy range, albeit the very lowest end of that range, and I have pretty much zero body fat except for my C-cup breasts, which in the right outfit I can pass off as pseudo D's.

Now that I've quit the company, I keep working out, but without the focus on the social aspect of going to the gym, I am able to concentrate more on what I want out of the experience. I realized some time ago that it would be a good idea if I took a few self-defense courses, and after that I found I was very interested in pursuing another sport. I was going to take boxing, as I am a big fan of watching it, especially the wiry male featherweights, but I find that female boxers are just too beefy for my liking, and I wanted to keep myself looking pretty much the way I do now; lean and mean. I finally settled on kickboxing because it was the right mix of boxing and martial arts, and it more fully worked the entire body instead of focusing my strength on one area.

After all, I have a few dangerous habits, and I'd hate to be caught off-guard some night when I'm on the hunt and come across some asshole who either doesn't take the bait or finds within himself the wherewithal to realize what's about to happen to him and fights back. So far that hasn't been an issue, but one never knows.

I also keep in shape so that I can run – run far and long. Being in good shape puts a damper on my constant pain. I jog around the city whenever I can, whenever the air quality of this polluted cesspool is good enough for me to do so and not do more damage than good. When it's too smoggy, like it has been lately – looking out my window right now I can barely see the island, not to mention the condos less than half a kilometre away from me – I just use the treadmill in the workout room. This condo is really all anyone would ever need, except safe haven from prosecution if I were to be found out.

Perhaps when I finally do go away permanently, it will be on foot. A long walk, so to speak.

3.

There is a *Simpson's* episode where little Lisa Simpson is upset because the new talking Malibu Stacey doll (their version of *Barbie*) only says stereotypical chauvinistic things like, "Don't ask me, I'm just a girl!" and "Now let's forget our troubles with a big bowl of strawberry ice cream!" and "Thinking too much gives you wrinkles!" Lisa convinces her mother to take her on a tour of the Malibu Stacey factory so she can confront the corporate executives with the doll's sexist slogans. The person they get to meet, however, is a woman, an executive sent out to placate the little girl and talk her out of her accusations. She assures Lisa the doll is for fun and that there isn't any sexism intended in the phrases she speaks. The interview ends when a male executive opens a door that leads into a boardroom and says, "Hey Jiggles, grab a pad and back that gorgeous butt in here", to which the woman giggles and follows him, closing the door with a sensuous swing of her hips.

That corporate female stereotype does exist and she is an affront to justice and equality. A version of her, in fact, was the executive in charge of the department Paul and I worked in. She had managed to get herself into a position of power, but the position itself was not very important, overseen by yet another executive, and she was hardworking and sweet, but largely incompetent, always asking others for help, nervous to take the initiative, but fluent in the language of business, the condescension and pretension of being an executive in Internetland. At some point in her life, she thought she was making a great contribution, that she was breaking down barriers, but along the way she realized she could not break through the barriers of sexism and she chose the route so many "feminists" choose: imitation of the capitalist male. Which ended up translating into being suspicious of and easily threatened by other women, especially women who did not conform to this model.

So when I was having trouble with the head designer, being treated like his lackey, she saw this as the "hoops" all young women have to go through to progress up the corporate ladder. She thought I should be happy to have the title of Manager, period, and ignore being treated as an underling. It was her opinion that the head designer, a big-talking moron whose best designs were the ones he stole (a common occurrence), was more difficult to replace than me. And although she was his manager, she was uncertain of her ability to properly discipline a man who clearly thought himself to be above all women, with the full support of his industry, and so when I approached her with the problems, demanding the head designer be reprimanded for his behaviour which was inappropriate at the best of times, she refused.

Even Paul was surprised at her reaction; he personally thought that is how a woman should properly act, but his experience was that women were crazy and did what they wanted, no matter how ineffective and inappropriate and he felt sure that the head designer would be in some trouble, a nuisance really, for all it would ultimately affect him. He told me that it was really for the best, though, that if I were to continue to push the limits like this, to ask for better treatment than I deserved, I was going to lose my job and get blacklisted. Certainly not the first time I'd heard that.

Luckily for me, my boss had a bit of a coke habit. She thought she was discreet, but it was well known amongst the women on our floor that she routinely slipped into the bathroom to snort a line or two. Like a Hollywood cliché, she even kept the stuff in a little porcelain container around her neck, with a tiny little spoon attached to the inside of the lid.

On my way home one day, I walked by a head shop and exclaimed out loud in my good luck when I saw the *exact* same tiny porcelain container that my boss kept around her neck. I bought it immediately. With a wonderful idea forming in my head, I went and picked up a gram of coke from a dealer I knew. Then I went to another kind of dealer I know, someone I met years ago in Ottawa and by coincidence saw again in Toronto, someone I will not describe even in an anonymous memoir, from whom I purchased a small quantity of potassium cyanide powder. Then I went home to play chemistry set. The next day I followed my boss to the gym. She liked to go on off hours, during the middle of the workday, so that there were fewer people around. While she was in the pool I went to her locker, which I opened deftly having watched her spin her combination more than once in the past. I found her little hollow amulet, which I verified was indeed full of cocaine, and replaced it with my own. I hoped she waited to snort some until she got back to the office, so I could be a witness to it.

Well, she didn't. She waited until she was in her car, driving. When the first seizure hit her she drove through the plate-glass window of a Yorkville storefront, injuring a salesperson. She was pronounced dead at the scene. The police identified that the cocaine was cut with potassium cyanide, but the conclusion was drawn that this happened at the dealer level and she was an unwitting victim, as many people had witnessed her in possession of the porcelain container and everyone knows it's hard to get an addict to leave their drugs unattended. There was no investigation.

I didn't kill her to get her job, but it did occur to me that I was logically the next person in line for it. The only difference between myself and her was that it was clear I was not going to conduct myself in any way short of how the men did, and I knew that might force them to pause before automatically granting me the promotion. However, I wanted the promotion and put a bit of work into it.

I had written up the architectural framework for a CMS that could be run on a Flash engine, which at the time was a ground-breaking feat as most CMS systems ran on a very complicated back-end, forcing connectivity to a particular server, making functionality much heavier and less interactive, basically not the way of New Media. This idea also allowed a company to update a Flash web site; something that until now had been impossible under conventional methods by a non-technical person. In order to verify some of the technical requirements I was proposing, I ran a few things by Paul. We worked on one small portion of the proposal together, for which I gave him total credit and recommended him to be the core developer of the actual engine. I did not know at the time most of the "core development" Paul did was pilfered from other people's code. I planned to present this new concept to the powers that be later that week at a meeting I had set up.

I'm not usually sloppy, but every once in a while I am. I didn't realize Paul would open up the document and read the whole thing one day when I was quickly called away from my desk to solve a problem for someone in another department. I didn't think he had the wherewithal to redo such a proposal and beat me to a meeting. I also didn't think he was the sort of corporate piece of shit who could have convinced himself thoroughly that it had originally been his idea, that it was a coincidence I had a similar idea.

So, before my meeting even came to fruition, Paul was being symbolically sworn in as the new executive in charge of our department, a first in the company to make such a big hierarchical jump in the ladder, no one noticing or wanting to notice that this only ever occurred when the rung-jumping was over women. His new CMS idea was being celebrated as an industry break-through, sure to win awards and catapult the company into a new era of success. All hail Paul.

4.

In order to understand just how silly this industry is, you're going to have to bear through a bit of boring instruction, which I'll make easy for you. A CMS is short for a Content Management System. In Internetland a CMS is a piece of software that runs on a server (over the Internet) and allows people who don't know how to do confusing and complicated programming to update their own web sites (or other web-based applications, like e-Learning).

From a user's point of view a CMS is a lot like using a program such as Microsoft Word. It reads your web page like a document. Old-style CMS's had several templates built into it, so you could choose from making a web page that was all text, to a page with text and images, to a page that acts like a news feed, or updates information in tables, or allows people to download complimentary documentation such as PDFs or Word documents or images. The user would log in to an administration screen and build their page from the series of choices given to them. When they choose the template they want, the CMS software would automatically translate their request into HTML code so it could be displayed on the Internet, and it would automatically write the accompanying code needed to make it work (which could be a number of languages, like JavaScript, ASP, PHP, Java and so on). When you finalized and saved your work, it would automatically send it to the next person in your workflow process for review and approval, or it would instantly publish your work live to your web page. Basically a CMS is the electronic method by which you build a web page in a busy environment where several people are involved in the process, in the same way Microsoft Word with the "Track Changes" option turned on is the electronic method by which a group of professionals would create an eventual actual paper document.

CMS software is usually pretty expensive and is used mostly by companies that run really complicated web sites and web applications, like the Heart and Stroke Foundation, or the government, or health industry web sites, or insurance companies, or banks. There are less robust, cheaper CMS's that smaller businesses use, but the real money is in the big ones for the big companies, as those CMS's can run you upwards of a million dollars.

How does one create CMS software? Well, it's a lot like building a house. You start with an architecture design of how the whole thing is going to function; what is the foundation of the program, what ends need to be satisfied and how does one support that? If you build a house with 4 bathrooms, all in different corners of the house, well, you're going to lay pipe in a different way than you would if those bathrooms were required to stand directly above one another, and so on. If you want a three faucet system with one master tap and three lesser controls like I have at Paul's condo, then you're going figure out the best way to get the handle to activate the right taps and still allow them to be adjusted individually. Except, instead of handles and taps and water, you have buttons and forms and results returned. Same difference.

Usually, in the old days, a CMS would work by having to use those pesky little drop down boxes, or typing a filename in a text field and pushing a button to upload your file. When you typed in your text for your web page, it would come up with no visible font, just plain text, and it wasn't until you asked the program to allow you to preview the page that it would show you the results of all your hard work. If it was wrong, the wrong picture, the wrong size, the text was formatting funny, you went back into the ugly page with all the text fields and did it again, waiting for it to build the page again so you could preview it and so on until it was error-free and you could publish it.

However, in the past few years a web application called Flash started becoming really powerful. Flash is a program that works in two ways. First and foremost it allows you to do really simple animations for the Internet; the cartoon *South Park* was first built in a program a lot like Flash and web pages everywhere do similar animations using Flash every day. Secondly, it allows you to program the functionality of everything on your page with some code called ActionScript. This means you could use Flash to build a web page, complete with buttons and forms and everything a regular web page had, but you could make it interesting like an animation, with moving backgrounds and integrated video and audio effects and all sorts of other things. Furthermore, you could get ActionScript to talk to other programming languages and databases, meaning your Flash page could suddenly do everything a CMS did and better.

My idea, before anyone else had done it, was to build a CMS using Flash. Instead of picking your image from a list and waiting to preview it, you could just drag it right in from a series of thumbnails, resize it on the fly, see the page as you're building it. You're no longer confined to the grid layout of HTML, you can move the image over a pixel, if you want, it doesn't have to all be the same size, you have much more freedom with what you want to accomplish programmatically.

The other brilliant thing about a Flash CMS is that it can look so good. Although it is not a requirement that the back end of an application be exceptionally attractive, the types of companies who spend millions of dollars on web applications seem to want to think of themselves as are cutting edge, that they are hip and cool and they enjoy working on something that looks slick, that looks top of the line, that is original, branded and enviable. People who are obsessed with functionality, as so many are in Internetland, forget people's attraction to beauty, their ability to be swayed by something shiny and pretty to the detriment of their productivity. People are actually more apt to work on something that looks good but doesn't work well than they are to work on something that works well but is hard on the eyes, if given a choice. If not given a choice they won't know what they're missing and won't care, which is how the industry had gone up til this point.

The first company to come up with a Flash CMS was going to be rich and the person who came up with it was going to be a hero. This is the idea I unwittingly shared with Paul, and was the basis of his promotion.

Needless to say, it was the first time he and I stopped seeing each other.

5.

I took on a new contract after that. It turned out to be a short one.

It isn't really that big of a jump to be able to go from Internet to video, really, especially not when you're one of the prodigal children of new media. If you use an Adobe program such as Photoshop, you have the basis of knowledge to jump to any of their other software, such as Premiere, After Effects, or Encore (all for video or DVD production), Audition (for audio production) or InDesign or Illustrator (for print production). They all come from the same foundation of logic.

To prove to myself what I already knew, that one could move

seamlessly from one technology to the other, I applied for and was hired at a very small company to make low-end television commercials for low-end local businesses. Very small companies are good places to acquire new skills, because you are hired on merit for your existing skills (in my case, mostly design and project management) yet are expected to wear many hats because of the financial constraints of small business and the inability to hire a task-oriented team. If you have confidence in yourself and about a half a day in an office alone to acclimatize to your new surroundings and new software, you can do just about anything these days in corporate Toronto. Another thing I learned while on this particular job was that the lines were blurring so completely between New Media and the regular "Media" that companies originally focused simply on television now had an eye cast towards the integration into Internetland. Therefore people like me, with cross-industry experience, could quickly become hot commodities.

Tony Davis, the man who ran this company, *RunSpotRun*, a parody on his cross between radio and television spots, was insane. I'm pretty sure, though I can't prove it because we don't really share our adventures like other like-minded people do, that he was also a serial killer. I did a little digging and discovered that three of the five women he had hired over the past five years had all died in seemingly unrelated incidences, similar only in that all of them were raped and there was no evidence left at the scene. He was a type of sociopath that was very different from me; though he clearly had no morals in reference to anyone else, he was a very dramatic, very loud, very emotive, almost bratty sort of a person, who demanded full control over everyone around him. I recognized him immediately, but it wasn't until later that he realized all we had in common.

Tony's usual course of action was to hire very young girls to work for him, girls he could underpay and explode around and generally treat like shit, of whom he could be sure weren't going to complain or go anywhere, as he knew the state of the industry. Television is even more of an exclusive Boy's Club than Internetland when it comes to the technical side of things; women are generally relegated to administrative and public relations roles even still. Therefore, in hiring young girls in technical roles, Tony and anyone who thought like him could wield more power and save more money. In my case, he grossly misinterpreted my age, as I can look very young.

I started working there without a hitch, warming up to my clients and managing my projects and getting glowing reviews for the work I produced. Tony seemed delighted in my performance. The one other girl who worked there (outside of another woman who came in once a week to do the bookkeeping) and I got along very well, and she seemed wary of Tony's response to me, always warning me that he could change at any moment. It didn't take me too long to see what she meant.

He would come in some days so energetic he was almost electric, bouncing off the walls with an insane level of happiness and confidence that instantly made me want to wring his neck. Then he would go into his office and become very quiet. Sometimes leave early. Sometimes barge into the office I shared with the other girl and accuse us of things, like moving objects and forgetting non-existent deadlines. I chose to ignore him.

One day, about three weeks in, he called me into his office. He said that some of his clients were going south on him and he wasn't going to be able to keep me on full time. However, he told me he wanted to venture into Internetland and wanted to "partner" with me to make that happen. He said that he wasn't going to be around forever and wanted to have someone to leave the company to, which made me realize he wasn't completely connected with reality, being that he was only about ten years older than me. But I accepted his offer; if it went the way he was planning we could both make some excellent money.

I asked for the weekend to think about it and get some things on paper. He agreed and said he was excited to talk to me on Monday.

Strange. That Monday I came to work, fully anticipating accepting his offer, but Tony seemed "mad" at me. He ignored me all day and feigned business when I tried to set aside some time to speak with him. He kept appearing in the doorway of our office and staring at me suspiciously before skulking away, at which my officemate gave me a knowing look. He went out abruptly for a haircut and didn't return for two hours. When he did, he came barging into our office with a DVD in his hand, a demo reel I had given him before I was hired there, and whipped it at me like a Frisbee, bouncing it off my breasts, hissing, "*This doesn't work*," and stalking out. Fuck this shit.

The next day I came in and sent him an email demanding a meeting. At some point after lunch he went into his office, clearly read it, shouted some expletives and demanded I come into his office. I meant to quit and leave, something I've done before and am quite good at, speaking of commanding a room, but this guy got the jump on me.

"I know what you're doing!" he yelled, jumping up and down and reminding me of a bizarre Willy Wonka. "I know what you're doing! You're going to steal my clients, you're going to steal my company! I know you! I know you!"

I told him to shut the fuck up. We had a little argument, during which I took the calm role, smirking, sarcastically telling him to calm down and therefore continuously riling him up. I waited for the perfect opportunity to point out what a child he was being and informed him I was quitting as of that moment. I went and gathered my things. I demanded my final paycheque, citing several laws entailing my rights. He begrudgingly went and drew up a cheque. In delivering it to me before I left, he tried to get me to sign a piece of paper saying that if I cashed the cheque (of money already worked for and owing me), I was agreeing to never mention his name or anything that had gone on between us in the office that day. Imagine, trying to blackmail me with a cheque I had already earned! I took the cheque, refused to sign anything and left.

Before I'd even gotten home that day, Tony had sent an email to my personal account, hatemail, telling me how much he knew I was out to get him, how he wasn't going to let me, how he was going to get me. He told me he had cancelled my paycheque because I didn't sign the document he wanted me to sign, prompting me to make a call to my lawyer to draw up a letter that would make short work of the situation. He even called me ugly, which made me smile.

I walked into my closet and tried to figure out which wig to don that night. Let's see how ugly, shall we, Tony?

6.

Birthdays have never really meant much to me. I enjoy receiving presents, being that they're things I like, but I have a hard time with emotions like appreciation and I find it stressful to spend time with people when I'm expected to be "on" all the time, not to mention that I don't have many friends. It's fairly easy for me to see a birthday slide by without notice unless someone reminds me. Inevitably my parents and siblings send me a card or gift, except the sister I despise, and sometimes Renee forces me out for dinner, but I try not to do anything that day.

This year, though, I was what I could only describe myself as particularly hollow. Perhaps it was the experience with Tony, the contemplation of having met another serial killer, but I was, more hollow than usual, like a shadow. It's very quiet inside me when nothing is stirring, not even the need to formulate a forensically fool-proof plan to rid the world of one more capitalist pig. This sensation, I believe, is the closest I ever get to being truly depressed. On that particular birthday, I was feeling very much this way and planned only to drink and chain-smoke.

I definitely wasn't expecting Paul of all people to show up at my townhouse. He did, however, and gave me a very nice massage while under the pretense of catching up. He didn't mention the events that had transpired between us last and neither did I. I found myself thinking it was good to have him within my line of vision, that there was something, something, about him that had ingrained itself as familiar.

Paul remembered it was my birthday and had prepared a surprise for me at his house, which was not far from mine. He convinced me to put on my coat and follow him. When we got to his house I found he had simmering on the stove a delicious meal of haddock, coconut milk, red chili sauce, hot pepper and rice, garlic bread on the side and Caesar salad. It was all of the food in the entire world that we had in common, as Paul and I had little in common outside of the physio-chemical realm.

He finished off the night by presenting me with dessert. Though I could not recall the moment, I had apparently admitted to him once that my favourite dessert as a child had been ice cream floats made with vanilla ice cream and Diet Coke, which was what he had prepared for me for my birthday that night. I hadn't had one in years and it tasted divine. I remember sitting across the table from him, that night in his kitchen on my birthday in the candlelight and feeling something, something that didn't register with any sort of tangible description but did cause me to cock my head to one side and discover a small smile dancing across my lips. Paul, absent of the sort of emotion that irritated me and made me feel like an outcast, had managed to make something come across which was exactly what I needed.

I finished my cigarette and got up and walked around the table and caressed his cheek with the back of my hand. *Thank you, Paul,* I said in my head and smiled at him, saying nothing. He just looked up at me, somewhere between total deadpan and a puppy dog, lifting up my blouse and wrapping his mouth warmly around my nipple, my hand moving to his hair as I closed my eyes and let my head slowly fall backwards.

Paul was such a big man, it was always so nice, made me feel all petite and fragile and, well, the opposite of how I felt usually, and it was part of his thing to pick up the woman he was about to have sex with and carry her over his shoulder to wherever he was going to lay her. In this case he wasn't going far; he hoisted me over his shoulder, pulled up my skirt and forced two fingers into me hard while with a dramatic gesture he swept the contents of his table onto the floor, plates and glasses crashing delightfully as he laid me down on the cold, hard surface, undoing his pants while he lowered his head between my legs.

7.

Maybe it was because his relationships had been so short-lived, or because he was raised in a small town, or because he was so selfish, but until me, Paul claimed to have never known that sex could take so long or feel so good. In other words, until I forced myself on top of him and would not let him come, but made him pant and work and beg for it, he used to fuck girls like a jackrabbit with only his own orgasm in mind. Knowing this, it made the whole experience even hotter when he demanded I "ride his hard cock" and yelled and slapped my ass as I did just that.

For the next couple of weeks, off and on, Paul and I saw each other more frequently than ever before. I realized suddenly we were seeing each other every night. The sex was great, but I wasn't getting things done, I was losing my purpose and I knew: soon enough I was going to kill Paul.

But I didn't want to kill Paul, not then, and it wasn't because I felt attached to him or thought it would be wrong to do so, but more like he was a becoming a favourite pair of underwear I didn't want to get rid of. I enjoy sex, I enjoy feeling hot, and being close to him, looking at him, fucking him, involved a wonderful sort of electricity I had rarely felt before. I had no reason to want this to end.

Luckily, Paul had no shortage of attachments to a variety of moral compasses, those that suited his misogynist needs. For instance, if you were to just dump him, tell him that you wanted someone else, that he didn't measure up, he would be hurt; it would lead to a period of time where he tried to discover what it was about himself that had ended his relationship this way, and he would strive to grow from it. And ultimately he would want to make amends. But if you could convince him he had made some sort of moral error that resulted in you *having* to leave him, his personality intact, as a kind of punishment for his behaviour, he would readily agree he should just go.

He admitted a few weeks later how he had plagiarized yet another idea for a concept, this time for e-Learning, from another woman he had dated. He didn't even notice when or where she went as his career catapulted forward another several thousand dollars a year after unveiling his newest "idea". Through the telling of this tale, he was still clearly in denial about what he had done concerning my CMS; he quite obviously still thought of it as his own idea. It gave me the perfect out.

I acted like I had seen so many women act before, in real life and on television and movies. I told him how terrible he had been, how horrible he'd taken that woman's idea, how he had insulted me with that, how I wanted him to leave. And being the uninteresting bastard he was, preferring to take a burden unto himself to make something right and crawl away wounded and condemned to failure, like so many man-babies, he was exactly who I needed him to be. He realized how this came across to me and how it would have morally offended a [normal] woman to her core. Despite his misogyny he could still fairly accurately place himself in the shoes of someone else; that was why his career and social life were such successes. He left with clean lines. There was no need to kill.

Enter Paul, exit Paul. Welcome to me and Paul.

8.

Communication on the Internet, in the way we understand it today, started with the birth of the CBBS in the mid-1970s, or Computer Bulletin Board System, soon referred to as a BBS. Much like a message or comment board works today, it allowed people to have conversations with each other over their computers anywhere in the world if they had access to a telephone line. The information shared on the original BBS's, however, was just text and the content was mostly technical. Revelations about how they were programming something or equipment recently acquired or how the BBS itself functioned; it was what most people would think of as the boring technical ramblings of nerds and for the most part they would be right.

Bulletin Boards, however, soon found more uses. I mean, what a great way to accumulate opinions, to start discussions between large and diverse groups of people? By the late 1980s, BBS's were becoming a common tool of communication between students and teachers at universities, engineers and military personnel, or certain sectors of the soon to be burgeoning Internet community. By the 1990s, the term Discussion Group or Discussion Board became common knowledge, and talk shows and newspapers and other data-accumulating businesses that wished to keep customers or viewers or readers engaged with their product further harnessed its use by providing them with an online community to become an active part of.

This soon spawned a new beast, the virtual community and the portal sites, very popular in the late 1990s, where people could join and either for free or at a very low cost build and maintain a public or private web space that involved sharing discussions, real-time chats, calendars, events and resources with other registered members of their communities anywhere in the world. AOL was a good early example of this. These communities were viral, meaning they spawned off of each other – my friend has an online community and by becoming a member I suddenly have access to creating my own online community, linked to the one I was first a part of, and on and on they'd go. The online community and portal sites (web sites that had no purpose but to send you to other web sites of common interest) made their money off of advertising.

Discussion groups and viral communities became extremely popular and accessible by virtue of the first versions of a CMS – a one-template sort of deal where you could "personalize" the information on a web site to suit the needs of your online community. Slash-dot for programmers and CommunityZero for laymen comes to mind as two examples of early versions of these, and became the original inspiration for things like Facebook.

Discussion groups were one thing, but they didn't allow you to actually fully delve into the mysteries of your own naval. They forced a person to still actively communicate with others, to maintain a certain civilized manner, a certain decorum and not do what we really all wanted from these things – a place to showcase our own individualism and either be admired or coaxed into a fight by our fellow human beings.

Enter the web log, or as it is now commonly known, the blog. Rather than a discussion, it is an interweaving community of people's own selfish vomitous ramblings. They're basically online diaries with links to the online diaries of the person's friends or online acquaintances. It takes the definition of "viral" to a whole new level. Now, through a robust CMS that allows people from anywhere to create on the fly fully-customizable web sites as often as they please, people are able to post, throughout the day, the mundane ramblings of their often feeble minds. What they ate, what albums they bought, what problems they have with which groups of people, how much they want the world to heal, how much they want the world to burn, it doesn't matter, whatever they're thinking, it's there. Whether for gossip, activism, political discussion, technical information, pornographic sex-talk, business dealings, racist propaganda, justice organizations, what have you – they all have an active forum on the World Wide Web.

Nowadays even journalists and politicians are keeping daily blogs; reminders of how many of us are narcissistic drug-addicted simpletons who should always be under some sort of supervision. More than a few people have destroyed their own or someone else's career or life due to a blog.

Victimology has found a home in the blog as well. Small support groups for "survivors" of all sorts of traumatic events – alcoholism, abuse, mental illness, over-eating, torture, to name a few – find far more numbers and far more comfort in each other due to the uniting and anonymous powers of the Internet. People who might have put their pasts behind them or allowed themselves to heal are now enabled to spend the rest of their lives dwelling on their hardships amongst others who have shared similar experiences. People can talk forever about what's ailing them if there is someone to listen, and talking forever will always trap them into being unable to move on from their current experience; the Internet has provided exactly this sort of environment for exactly these sorts of people.

Much to my chagrin I realized one day that many people actually *write a blog for a living!* This ridiculous instrument of self-indulgence has actually become a career, and not a very glowing one. People are hired for online newspapers, at an excellent salary, to walk around with their laptops or Blackberries and ramble on about what they see around them, for the "entertainment" of those [slack-jawed morons] who find this interesting.

Most people who either keep a blog or join a discussion group are smart enough not to give away enough information to allow someone could track them down and kill them. Most people know their identities are relatively "safe" when they choose to send their opinion to others over the Internet. Yet still, moments into any discussion on any discussion board, you will find someone who is clearly *angry*, clearly *insulted*, in need of *lecturing* everyone on what they know to make their point. Recently it was even reported that someone had nearly killed someone else in the first incident ever of "web rage".

No, no the blog is better, it's all about *me* and if someone 'disses me about it, I can write back, with the power of One Who Owns This Blog, and insist these strangers do not *know me* and cannot *comment* despite the fact that I have actually described myself to them and have a link at the bottom of each post entitled "Comments".

9.

I am sitting on the leather armchair in my living room, smoking a cigarette and staring at Gable. He is staring back at me, unblinking, and his eyes tell me that he knows, he knows what I have done and what I will continue to do. He knows I am losing control over myself and he is judging me for it. Damn German Shepherds, they're too smart for their own good. Gable knows that a good dog is supposed to take on the traits of his owner and he's refusing to do so. He's better than me.

If it could be said that I love anything in this world, it's Gable. As I look into his dark, sweet eyes I find I don't mind that he's better than me. I realize he is what he is, a good dog that is better than a sociopath, better than most people who have the choice and ability to make good decisions. *I know what you've been up to and I don't condone it*, his eyes are telling me. *If I can figure out how, I will turn you in*. And I believe him. I spend a few minutes trying to decide if there is a way he could turn me in, to whom he would do such a thing, what sort of evidence he could lead someone to and a growing silent hysteria in me makes me start to fantasize about killing him to save myself. But that's not what I do. I don't kill things that are good, I don't kill to save my own skin and I am certainly not cruel. If I am caught someday I am caught; I will not kill this lovable animal who for all intents and purposes is the only comfort and companionship I have on a regular basis.

I barely see Renee anymore and I foresee our visits getting more infrequent as time continues to go on, which is probably for the best, at least from the viewpoint of her safety. It started a few months ago, right after that cop, the detective, came to see me. I had gone to see Renee to take the edge off that encounter, pleased she seemed to have finally disassociated herself from Jack, having even begun dating a new man, a nice man, a good man. How rare those creatures are! I met him and regarded him with a certain fascination. His name is Jeffrey and he is an insurance adjuster with a penchant for fine art and he absolutely adores Renee. He's not breathtakingly good-looking, the way Jack is, but he's definitely attractive and gets more attractive because of his personality, whereas Jack's looks fade quickly to ugliness as you get to know him. I noticed right away, however, that Renee doesn't seem particularly happy with her new relationship and her aloofness strikes me as having very shallow roots. I could see she was still pining for Jack, despite all her condemnations of him and her increasingly weak declarations of growing sick of his antics.

It was shortly after my second or third meeting with Renee and Jeffrey that I felt a certain coldness creep up between us. She began to express a rather childish and tiresome jealousy at the state of my life; that I was free to do as I pleased and lucky to not be "tied down" in a relationship, which is ridiculous considering all Renee ever claimed to want was to be in a fruitful, supportive, kind relationship with a good man. Not being particularly patient with anyone who plays games with themselves and uses me as a tool to do so, I bluntly told her to either dump Jeffrey or participate in the relationship fully, that she was boring me with this silly banter, she needed to make a decision and unless she really needed advice or had something of interest to say, to keep me out of it. It's not like it's the first time I've said something like that to her, and generally she would come back saying it was just the ass-kicking she needed to force her to think clearly again and get out of whatever rut it was she felt she was caught in.

Not this time though. She got petulant and stalked off to her bedroom (we were sitting in her gallery) and I gathered my things together and left.

I didn't hear from her after that for several weeks. When she did finally call me it was a polite, clipped conversation in which she invited me to a dinner party she was having, mostly for Jeffrey's friends, that she felt she needed to stock a little with her own people. I agreed to go and was once again struck by what a nice man Jeffrey was. After having seen Renee be treated so shabbily by Jack for all those years, I was, to the greatest extent I could be, happy for her. She, however, seemed irritated by Jeffrey's kindness. When he pulled out her chair for her, she shot him a dirty look and said she could do it herself. When he asked if he could get her another drink, she cut him off, shot him a look and went to get her own – without refilling his glass. The guests at the table seemed rather embarrassed, the way any good guests would be when they realize they're stuck experiencing a relationship on the rocks. I lit a cigarette.

Don't get me wrong; I know how annoying it can be to have someone dote on you too much. It's suffocating. But let me assure you Jeffrey was not that sort of person; he was, plain and simple, a sophisticated gentleman. What Renee was doing was uncalled for and cruel and it was clear she had put no thought whatsoever into what I had said to her the last time we had spoken, when she had gotten so angry and stalked out. I was growing increasingly irritated and was once again entertaining the idea of putting Renee, and by extension Jeffrey, out of their misery. I wasn't a bit impressed with the sort of person she was becoming; it was as though she had grown only to a certain point and then ceased the process altogether.

I had invested a lot of my life into my friendship with Renee. She was, after all, the metre against which I measured how people who were lucky enough to have been born with feelings and morality should act. Now, it was as though she had devolved into behaving like some spoiled brat.

After that dinner party we didn't speak again for another several weeks. I saw her on the street one day and she clearly couldn't get away from me fast enough. I knew I hadn't done anything wrong, but it still gnawed at me. If Renee wanted to salvage our friendship she had to smarten up and make a decision pertaining to Jeffrey before their relationship went any further. But my senses told me something deeper was going on, that Renee was acting like this towards me out of some sort of guilt – for what, I don't know. But I was going to find out.

Gable stares at me and sees all of this. I suspect he knows not only what I am thinking, but also what is going on with Renee.

"What is it, boy?" I ask him, lighting another smoke, actually harbouring some insane hope that he will answer me. "What has that girl done now?"

It has something to do with Jack, Gable answers. *I don't want to be the one to say it, but you should have done something about him when you had the chance. I'd still turn you in for it, though.*

10.

There has to be a group of people in this world who feel the same way I do about justice. There has to be. The distance between Renee and I has grown into a chasm and the hollowness inside of me has expanded right along with it. Corporate life has shown me nothing but the worst side of people; even those who claim to want to do well succumb immediately to ego and laziness and backstabbing and corruption. No one is safe from it. I can't kill everyone, but I can't help but think that something soon will. People have such a capacity to make good decisions and do good things, to live in harmony with each other and this planet, but it is becoming increasingly apparent that at each point that they are faced with a decision to do right or wrong, they choose wrong, then lament their own misfortune.

I am thinking this as I take a walk down Queen St. with Gable, looking for my homeless friend, Shaun, who has long promised to enlighten me with some of the many survival skills he has acquired during his years of living on the streets and hitchhiking across North America. I am feeling that it is time I take him up on his offer and get the hell out of here. There is nothing left for me here and the longer I stay, the more in danger people are. I feel my own sense of justice beginning to erode under the corrosive effect of the knowledge that nothing I do is going to make this world a better place, and that even if I could, ultimately I will never really care. There are just too many of the motherfuckers. Still, I have to try. If I could just find that elusive group of people who really do care, who really do have a chance at making the world better, I could disappear. I am, however, losing faith that such a group of people exists at all.

As if to prove my point, my eye is drawn to a scene unfolding about 500 yards away in a park across the street. A corporate fuck about my age in a three-piece Harry Rosen is walking through the park toward a homeless man who is asleep behind a bench, near some bushes. As he passes the homeless man, he veers off the path towards him, kicks him in the mouth, hard, and just keeps on going as though nothing had happened. The homeless man immediately sits up, emitting a howl like a hurt animal, blood running down his chin and a gaping hole where his four front upper teeth were just moments before. The street is crowded and there are a few people in the park, but no one makes a move to go to his aid. A couple on a nearby bench gets up and quickly leaves the vicinity.

"Holy Christ," I mutter, twisting out my cigarette under my left Ked as I cross the street towards the guy. "Are you okay?" I ask him as I get closer. The man has stopped howling and is just sitting there, crying, wiping his mouth with his sleeve, blood everywhere.

"It phlucking herrrrts," he cries to me, adding something else I cannot discern.

"You need some gauze and probably some painkillers," I tell him. "I'm going to call the paramedics."

He looks at me gratefully but slobbers that they won't do anything for him. "Damn straight they will," I say, "I'm going to make sure of it. And trust me, buddy, if I ever see that guy who did this again, I'll kill him." I take out my cell phone and call 911.

The homeless guy, Frank, is right. The paramedics initially don't want to do anything for him. They tell him they won't use any materials or take him to the hospital unless he can prove to them he can pay the bill. I watch for a while in silence and then intervene, threatening them heartily and reminding them that this isn't the case. Frank doesn't want to go to the hospital anyway, but he does need some basic medical assistance. Shooting me an angry look, the one paramedic finally and grudgingly goes back to the ambulance and gets some gauze, puts on some gloves and roughly mops up the mess on Frank's face. His partner, a butchy, unattractive woman, does nothing but glare at me. I make a mental note. I won't forget these people.

I sit with Frank until the bleeding has slowed. I go and get him a bottle of water, a big one, and a roll of paper towels, from the little convenience store across the street. I would have liked to get him some food but figure he probably won't feel like eating anything at the moment, so instead I shove a couple of twenty dollar bills into the breast pocket of his disgusting, stinking jacket.

"Thank you lady, really, thank you," Frank says to me. "I really appreciate you helping. I didn't think there were nice people like you left out there." He pets Gable on the head.

I smile, thinking if only he knew. Out loud I say, "Oh, I'm only nice to those who deserve it. I didn't think there was anyone left out there who did." I light a smoke.

Frank tells me he hasn't seen any kindness in the whole three years he's been living on the street. He proceeds to tell me how he got there, in that sort of apologetic way a lot of homeless folks I've talked to try to explain their situation, as though to justify it. Whether or not these stories are ultimately true makes no difference, but I have always believed that most of them are. Something about living in squalor on the streets makes a lot of people incredibly self-aware and honest. What else have they got?

Frank explains to me how he came home one day to find his house was no longer his own, the government having possessed it for his failure to pay taxes for over a decade. Locked and chained, with all of his possessions inside and a cop outside to make sure he didn't come home and try to break in. The cop asked for his ID and then took it and refused to return it. Frank knows he hasn't got a leg to stand on and will never be able to afford to pay off the government. He has already tapped his friends and family for it and they were either unable or unwilling to help him out. Too quickly, in my opinion, he has accepted his fate and knows that he is to live out the rest of his days on the streets.

Suddenly it becomes clear to me. I will volunteer with some social services program and help people like Frank. Surely there is a group of people who sees the better side of humanity and has chosen to work for the betterment of society. Surely there I will discover something that cleans the tarnish off my worldview.

I ask Frank if he might like to get off the streets for a little while. I tell him there is a hotel a few blocks down the road that rents rooms by the night or the week, and that I have more money than I need and have absolutely no problem buying him a few weeks' rent. At first he looks at me suspiciously, as though there might be strings attached.

"What do you want in return?" he says. "I'm probably never going to get off the streets, you're not going to change me, I've lost everything and don't even care anymore. I'd rather drink and have no place to live and numb the pain than get back in there and work or change."

"Suit yourself," I say with a shrug. "I really don't care. I don't want to change you. I just thought you might like to get off the street for a few weeks. Use all the money I gave you for booze; I don't give a shit. It's not really fair to give a person a gift and then try to control the way they use it, don't you think?"

Frank just sits and stares at me for a few minutes. I know what he's thinking. This sort of logic always boggles the mind. It's rare to come across someone who doesn't want something for their efforts, however large or small. He just doesn't get that I Really Don't Care. It's the right thing to do and so I do it. Finally, though, he does what I knew he would. He agrees to accept my offer and a cigarette. I light them both. We get up and walk down Queen St. together towards the hotel I mentioned. I tie up the dog, go in and pay for the room for him. The woman at the desk takes one look at Frank and I can tell she really doesn't want him staying there, but after taking one look at me she clearly decides not to say anything. I tell her I'll be keeping an eye on the place and will react very badly if I hear that Frank is getting a hard time from her or anyone else at the hotel. The look in my eye convinces her I'm serious.

Frank again thanks me and I brush it away. "The last time someone was nice to me was when this cop, Beech, told me where on the street to sleep the safest," he says.

"There's a liquor store across the street," I point out to him and I leave the hotel. A shudder moves through me as I remember that Beech is the name of the detective who questioned me about the explosion.

Gable and I make our way back to the condo. About forty-five minutes later I am sitting in the hot tub on the roof, checking my voicemail on the cordless. There is a message from Renee.

She's pregnant and marrying Jeffrey.

You know she's still seeing Jack on the side, right? Gable asks.

"Yes, I know," I say.

11.

Detective Gerald Beech knows I blew up that boat. I could see it on his face when he interviewed me, now several months ago. I could also see on his face that he was supremely attracted to me and was plunged immediately into a conflict of conscience that he would so want to sleep with someone he knew instinctively was guilty of what he believed to be such a heinous crime.

Oh, and he was a hot cop too, all bone structure and attitude and muscles.

When I came home that day to discover Detective Beech at my condo, I had no choice but to let him come upstairs for our interview. He did not initially sit down, but instead walked around my large living room looking, presumably, for details that would tell him something about me. I immediately realized that in not expecting a cop to show up at my home I had not taken any precautions to ensure no hint of my sociopathy was present; there were no photos, no knick-knacks or any other objects to convey any type of a personality. The only hint of me was the G-freak, attached to my refrigerator by its suction cup, which I immediately threw in a drawer upon going into the kitchen to get Beech a glass of water, and the photo I had taken of the scene of the crime, hanging on the wall in the living room, which was what he was looking at when I returned with his drink. Idiot that I was in my pride of the photo, I had actually signed the corner of it, so was now unable to pretend I had not taken it.

"How may I help you out, Detective?" I asked sweetly as I settled into my leather armchair, legs slightly askew, sexy. I lit a cigarette and blinked up at him through my lashes. "I have already told the police everything I know about that day, which isn't terribly much, considering I never made it to the cruise, thank goodness."

"Well, we have to cover every angle," Beech said, looking at me with a penetrating gaze I could not remove myself from. I had the urge to roll my eyes but restrained myself and concentrated instead at making a wave of pain cross my face.

"I realize this," I answered in a purposefully choked voice. "It just hurts me to bring up the memory of Paul's death like that. I miss him terribly." Remembering the day I really did miss him, Emotion Day, I felt this was very nearly the truth. "Paul and I had a very tumultuous relationship and I am constantly battling an overwhelming sense of guilt that I not only lived, but that he left me everything. You can't imagine my surprise when I found that out."

"If you feel so guilty about that, why do you choose to live here?" Beech asked me, his gaze unwavering. "Surely it would be more painful to live in this place and be reminded of him than if you had sold it and moved elsewhere."

"I suppose it's a type of penance," I answered without missing a beat. "The pain is somehow necessary to assuage the guilt, I think. I can't seem to stop myself."

He walked across the room and sat down on the couch perpendicular to me, opening his briefcase and putting a file folder on the glass and platinum coffee table that lay between us. He opened the folder and I could see there was a small pile of 8x10 photos inside, the top one showing the initial wreckage of the boat.

"What else do you have such a lack of control over?" he asked, looking at me hard.

I felt a flicker of irritation and was sure he noticed it as well. Instead of answering, I simply smiled. Fuck him. He already knew. There wasn't any point of playing, but I wasn't going to confess. If he had evidence against me, he would have to produce it.

"Do you do much plumbing, ma'am?" Beech asked me.

"Plumbing?" I asked back, feigning a confused expression.

"You know, replacing water pipes? How about hunting? Do you own a gun? Do you work with gunpowder? How are you at working with wires?" He was playing with me; I wasn't giving in.

"I quite frankly don't know anything about any of these things, and fail to see what it would matter if I did," I replied. So, they knew the explosion had been triggered by a series of pipe bombs. Even if the water hadn't washed them clean, I had taken great care to ensure that neither my fingerprints nor my DNA had gotten on any of the material, and I had purchased all the supplies I had needed in disguise from a variety of different locations around the city, weeks before the event took place.

"There were forty-five people on the boat that night," Beech went on as though he hadn't asked the previous question and I hadn't responded, "forty-three invited guests, the captain and his son, an ex-con who had been helping his father out for the past 6 months since he was released from Kingston Pen. Initially we thought the bombs might have been set to settle some score with him, but he had been a model inmate, incarcerated for grand theft auto and from what we can tell had no enemies whatsoever. However, the more we looked into the guests on the cruise that night, the more we discovered that nearly every one of them had a long list of enemies, corporate, personal and otherwise. Not a great group of people you are associated with, your benefactor being among the worst of them, if you don't mind my saying so." His eyes bored into me.

"I don't disagree with you," I said seriously. "They were a bunch of assholes, if you don't mind *me* saying so, and the world is a better place without them." Too late, I realized the trap and added lamely, "Not to speak ill of the dead."

"Yes." Was that satisfaction in his eyes? His face was otherwise expressionless.

I glanced at the pile of photographs. I was dying of curiosity. I really wanted to see the carnage I had caused. I knew I couldn't ask though and would have to act as though they upset me when he finally showed them to me, or else I would give myself away entirely. Noticing my glance, he put his hand on the top photograph.

"I would like to show you these photos and see if you recognize anyone," Beech said. Sensing another trap, I hesitated. It wasn't normal for a cop to bring such photos to a woman's home and show them to her, suspect or not, was it? I was starting to get nervous, but I pushed it aside and moved to join him on the couch.

It was then that the most unexpected thing happened to both of us, and luckily for me it resulted in giving me back the upper hand. The moment I sat down next to him, close enough that our thighs were touching, we were both jolted with the strongest shock of attraction I had ever felt. The chemistry between us was palpable. I could barely catch my breath; all I wanted to do was lay back and let him take me, push him down and fuck him like he'd never had it before, rip off my clothes and let my skin, suddenly burning with desire, find its way to his. I was throbbing all over. I heard his sharp intake of breath and I knew he was as affected as I was. We both just sat there, breathing, waiting, but the sensation didn't go away. Finally Beech stood up and moved to the armchair I had just left. When our eyes met again it was a different sort of gaze. I lowered my eyes to his mouth and subtly bit my lower lip. I spoke and discovered my voice was shaking.

"What were the photos you wanted to show me?"

Beech didn't say anything for a full minute, just continued to look at me, through me, into me. Eventually he closed the folder and said, "Maybe another time."

12.

This is my first surprise, sitting around a boardroom table in a dingy office in a ghetto rec centre, which serves the Off the Streets downtown chapter. I have just donated $25K to their cause and as such have been immediately invited to be on the board, something I must admit I was initially very curious and even a second or two of excited about. I am no longer any such thing. Bored, disappointed, angry, belligerent; this is more along the lines of where my mind is at now.

Today the board of Off the Streets is sharing their meeting, for "collaborative framework composition", with the nearby chapter of the Salvation Army. So far what I've heard is a shocking amount of condescension, religious empathy, judgment and pessimism disguised as more condescension disguised as compassion, a whole lot of short-sighted, small-minded thinking and bitterness sharing space with defeat. The beginning of the meeting also seemed to include a lot of ass-kissing, much of it for me, since it is apparently a very strange thing for a person to donate a great deal of money *and* want to actually sit on the board. I could not tell them the biggest reason I did so was because my fantasy life was looking for a kindred spirit; it took not but a glance to realize none were to be found in this room.

I came to the table also wanting to know precisely how the money I had donated was going to be spent, and how that worked in tandem to the government funds Off the Street had received a few months earlier to the tune of $1.2 million.

"The idea of purchasing a building and opening up another shelter is a good idea," I say to the group around the table, "but I see a few conflicting factors. First of all, purchasing, fixing and furnishing a brand new shelter will pretty much use up all of your governmental funds, and since your plan is to open the shelter based exactly on the models of the other shelters in the city, even you must realize that it is only going to serve the same demographic of people in need, that being less than 20% of the actual homeless population. In smaller towns programs like this can really help, but in Toronto this only ever seems to scratch the surface."

"Excuse me, *madam*," sniffs a long-nosed angular woman across from me, "but I don't think the fact that you have barged in here with your money gives you the right to tell us what to do. I think those of us who have sacrificed our time and experience for years have a little more to say on the matter than you do."

Summoning up my entire corporate demeanor and donning my most diplomatic tone of voice, I smile at her, saying, "Of course, ma'am, I heartily agree with you, which is why I am bringing up points of criticism in the hopes of sparking discussion and debate, which tends to be the only way groups of people can come to any sort of conclusion that benefits not only our ideas, but those we're trying to serve." I reach into my handbag and feel around for a piece of nicotine gum, finally finding one, unwrapping it and subtly popping it into my mouth. We are quickly approaching hour two of this meeting and the discussion has been going in similar circles the entire time so far.

"I agree," pipes up an excitable young man about four seats down from me. "I've been doing this for going on three years and every meeting is like this; I don't feel like we ever get anything done. People are out there dying for our help and all we do is talk talk talk!" He finishes, his voice getting higher and higher, gay little thing.

After fifteen more minutes of wrangling, they finally decide to finish off hour two of the meeting by going around the table person by person and letting everyone speak for approximately two minutes about what they had been working on, their recent experiences and what they thought we should implement to do better. Having never been to one of these meetings before, I cannot say for sure, but I suspect it had been a familiarly fruitless experience at each meeting held for the past ten years. The conclusion is the following: we need more volunteers (how to get them, no one says); we need more supplies (how to get funds released or decide on exactly what constitutes "supplies", is to be left to a future meeting); we need to have another meeting.

13.

Sometimes I forget that I am mind-blowingly wealthy and that if I'm really going to disappear off the face of this planet sooner rather than later, I might as well spend my money soon; I have no one to leave it to.

I remember how I always had a dream of buying those twin Victorians and making them into a fast moving, one stop, get off the streets if you want to transitional housing. I remember that it was my first idea after inheriting this money that I would make this plan a reality. Somehow I had pushed it aside and forgotten about it. My initial plan had banked on volunteers, but no offense, volunteers aren't reliable. I've also had some additions to that overall plan over the course of the past few weeks, watching people who employ themselves in this game the way I have been and becoming less and less impressed. I am often glad at my lack of conscience and in this case moreso; I have no moral dilemma arising over having to temper the knowledge that these people just want to help, while knowing they are largely stupid and useless in their approach to doing so. I can just think what I think and be done with it.

I leave the meeting as soon as I can extract myself, go outside, spit out my second piece of nicotine gum and light a cigarette. Buttoning up my coat against the wind-tunnel I find myself in, I walk a block to Spadina, finish my smoke and hop in a cab back to the condo. As we go under the Gardiner at Bay St. I see two homeless guys, each about thirty years old, setting up to take a nap in the little roundabout. I stop the cab, get out and walk over to them. I snap their photos with my phone and tell them that if they want to have a room for the night there is one standing rented at the Parkview Arms; all they have to do is get there. I tell them they can believe me or not and I throw $50 at them and suggest they buy some booze and have a night off from the bullshit. If they take up the offer, they will be the fourteenth and fifteenth people respectively who have taken a night or two in the now four standing rented rooms I have at that hotel where I had put up Frank for the night. And apparently the story of Frank has preceded me; these two men seem sure I am that person and I don't say either way. Funny thing is, when I see any of these people again, they never ask for anything more than that one night of reprieve and many earn enough panhandling to get their own room. It works out to $22/night per room. You don't even have to be rich to afford that. Most people I used to work with, even the peons on the bottom rung of the corporate ladder, spent more money than that a day on designer fucking coffee.

This day has really gotten on my nerves, I reflect as I enter the condo and give Gable a scratch on the head. Out loud I say, "This day has really gotten on my nerves!"

Gable looks at me, saying, *I don't agree with what you're about to do, but I understand you need a stress-reliever.* I smile at him appreciatively, going upstairs to don a suitable outfit.

While I'm getting dressed I plug my phone into the computer and transfer the two newest photos into my growing gallery of the homeless men and women I've been putting in the hotel for nights here and there. I like to study their faces.

14.

It's been a few weeks and I am walking home from my lawyer's office where I sealed the deed on the two Victorians. I have just hung up my cell after giving the foreman of the construction team I've hired to renovate the two houses the go-ahead to start with the demo. I had expected to feel somewhat elated, but instead I am simmering a sort of anger about the utter idiocy of people out there, even the good ones, even the supposed smart ones. Really none of us deserve to be here. It's just all so fucking boring.

And then in one of those divine coincidences, I see someone I recognize going into a store ahead of me. It is the man who kicked in Frank's teeth; the kind of jock-executive who likes to lecture homeless people when he's sober and then goad them on and beat the shit out of them when he's drunk. I duck into the store beside him, an empty, crappy, Chinese antique shop and pull out a wig I have in my bag – black, shag-bob cut, really realistic looking. An ancient, Chinese apple-doll woman rocks back and forth and stares at me with a simple grin as I masterfully whisk my hair up and don the wig. I glance at her and wink as I turn to leave the shop, putting on my sunglasses as she calls out, "Yes, yes, okay!"

Then I go into the store next door, a high-end pillow boutique if you can fucking believe it, and see that Mr. King-Ass Jock is still there, snapping condescendingly at the saleswoman as he instructs her on why this particular silk-covered goose-down pillow is not up to his personal standards and needs. I move closer and glance at him coyly through my shades, all insinuation and head cocking. He notices me immediately and cuts short his bitchfest at the shopkeeper. Sidling closer to me, he picks up a nearby pillow with the manicured sausages he has for fingers and asks me what I think of it. I let myself get caught up in this silly game of a conversation and participate until he asks me to dinner. I tell him I'm going out of town tomorrow morning and if we are to go to dinner we must go this evening, early would be better. He agrees.

I leave the store and go home to change, with plans made to meet him at Bar Italia at 7 o'clock. I look at my gallery of street folk and tell Frank's picture I'm getting him retribution tonight. Gable has followed me into the room and stares at me with parental disappointment in his eyes, but I don't care. "Shut up," I tell him as I grab my coat and bag and walk out to get an elevator.

15.

King-Ass Jock and I have a long dinner and many, many drinks. He is feeling even more drunk than he should be due to the hit of GHB I dropped into his rye and ginger while he was in the washroom about a half hour previous. I am starting to tread the fine line between getting him as drunk as I need to him to be and making sure he doesn't start making a scene, as assholes of his type are wont to do when they get too much in them. Another half hour and I suggest we go and take a nice long leisurely down through the park.

"I have a flask full of bourbon," I tease, giving him a wink. "Let's drink it on the way back to your place." He emits a drunken laugh and starts saying something crass; I have ceased to listen to him because as look past his bullet-head I notice that Detective Beech has just entered the bar, clearly off-duty and with a silly-looking blonde on his arm. He is staring at me and I can tell that he is searching his mind trying to place me. My usually non-descript light brown hair and alabaster complexion is completely hidden by my disguise and I look more like a Persian beauty-queen this evening, but nonetheless he has immediately found me familiar.

"Let's go out through the back patio," I say with a bit of a sense of urgency to King-Ass and he follows me back through the bar like a dog.

A half hour later I am standing over his limp body in the park, against some bushes, in a scene suspiciously like that wherein he had kicked in Frank's teeth. I nudge him with the toe of my shoe and he makes no sound and does not move; someone less experienced than me might think he was already dead, but I knew he was just in an unconscious stupor. I leave him there and walk about a half a kilometer across the park until I come upon a few bedraggled men who scramble to hide their crack pipes; they are exactly who I was looking for.

"Hey guys, did you hear about the bum who had his teeth kicked in a few weeks ago?" I asked them.

They laugh loudly and say, "Which one?"

"It doesn't matter," I answer. "All you need to know is that the guy who did it, some asshole executive, is passed out at this very moment on the other side of the park. I'll give you $20 if you finish him off."

"Each of us?" one asks me suspiciously.

"Sure, why not?" I turn around. "Come on, I'll show you where he is."

They follow me with trepidation as I lead them back to what I hope will soon be King-Ass's grave. He's still lying there, passed out. I wished I could kill this asshole myself, as I had planned, but having seen Beech in the bar I don't want to take the chance that any evidence of myself is left at this scene. I hand each of the two men a $20 bill with my gloved hands.

"Come on, now, kick out his teeth," I tell them. One is nervously taking a haul off his crack pipe, the bitter smoke wafting over to me. He exhales, shakes his head and yells, "Fuck yah!" running and kicking King-Ass in the mouth.

Amidst the yells, I walk away. In a moment I find myself catching a cab on Dundas St back to my condo.

16.

Can't say that I was a bit impressed the next morning to read in the newspaper that those two little druggies didn't have the guts to actually kill the guy. They only beat his face into an unrecognizable pulp and took all his money and credit cards. Even worse, the poor crackheads were stupid enough to use the credit cards and one of them was caught within days. The community howled for their heads on a pike and a wave of sympathy rolled out in the form of gifts of money and vigils for King-Ass Jock. I should have finished him off myself. I had a moment of even feeling a little unsettled that I had gotten those kids mixed up in this; they weren't the problem, they just wanted crack. Lucky for me the one they caught either had the foresight not to mention, or had already totally forgotten, that I had approached them and given them money in exchange for beating this guy up; at least, the information was never published if he had said something.

So what are you going to do about it? Gable asked me with big eyes many times over the next few days. *You know what you've done, don't you? You've just given that man justification to keep on abusing street people. No panhandler is safe because of your mistake. You've let a criminal run free amongst them.*

"I know," I would snap at the dog, irritated. I could already picture

King-Ass littering the city with the teeth of those he had condemned, not because he knew they had done anything wrong, but just because he hated them through his own need to feel better than someone else.

I waited a couple of weeks and then, in the same disguise I had worn on our date, I went and visited the shameful little fucker in the hospital. His face was still swollen beyond all recognition, partially because of the initial beating and partially because of some surgery to reset his nose and one of his cheekbones, but otherwise he was about ready to go home.

"Hey," he said weakly, recognizing me immediately. "How did you ever get away that night?"

"Oh thank goodness you're such a gentleman," I told him. "I was too drunk to think straight and you put me in a cab and sent me home right after we left the bar. What were you doing going to that park all by yourself?"

"I don't know," he said, looking confused. "I guess I decided to walk home."

We chatted for a little bit and I left, not before making sure he entreated upon me to come and visit him that weekend when he got home.

"I know it won't be as much fun as if you'd come home with me that night," he said wryly, "but with your help I know I'll be my old self in no time. I could really use your help with the cooking and cleaning."

I smiled at him while digesting the fact that this near-stranger had just recruited me for "cooking and cleaning", and warmly agreed to visit him at his home in two days. He gave me his address and the guest code needed to enter his keyless condo building, after unwittingly letting me know the doorman would not be present after 10pm.

Tonight at 11pm, wearing a long, red braided wig, dressed as an independently wealthy arts charlatan, I enter his building. I get off the elevator on the second floor and find the garbage room, where I switch wig and alter costume, sexy black with gloves, becoming again the woman that King-Ass wants to see. Then I get back in the elevator and proceed to his condo. I knock and wait as his shuffling footsteps slowly make their way towards the door.

"So glad you could make it," he says, moving to hug me as I step out of his way to avoid his touch and transfer of DNA or fibre evidence. I walk into his place and he follows me.

Once in the living room I turn to him, reaching into my bag. I pull out a plastic bag containing a pre-tied noose and a gun. Cocking the gun at him, I toss him the bag. He is surprised and doesn't know what to say.

"Take the noose out of the bag and tie it up there – there, where the banister extension juts out into your living room," I say, pointing at the area I mean and making sure all his blinds are securely closed.

"What the – what the hell are you doing?" he cries, coming at me.

"Not another step unless you want your brains blown out all over your condo," I say. "Now, do what you're told."

He does, which I find interesting, amusing and boring. I mean, if the tables were turned, I would certainly not do it. I would let them shoot me first. In fact, if I were going down I would be doing everything I could to take them down with me. But not this guy, he dutifully goes and ties the noose up where I tell him and waits there, as if waiting to see if he should hang himself immediately or find out if I have further instructions for him.

"Get your ass back here," I growl at him, and he comes back down the stairs. "Get a piece of paper and write a note, saying how you can't live with yourself any longer because you have beaten up so many defenseless homeless people and you know it's just a matter of time before they come for you." He looks at me, amazed that I seem to have known who he was all along. "DO IT!" I thunder at him.

He scrawls out a note, which I demand he read back to me. Satisfied, I turn back to him. "Now, go put yourself out of your misery," I say, deadpan.

Surprised again at his convalescence, I follow him as he takes his last walk up the stairs before putting the noose over his head and climbing up on the railing. At the last minute, however, some human drive for survival makes him stop. Maybe he had planned this as his escape the entire time. As I stand behind him still holding up the gun, watching him teeter on the railing above me with his hands on the ceiling for balance, he suddenly spins around to face me and attempts to do what he does best: kick me in the mouth. My quick reflexes save me and I duck out of the way in the nick of time, both hearing and feeling his foot whiz by my face.

"You little fucker," I shout, making a move to push him over the edge myself. In the end I don't need to, though, because his last ditch effort to save himself has thrown him off balance. Time turns into slow motion for a moment, both hands and feet searching in vain for a better grip in an attempt to re-shift his centre of gravity, and he falls over the side of the railing, noose tightening as his body falls to the living room below him.

There is a snap and a thud as his neck breaks and his body hits the wall simultaneously. The unmistakable smell of urine hits my nose and I realize how scared the disgusting little coward must really have been. With no urge to wait while his face turns black, I walk across the room and pick up the plastic bag that had contained the noose, turn and leave.

Back on the second floor I turn again into a red-headed age-inappropriate wood-nymph and I proceed to leave the building. Two or so blocks away I duck into an alley, remove the red wig and the ridiculous skirt, revealing the mini-skirt beneath, change my shoes, deftly put my natural hair into a French twist and emerge out the other end of the alley towards King St. and a cab.

There I run into Shaun, who I had been looking for the day I had met Frank and witnessed King-Ass's crime.

"Oh, hey!" he greets me warmly. "I've been looking for you for months!"

"Me too," I admit. I like this kid; it is good to see him again. "Do you still want me to teach you survival skills?" he asks. "Absolutely!" I exclaim. Yes, yes, get me the fuck out of here! "Okay," he replies, "Just come find me down in this neighbourhood and we'll make a plan. Or better yet, why don't you just leave a message at the Arms and let me know when and where?" He stops for a moment. "I know what you've been doing at the Arms, you know. Word gets around. It's really amazing. I really have never heard of anyone doing something like this for so many people. Anyway, we've got your back. Some of the guys have started a pool to make sure we have enough for an extra room if too many people show up. Sometimes there's four or five in one room. But it's weird. They're all good about it and they're all clean. It's all good." Shaun had been on the streets since he was thirteen years old; he was now twenty-three. He shook his head again. "I've never seen anything like it."

17.

I toss my copy of the *Metro* into the large newspaper-recycling bin on the subway platform and make my way out to the world above. I have just come from visiting the twin Victorians on the east side and meeting with the man I have hired to manage the operation when the renovations are completely finished. I am pleased with the progress. The construction firm I hired is doing an excellent job and I will highly recommend them to others. The man I hired to manage things, Duncan Westbrook, has a Masters in Social Work and has worked for all three levels of government as well as a few NGOs, nearly leaving the social work industry altogether as he suffers from many of the same disappointments and disillusionments I have experienced in the area. He thinks this new gig is a gift from the gods, and has given my executive summary of the operation his seal of approval. I leave it to the expert to perfect it.

Besides my original idea of having this safe-house for people who want to get off the streets, we are going to implement a sort of mentor program whereby if you manage to pass the requirements to get into the building to begin with, you will find after your six week grace period that you will be offered a job mentoring others, your pay consisting of six months of free rent and basic food allowance at your own apartment. After those six months, you will be given an actual salary to mentor those who had moved into the stage immediately before yours, which will last for a year, at which point you are on your own, though a lucky and successful few may find themselves further employed in and amongst the twins in a variety of possible areas. If you fuck up at any point along the way, you're fucked. This is for serious applicants only. However, the overall point is to take the pressure off of the suffering public and government-assisted programs that are inundated with too many people who are looking for help with no real intentions for the future. Duncan is in the process of hiring a basic staff and setting up what will be the original board of directors so that we can finish off the proper paperwork to make this an official charitable organization. Naturally there is much more to this, but that's it in a nutshell.

I am making a quick stop at the Parkview Arms to leave a message for Shaun. I want to make sure he is in town at the end of the summer so I can take him up north for a week and we can have our survival skills training session. I think the twins will be operating smoothly under the knowing guidance of Mr. Westbrook by then and I won't have to involve myself anymore. By next summer I expect I'll be gone forever.

After leaving the Arms, I head back towards Queen and Bathurst to the drop-in centre there to see if I can happen to find Shaun in person. No such luck, but I do run into this smarmy little social worker whose name I believe is Christian, ironically, seeing that in practice he is anything but. Maybe it's not that ironical.

He walks up to me in the lobby with a mock-serious, mock-concerned look upon his face, tells me he needs to speak with me directly and am I free to take a walk with him around the block? I begrudgingly agree.

We walk down Bathurst and turn into the alley just north of the addictions centre. It's a cloudy day that is threatening rain and the alley is empty. We follow it for a few blocks and he leads me into a smaller offshoot I hadn't noticed before, indicating for me to sit on a disgusting old crate amidst undelivered stacks of newspapers. One of the newspaper pile's ties are coming undone and I unthread the plastic, winding it around my hand and snapping it impatiently on my knee.

"I've heard about what you've been doing," Christian finally says, a slight sneer creeping across his face. "And no one's too happy about it."

For a fleeting instant I wonder if he's going to call me on one of my many crimes, but I quickly become aware that he's talking about the Parkview Arms.

"So what?" I say off-handedly, getting up. I don't need to listen to this. I had thought perhaps he was going to tell me something interesting, but now I realize there isn't anything interesting he could possibly say. "What's it to you if I'm putting people up in a hotel?" Damn, you'd think I'd committed murder! I smile inwardly at my own joke.

"Listen, I know you're new to social work, but if you think you can just throw a lot of money into some program and then take over and ignore the *protocols*, you can think again, lady," he says callously. "We have a very well-thought out system in place and we don't need someone like you coming in here and messing the whole thing up."

I stare at him, growing deadly calm. "Is taking a woman into a dirty alley to confront her in this fashion part of your protocol? I'm afraid I neither understand what it is that has riled you up, nor do I care in particular."

Christian's face grows red and his mouth contorts into a grimace. "You can't take money and help the people you choose to help!" he told me, his voice rising. "You can't set aside rooms for certain people; they have to go through the *system*, and the *system* treats them all equally! The money you donated – "

"Don't tell me about the money I donated," I retort sarcastically. "In the months since I made the donation I haven't been able to get one of the Off the Streets people to give me an accountable representation of where that money was invested or spent. From my own observations and calculations I can only surmise that they were largely spent on administrative fees, despite the fact that 90% of the people working for them are volunteers. The last industry-wide public report claimed that sometimes less than 8% of every dollar donated to any charitable organization actually gets to the people or point of that group. Why don't you just admit that what you're really pissed off about is that the money I am using to help the people I want to help is actually helping them, instead of securing your worthless ass for another year's contract?"

"You *bitch*!" he gasps, lurching off his crate and making a move towards me as though he is going to punch, or his case probably slap, my face.

I am too fast for him. As he comes within reach I whip the plastic newspaper tie out and around his throat, pulling hard enough to cut his skin and injure his windpipe. The move has spun him so that his back is to me, while his arms flail out wildly at his side he is unable to scream or hit me at all and I calmly continue to bind the plastic tie tighter in my hands. I am initially unprepared for the force of his struggle, but luckily due to my constant working out and kickboxing I am freakishly strong for a woman. In a surprisingly short time, he stops moving altogether and his body slacks downwards, but I keep the tie tight for another two full minutes before releasing him and watching collapse amidst the refuse of the small sub-alley. I pick up a newspaper and wrap the plastic tie in it thickly, so as not to let any of the traces of blood seep through, pull a plastic bag out of my purse that I have there for walking Gable and tie it up tight. Putting the package back in my purse, I carefully walk out of the alley.

I don't usually kill out of uniform. I hope I haven't left any evidence behind. Part of me, however, no longer cares if I am caught. This thought, naturally, is immediately followed by renewed pressure to get out of town. I don't even understand my own mind anymore.

18.

How many pretentious and pointless poems, songs, stories, art and now even blogs have been called *Untitled?* This is what I am thinking as I smooth out my gold satin dress with my long-black-glove-covered hands and roll my shoe carousel around in my closet looking for the strappy gold heels I know go best with this particular ensemble.

Gable is sitting staring at me quietly and answers my unspoken question. *Countless, from time untold until time itself stops the trend. You can never stop them so don't even try.*

"You're probably I right," I admit ruefully. "But even you, Gable, will not stop me from trying." I am ready now, I decide, as I look in the mirror and approve of what I see. I walk past that infernally wise animal, down the stairs and out the door.

I had been looking forward to this night. It's the first large-scale fundraiser I have ever planned and executed, but after working with the arts community for the past four weeks planning this fundraiser for the Factory Theatre, there are several other people I now wished to execute instead. I got myself into this through 'Cat' (Catherine) Laflamme, a friend of Renee's, who was the PR director for the theatre. After a lifetime of hanging out with Renee, and with her father before he died, I had met a great many of the characters who made up the Toronto arts community, but it was usually one or two at time. Let me tell you, these people smell a whole lot different in a big group, especially one in which they feel particularly empowered. To them, corporate capitalism, the world in which I had garnered most of my life experience, was the enemy; however, it was not an enemy they particularly wanted to vanquish, but moreso one they wanted to conquer and replace.

Like corporate capitalism, there are all sorts of different levels within the arts community, from the dirty perpetual student-minded small-time artist who mingles with activists and spews witlessly about Marx, to the Queen St. art show circuit who define themselves as the champion of festivals, the definers of fashion, the yuppies of the future, to the large scale galleries and theatres that attract the more "grown-up" caviar and champagne crowd.

I know quite a bit about that last crowd, as they are at that point often inextricable from corporate capitalism, but the middle and bottom threads of the arts community were still a bit of a mystery to me. I thought, why not bring some of my higher standing to them in the hopes of discovering there what I had been unable to discover in corporate or social services? To that end I had sought out Renee's advice in one of our less and less frequent visits with each other; I had even feigned interest in her burgeoning belly in order to get her help and see her again. She had suggested I get in touch with Cat, which I did, and Cat immediately set me upon planning this fundraiser. It was a relatively easy thing to do, as all I had to do for guests was tap into my corporate Rolodex, specifically those in advertising that fancied themselves as profitable artists in their own rights.

I had also started helping Renee in seeing out her father's dream to have the studio on Markham St. cater more to helping previously unknown artists get their foot in the door. Together we worked for a week or so planning and executing a contest that resulted in a few shows that highlighted the work of the unknowns and ensured that the guests were of the sort of means to spend money on the art.

Me, I don't really appreciate most art. I know what I like and I understand *real* talent when I see it, but some of the crap people put out there and claim to agonize over is nothing more than a ruse, in my opinion, to cover up the fact that they aren't really doing anything with their lives. Such as those who do nonsensical abstract, empty canvas work, pithy lines, blood and urine on multimedia backdrops, video installations of blinking eyes or flexing fists... you will never convince me that one is brilliant to see the beauty in a piece of shit, but somehow lacking in intelligence or understanding because they can see through it, to the shallowness and meaninglessness in the lives of many who devote themselves to the trade. I have discovered to my disappointment that much of the measure of being a "successful" artist in the Toronto arts community is insinuating yourself into the right clique and convincing people you are good at what you do by moreover following the norm, making no change to your craft more significant than GM adding an extra cup holder to a "new" model of automobile, rather than actually being innovative, rather than actually trying to improve oneself.

But isn't that the truth in everything? I more and more believe that Machiavelli was right when he said, "And let it be noted that there is no more delicate matter to take in hand, nor more dangerous to conduct, nor more doubtful in its success, than to set up as the leader in the introduction of changes. For he who innovates will have for his enemies all those who are well off under the existing order of things, and only lukewarm supporters in those who might be better off under the new."

19.

So there you have it, and that is the mindset I am in after leaving the fundraiser, that which I had facetiously called *Untitled,* taking with me in tow one of the aforementioned types of artists that I met at the event, beautiful to behold in his physicality but from whom the stink of his failure could not be washed away. I have initially gone with him to get myself off and pretend I was somewhat normal, but after spending an hour in his studio I start to have different ideas.

He lives in a big old warehouse building about a block north of the theatre, a building that had up until the past few years housed exceptionally cheap and moderately clean studio apartments for those who could not afford regular downtown Toronto prices, and had recently been renovated into exceptionally expensive and moderately clean studio apartments for those who could not afford to live in downtown Toronto without the class distinction of being an artist setting them apart from the rest. This particular artist, who I'm sure you will all have heard of within the next week or so due to what I'm about to do, is one of those tiresome and selfish creatures who believes that everything that comes out of his body, and his alone, is a demonstration of his immeasurable talent, a talent the world must and should bow before, and as such he had a chilled reserve of many normal bodily functions sitting in wait in large jars on the shelves that line his studio. He has nothing to offer the world and does not care to try.

In a dance that begins as one of seduction, I ask him to demonstrate his muse by dousing himself with what those jars held, and drunk and stoned he readily agrees. I sit back and watch as he prepares his parts, strips himself naked and first covers himself partially in black paint, partially in gold, "so we matched". Then, strutting around on the plastic sheet that protected the floor in his work area, he proceeds to put on a pair of heavy rubber gloves (so as not to get paint in the jars), dip into his reserves and sprinkle his body with an assortment of previously mentioned bodily preserves, finally taking off the glove and smearing it all over himself. Watching him laugh and wriggle like a fucking moron, I egg him on, telling him how brilliant he is until he's positively squirming, gyrating, almost masturbating in his filth, and look on with little surprise as he slips on the plastic and knocks himself out on the edge of the table.

Gingerly I step over to him. I cannot see through all the paint and shit and piss whether or not he is bleeding from his head, but having watched the accident occur I suspect he will not be out for long, and probably not at all if he wasn't already inebriated to the point of losing consciousness. Glancing over at the shelf I see a can of turpentine and just to make sure he doesn't harm anyone else with his idiocy, I walk over, grab a rag, knot it, open the can, soak the bottom half of the rag in the foul-smelling liquid, use the rag to close the can and wipe it down, go back over to the sleeping beauty and proceed to shove the rag into his mouth up to the knot. He awakes faster than a princess with smelling salts, but the turpentine is poisoning him at breakneck speed and I firmly hold the rag in place in his mouth while slowly choke him with my gloved hand. I admit I am surprised by the extent to which he does not struggle. Soon he is unconscious again. Leaving the rag in his mouth to finish the job, I get up and leave, walking to a block away and jumping into the first cab I saw, straight home to shower off the smells. Sometimes I think even murder isn't challenging enough anymore. People really disappoint me.

And now that I've told you this, I'm sure you'll know whom I'm talking about. Instant success I'm giving that man, now going down in the annals of artistic history as one so brilliant as to sacrifice himself for his art, to push himself to the limit and beyond, to give his life for the eternal life of all he had worked for.

Please.

20.

I arrive at the coffee shop about five minutes late and easily locate Deb sitting at a table in the back corner, laptop open in front of her. This is the woman who replaced me at work, who with the loss of me, and having to work with the man who came in as CEO after Jim Dieter's untimely demise, has been finding it very difficult to get the company going in the direction the board wants it to go. Generally speaking I kept meticulous paperwork, paper trails, methodology documents, contact lists, email archives, everything you would need, but what I didn't leave, due to the swiftness with which I was escorted off the premises, was the key to understanding everything I'd left behind. Deb had emailed me several times asking if she could meet with me so that I could help sort things out and when I could put it off no longer, I emailed her back and agreed for us to have a coffee together.

"So what's it like around there these days?" I ask her with genuine curiosity as I sit down with my extra large mocachino. "Business going well?"

"I guess so," Deb says. "We're rolling out the third iteration of our software next month, so development and project management is working overtime. Version 2.0 had some pretty terrible bugs in it and it caused us to lose several critical clients, so we had to let four developers go, which isn't making it any easier for them to get this out."

I smile. I had warned them for the past year or more that our quality assurance practices were not up to snuff, which of course they ignored, and which is precisely why a buggy product was released onto the market. I hadn't heard the details, but had noticed that our stock had taken a bit of a tumble in recent months. Lucky for me I didn't have too much invested in the company anymore, on any level.

"So is this new version going to solve these issues?" I ask.

"I hope so," she says. "They spent months hacking into the code of our competitors products and taking what were the best features from all of them, so what we're going to be releasing should be something that meets all of our clients' needs." She's talking about corporate recruitment software, not a particularly innovative concept for the past ten years, and even less so since people had stopped trying to come up with their own ideas and had reverted instead to the tiresome practice of trying to create a patchwork made up with incoherent pieces of what everyone else was doing. Internet software had become nothing more than a community of Frankenstein hackers, abnormal brains and all.

"What's really getting on my nerves is that Grayson has suggested that I spearhead the marketing strategies for the new product, with a deadline of yesterday," Deb went on, "which is an impossible endeavour on two fronts: first of all as COO this is not my area of expertise and secondly, Grayson and the entire technical department won't let me get in enough time to truly understand the product I'm supposed to be marketing. I have long suspected, and I know I'm right, that they're not really at all ready to release this thing and when it all comes down it's going to be on my head, as though I wasn't creative enough to dupe the clients and our shareholders into believing it was ready for market."

"Lovely, another demonstration of the quality and efficacy of Internetland," I say sarcastically. "You need to stand up to them and tell them to spend the money on a real marketing firm who will do this right, and let you focus on the job you were hired to do."

"I'd like to, but –" she lowers her voice, "there's more to it than that."

I lean in.

"Don't tell anyone I told you this, but they're doing the marketing in-house because the fat cats at the top are planning to pull out. They want me to pump up this product for a successful release, to drive their shares back up, and then they're going to sell and run for the hills before anyone realizes it's a dud. I can't prove this, but I'm sure that's what they're doing. I just don't know how much I'm going to be held accountable for that. On top of it, I have a lot of shares in this company as well and if I sold mine and then this happens I'll be the first suspect for insider trading. And if I sit back and let it happen and do nothing, I'm going to be out hundreds of thousands of dollars. Not to mention all the other shareholders that are going to be screwed, my parents and my brothers being among them."

I'm not surprised and I tell her so. I'm not exactly angry, either. I'm somewhere in between. This is exactly why these motherfuckers need to be wiped off the face of the planet; their motivations are only for self, only for greed, and it doesn't matter who they destroy along the way. Good people with families and homes… oh, this is like a repeat of Silacorp all over again. I know I said I was done with killing, but just a few more wouldn't hurt, would it? I mean, there is no escape from these people! I had started to soften in attitude towards the corporate world after my recent experience with social work and the arts, but this is a reminder that it is not only the same, it is getting worse. Worse because no one has learned from past mistakes, worse because nothing has come into place to make it stop, there are no consequences for the actual perpetrators, just laws to punish the scapegoats.

I talk with Deb a while longer and clear up some of the questions she had for me. Then I return to my condo and go to my closet and pick out a suitable wig.

21.

My mother is on the phone. I have made one of my rare telephone calls to her because she has left about ten messages, each one getting more and more frantic, so I feel if I don't call her back she'll just end up on my doorstep. I don't want her here.

Now that we're actually talking, though, any hint of her growing hysteria that was so obvious on the machine has evaporated; we're having a "normal" conversation as if we talked every day, as if she wasn't consumed with worry. Elise Keaton 101. Today she's talking about my sisters, one in particular, the one I don't like. Her daughter, my niece, seems to be having some problems lately.

"It's so sad, so tragic," Mother is saying. "Trudy's little friend, Chantal, was just killed in a car accident a couple of weeks ago. Those little girls did everything together, but Trudy doesn't seem to be reacting to her death at all. At first we thought she was in some kind of shock, but your sister says that it's as though she really doesn't care at all. It's been making her teachers and the other kids in her class extremely uncomfortable, and they finally sent home a note requesting that Trudy be taken in for some sort of psychiatric evaluation."

So, I think to myself, *little Trudy is a sociopath like me.* I had wondered if it was a genetic thing when I was a kid, but everyone in my family was so normal, so painfully normal, that it had left my mind a long time ago. I suppose if I cared at all I would want to spend some time with Trudy and teach her how to cope. But as much as I didn't care to make the effort, I knew that Trudy wouldn't care that I made it. If it was important to her to learn how to fit in and cover up her sociopathy, she would have to figure it out herself, same as I did. It might be nice to teach the little one to carry on my legacy after I'm gone, but quite frankly I don't think that most people, including her, are as smart as me when it comes to covering their tracks, and attempting to teach her would probably result in both of us landing in jail.

"It's not just about Chantal, either," Mother was saying. "Trudy's been exhibiting some seriously cruel traits lately. She beat up her sister until she was nearly unconscious. She's been killing animals around the neighbourhood and playing with their bodies. She's been setting cats on fire. And your sister says she really doesn't seem sorry about it, even when she's told it is wrong and is punished. Even getting a spanking does nothing; it doesn't make her better or worse. I'm really getting worried."

"Well you should," I tell Mother, stoking the fire. "Sounds to me like she's a little serial killer in the making. I wouldn't want her sleeping in my house if there were any knives or weapons around, that's for sure."

I can hear Mother go pale. "That – couldn't be true," she gasps. "You don't think that's the case, do you?"

"Well, you never know," I say, meaning it. I have no urge to see my parents stabbed to death in their sleep for no reason. "I'd keep an eye on her, that's for sure."

I find myself wondering how many other people in my family might have been sociopaths. The family that I had known growing up were all normal, but what about previous generations, or my cousins out east, or the ones still over there in Europe? It was an interesting idea that I hadn't thought about in a long time. But, having never found any pleasure or comfort in meeting others who share my "illness" I must say I am not too interested in finding out any more. In fact, it further makes me believe I should not be here any longer – yes, the urge to

disappear is constant these days. I want to disappear. I just don't want
to die. Not yet.

22.

"I have played all my cards but one," I say to Gable on a quiet Saturday
evening at the condo. I am again playing with the idea of getting
involved in politics.

You're an idiot. Gable tells me reproachfully. *As if that is the last
card left. The card you should be playing is turning yourself in and getting
locked up in a prison for the criminally insane.*

I laugh at him. "Dear Gable," I say, "don't you know that sociopathy
is not considered a suitable psych defense in court? They wouldn't send
me to such a place."

*Perhaps sociopathy is not a suitable symptom of insanity, but certainly
having hours-long conversations with an otherwise perfectly normal
German Shepherd is.* He blinks innocently three times.

I feel a knot gathering in my stomach as I realize that it is very
likely I am criminally insane, and I wonder sometimes how much of
my life is even real anymore. I haven't heard back from Shaun since I
left a note for him down at the Arms, and I feel some pressure to try
and contact him again as soon as I can and get my training down pat.
I need to leave; I need to leave and stop repeating that I need to leave
in place of leaving.

To distract myself, I think of the one thing I do know is real is that
the twin Victorian project is going swimmingly. So swimmingly, in
fact, that I was honoured with a Community Service Award at a gala
dinner at the 360 last week, along with Duncan Westbrook. Hilariously
enough, Christian the Social Worker was also awarded, posthumously
of course, for giving up his life in the "line of duty". I had to admit
even to myself that that was essentially what he had done, since it was
certainly part of his duty to stop up progress and keep the people who

really needed help from getting it. That they believed he was slain trying to stop a drug-deal in the alley behind the addictions centre was more than lucky for me.

At the gala I was approached by a man who worked in federal politics, for the conservatives, and who thought that my sort of corporate and wealthy background mixed with my off-handed, non-structured, Randian-type of altruism would look particularly good against the backdrop of his political party. Like all people, I have my suspicions about the ubiquity of the politician's soul, but like many people, I still harbour some hope that those who work in politics might be of a finer ilk. Maybe I can deconstruct some of the stereotypes I see from observing them from a closer distance.

I agree to attend the event to which he has invited me. It is a large-scale fundraiser at the Toronto Convention Centre, $500 per ticket, featuring the Prime Minister himself and a smattering of all those who wield power and influence in this country. In the past I have been invited to similar events by some of my former colleagues, but have declined, having had no interest in any of them at the time. Even Paul, dear Paul, was known to be a frequent, if undevoted, member of this circle of society, and it did him no harm in his rise to fame and fortune.

Of the two major political parties, I am not particularly tied to either of them from an ideological point of view, and this is nothing more than the first step into a brand new experience, one in which I will surely find what I'm looking for.

Either way.

PART 3

1.

It is an understatement to say I am not displeased when my concierge calls up to my place to tell me that Detective Gerald Beech is here to see me. I can push aside the temporary scare I had when he saw me at Bar Italia and may or may not have recognized me, but I cannot forget the electricity that passed between us when he was last in my living room. So pleasing is that memory that I am not even aware of whether or not there may be a disturbing undertone to this impromptu visit.

I can tell he is curious too, when I open the door to let him in the condo. I touch him lightly on the arm and sparks go off in every cell in my body as I lead him to the living room and offer him a drink, which he declines. I notice he sits in my leather armchair, presumably so that we cannot accidently come into physical contact with each other again; oh yes, there is a morality in this man, an intense, harsh, ruthless *good* that I find simply fascinating.

The fascination does not go away, though my mood sours considerably when I realize he is so close, so close to catching me. He has somehow gotten himself an eye-witness who saw a woman prowling around the dock the night before the cruise, a woman whose description didn't suit me at all but had sparked an interest in him to check me out again. Perhaps he recalls finding me familiar in Little Italy and realizes I am capable of changing how I look; maybe he isn't even conscious of it, but I get the impression he is not here to explore any possible chemistry between us. In fact, he seems irritated it exists and intent on ignoring it. No fun at all.

Glad as I was to have him show up, I find I am even more pleased to see him leave. Replaying our visit to myself I see that this man throws me off my game. He makes it so I am not thinking clearly about the matter at hand; I am lost in the interpretative giddiness of speculation when he is near me, and that is not a good thing for someone in my position dealing with someone in his position, no matter how many more interesting and exciting positions we could potentially... See what I mean? No, it's better I spend no more time around this man. For exactly one second I flirt with the idea of killing him, just ridding myself and the world of this beautiful nuisance, but I know I can never get that close to him; knife in hand I'd be more likely to rape him than kill him. And I go off on another tangent for a half hour or so. I take it out on the G-freak.

2.

Restless, still consumed by conflicting thoughts of Gerald Beech and fantasies about disappearing into the wilderness, I do something I have hardly done in recent years: I decide to go out and get a drink and collect my thoughts, dressed entirely as myself, being nothing but a woman going to a bar for a drink, maybe read a book and not kill anyone. Which in itself gives me a slight identity crisis; who am I if I am not indulging my habit and compulsion to kill, and yet who am I if I cannot enjoy doing exactly what I have been claiming in this memoir I am capable of doing (yet rarely do), which is demonstrate that I am in control of my own actions and I can, for one night at least, engage in a normal activity like a normal human being.

For a change I decide to go east and end up at this interesting dive of a bar I have a heard of before around Queen and Sherbourne, a piece of shit place that bills itself as a private club and lets its clients smoke after midnight. Wondering vaguely how they manage to stay in business without being busted by the cops, I go in and sit down and order a pint of beer instead of my normal vodka and tonic, for a change, pulling a book out of my bag, opening it and lighting a smoke. The book is *Memories, Dreams, Reflections* by Carl Jung, a book I love to read because I rarely dream at all anymore, which I personally believe is a side effect of having no real emotions to have to work through. Reading about other people's dreams gives me insight into the psychology of the majority, and this book has been a great companion of mine since my late teens.

I am sitting in my dimly lit booth, nearly done my second beer and sixth cigarette, ignoring the sounds of the door to the establishment opening and closing and barely aware of the changing tunes on the jukebox. Occasionally I look up to and stare indiscriminately at the back of the booth across the table from me, reflecting that it was a good idea to get out, to feel different, different moreover because I am myself and not in disguise. Eventually I become aware of the shape of someone to my left at the bar, and sense they are staring at me. Begrudging this intrusion on my thoughts, I turn my gaze in that direction and realize that it is Beech. I don't know how long he has been there, watching me intently. I make no motion of recognition and continue to eye him deadpan.

We stay like that for some time. He casually lights a smoke and continues staring into my eyes with me staring back at him, occasionally allowing myself to explore the contours of his face, ears, neck, shoulders, the little divot at the bottom of his throat where it meets his neck, the hint of chest hair peeking out from the v-shaped opening at the second from top button of his shirt. He is clearly off-duty, wearing a casual button-down, brown leather jacket, jeans and work boots. His short, dark brown hair is tousled carelessly. His face has the beginnings of that sexy weathered look that both stress and outdoor work gives a man as he stands with one leg in his 30s and 40s respectively. Oh, how I sometimes wish I were a real, live human, capable of something more than getting turned on or off when contemplating another person. In this case, I am getting increasingly turned on, literally touching him with my gaze, I can almost smell him from here, and I am growing ravenous for him.

After I don't know how long, he gets up and walks over to me, grabbing a chair and deftly turning it around to straddle it backwards rather than slide into the booth across from me. I light a cigarette and we continue to look at each other for another unfathomable span of time.

"Never seen you here before," he finally says, his voice low, lusty or angry or impatient or a combination of all three.

"Never been here before," I answer tritely and expressionless.

"I saw you a while back, at Bar Italia. You didn't look at all like yourself."

"Pretty sure I always look like myself."

"Touché."

"Yes."

We continue to look at each other. Finally I break the gaze and motion to the waitress to bring me another beer. He does the same.

"The man you were with hung himself two weeks later," he says, finally.

"Did he?" I ask without interest. "I suppose I wondered why he never called me back."

"Yes. Didn't seem like the right man for a suicide, but he left a note and it wasn't my case. Maybe it should have been."

"Maybe."

Radiohead, *Exit Music,* starts on the jukebox. It seems like a strange choice for this bar and this crowd. Outside of Nine Inch Nails, Radiohead is one of the few bands that can almost trick me into believing I can feel and this song is particularly good at it. Beech is still looking at me, I am still looking at him and we stay silent while the song, written for the movie *Romeo and Juliet*, plays out. It's like I can feel the music upon me, I can feel Beech's eyes penetrating me and I am pulled by the song to its haunting crescendo, its beautiful climax.

It is the most romantic moment of my life.

3.

When I look back at last night I find it is more confusing and convoluted than any of the crazy nights I've spent in the past, in strangers' beds, in strange locations, doing strange things to strange people in strange ways. Luring malevolent and unjust men to their deaths is much more natural to me than exploring the inside and outside of an actual connection to another human being. Nothing is more unfamiliar to me than something.

I'm not sure if we even spoke a word after that song, though of course we must have, because I'm sure we talked all night. There must have been some exchange of words otherwise I could not have suddenly found myself running, literally running, down the street with him from the bar, his strong, rough hand grasping mine, tumbling into a cab, tearing at each other in the back seat and then suddenly be upstairs in his century-walkup. Otherwise I could not know that Beech was that person I was looking for, that person who understands what is right and wrong, that person who believes in justice, the same justice, *real* justice, just as fervently and passionately as I do. Otherwise I could not know that he sensed the same in me and much more.

For hours I seemed only to be experiencing a jumble of limbs and tongues and lips and skin and muscle, a deliciously perplexing mixture of hard and soft, electricity so strong I could almost hear it humming, a cacophony of orgasm, guttural shrieks in the night. Then after, the quiet tracing of each other, discovery after conquest, words and thoughts and sensation mixing together before the weight of consequence could bear down on us. It was then that he told me – he *must* have spoken it out loud – that he knew, that he could see into me, through me and beyond. He couldn't know the details, but he knew, knew what drove me, why, what was missing, and that try as he might he could not wholly disagree.

"If I could do it myself, I would," he admitted in a whisper. "If I could disentangle myself from what I know to be right, if I could stop caring so much, I would have done exactly what you did and so much more. What I see every day on my job makes me want to go there, cross that line, be that person sometimes. I wouldn't have stopped at that one act, either; there are days when I feel I could burn the whole goddamn world down. But I don't. And I won't. And what's more, I couldn't. I'm afraid to even think about it; I'm afraid that maybe after all I *could* and then maybe I couldn't stop. However I admire the concept of justice, I am a slave to the law. And deep down inside I will always believe that people can be better than they are and deserve another chance."

I admitted nothing, which did precious more than avoid giving details of evidence that could lead to my eventual incarceration, for I also denied nothing. I merely held his gaze steady while continuing to map out the treasure trove of his body with my fingers.

"Someday," he went on, "you're going to fuck something up, I know it, and I'm going to be the one that catches you."

"I don't care."

"But I will," he breathed.

"Not as much as you think. You'll know it was the right thing to do, and the rest will fade like any other pain."

We laid there until dawn, neither of us sleeping or speaking. I could feel the foreignness of his feeling weighing against me as he pondered emotions he did not think he should have or speak of. I wondered if Gable was okay, if the dog-walker got my text message the night before and stopped to take him out or if there would be a mess to clean up when I got home.

Soon enough we got up; Beech had to go to work. I got halfway dressed before we caught hold of each other and tumbled back onto the bed for another episode, this one short-lived but more intense than anything I had experienced in my life.

As I was about to leave he caught me in his arms and gave me a long, tender, lingering kiss, the right amount of soft and hard, confidence and wanting.

"We can never see each other like this again, you know."

Yes, I know.

4.

Forget passion, patriotism, education, experience and devotion. If you want to get ahead in politics, nothing speaks louder or wields more power than money. And don't worry about caps on donations or laws or any trivial rules like that; if you have money and want to give it, they will figure out a way to let you.

Tonight I am a glorious, sophisticated, sumptuously voluptuous, porcelain-skinned redhead, for I know better than to ever show my real face around any of these people. Whatever hopes I had had of finding kindred spirits amongst those who devote their lives to "bettering" our country evaporated on first contact, back at the Factory Theatre fundraiser; the only way politicos resemble me at all is not through of love of justice, but through a disturbingly high propensity toward breeding fellow sociopaths. And I don't need to join a fucking club.

I look into the mirror one last time, adjusting my trendy Anne Klein bejeweled horn-rimmed glasses, grab my purse and head out the door.

This right-wing political fundraiser is like a buffet for a girl like me. So many greedy little bastards to choose from. This is why I show up in disguise and donate to their cause using a fake name. I plan to go hunting. I am welcomed with open arms by the little party-op I had met at the theatre fundraiser, who does not recognize me, and he shows me around the room, introducing me to people as a new member (which I am not), ogling my beautifully arranged breasts whenever he thinks I'm not looking and shamelessly even when I am.

The people in this room represent a fairly complete stereotype of the slimy side of republican conservatism. There is both the fat and thin self-stuffed fifty-something loudmouths, arriving with an overweight, over-dressed, badly aging woman whose family fortune is likely the basis of their relationship and which the male considers his personal accomplishment. There is the shallow male model-type with the fake tan and the whiter than white teeth, not only devoid of personality but actually sucking the personality out of others, active member of his community and church, complete with bleached blonde fake-titted arm-candy too-young-to-be-a-soccer-mom-but-will-be-soon, who is likely having sex with the first fifty-something stereotype while her boyfriend/husband buggers the hell out of another waxy rendition of himself in the bathroom at the gym. There are the single men, mostly shorter than your average male, oozing with self-esteem issues generally masked by an arrogant over-confidence and as a result amplifying their innate nerdiness. There are the single women, some Christian stereotypes whose fear of all things "liberal" is stamped clearly on their faces, some resembling nothing more than high-priced prostitutes. Nearly everyone is white and those who aren't are trying very hard to be. This is a crowd that abhors originality, education and poverty; there is a need to demonstrate that they are better than everyone else, borne of a deep-seeded fear that some people might not think they are good enough, or "cool" enough, with an immature and mean-spirited hate-on for anyone who feels comfortable in their own shoes, or skin. Shallow judgment and prejudice hangs heavily in the air.

In this room, everyone bears a grudge against another person or group of people. Most of it is partisan, with few being able to carry on even a short conversation without demonstrating not just disdain, but all-out hatred for what they call the "bleeding heart loony leftist socialists", which includes not only partisan liberals, but also gays and lesbians, academics, scientists, artists, immigrants, activists and every other person or thing that makes life on this planet diverse and interesting.

I speak to a couple who is currently outraged about youth petty crime, who have convinced themselves that their way of life is in imminent danger because teenagers exist, and that all children should be treated and tried as adults, locked away forever – except for their own children, who, if they were to commit any crime whatsoever, would only do so under the influence of impoverished gangsters, rock music, or video games. I speak to another group of people who complain about the science of global warming, who consider it a leftist conspiracy meant to persecute Christians. I speak to several people who think that artists are nothing but slaves to the elite of society, who should only crank out their work for the pleasure of others and never allow themselves the slightest in self-expression. I speak to a whole slew of them who truly believe that homelessness should be considered illegal. Backward, fearful, ignorant people wearing expensive suits come at me from every direction, all of whom express a deep desire to rid the world of those they disagree with in the cruelest, most unjust way. To them, both life and politics are a war that they must win at any cost; their grudge against their perceived enemies is void of any sense of acceptance or forgiveness and will carry on beyond eternity.

By the end of the evening I am convinced these people are insane, in a way I am not and never will be. They are not sociopaths; they care too much about how they themselves are treated in their imaginary and paranoid world. They have made a clear and decisive choice not to not be immoral, but to rewrite the definition of morality until it suits their warped and twisted minds. It is not wrong to kill a good, innocent person, not if that person is representative of another system of belief, religious or political, one they have convinced themselves is an enemy to their own way of life. It is not wrong to treat everyone with disrespect if they fall into a category that an elitist interpretation of some holy text or creed has deemed unworthy. All humans are not created equal, not to these folks, and morality only applies to their category, real or fake. Those who belong in which category is an ever-changing, interchangeable set of definitions that serves only to make excuses for them having to take any responsibility for their actions. God is guiding their hand.

I am rightly seething when I leave the fundraiser later that evening. In the parking lot I wait for my cab to take me back to my condo and am accosted by a slightly tipsy motherfucker in his late forties, one of the ones who thinks the army should violently remove the homeless from the streets and shoot the dirty gays in their sleep, slurring to me how beautiful I am and how we should make great babies together, repopulate the planet with the *real* version of the chosen people, white people. I think about what Beech so deeply believes, that people can change, deserve the chance to change, and I find as usual that I do not care. Life is too short. There is only justice in the here and now.

I can't not take this asshole out.

"Oh honey, you're breaking my heart," he says mockingly when I tell him I only have a couple of hours and that we'll have to go to his place. I present him with a sexy smile.

"You don't deserve to have a heart," I tell him with a smirk as we head towards his car.

5.

I am sitting in the park across the street from the Parkview Arms, waiting for my homeless friend Shaun to show up. Gable sits obediently beside me. The car is parked at the curb, packed with the few things that Shaun said I should bring with us, including a newly purchased Wrist Rocket Pro slingshot, a new hunting knife and a 7mm Map flat shooter deer rifle, all purchased under one of my several aliases, though not the one used at the Tory fundraiser.

I have today's newspaper, and am looking with something close to fondness at a picture of Beech before proceeding to read the article about the ongoing investigation into the shocking murder of Shannon Giles, self-professed reformed Pentecostal minister, political lobbyist, professional moralist, pillar of his [white fundamentalist] community and headmaster of his own so-called Christian "college", who was found dead in his home the day after a political fundraiser with his heart cut out of his chest. Forensic analysis of every item at the crime scene turned up no viable clues as to the identity of his killer. Giles was last seen leaving the fundraiser with a woman described as a new member, whose name is found on the list of donors but whose identity and location cannot be confirmed.

"The police are doing everything we can to track down this woman. As of this moment, she is not a suspect, but we believe she can give us valuable information as to the last moments of Reverend Giles' life," Beech is quote saying in the article. "However, as our investigation continues to turn up details of the minister's life, we are finding that his list of enemies is too long to claim right now that we have any one suspect, or even any one motive. We will track down every lead and keep the public informed, but as of this moment we do not believe there is a risk to the community. Despite the sadistic nature of the crime, we believe this was a vendetta killing."

He knows it's you. Gable says to me. *And he's looking for a way to find you.*

"So be it," I say under my breath. And quite frankly I don't care. It is without a doubt the most gruesome and ritualistic murder I have ever committed, but he had been such a deserving candidate.

Shannon Giles had taken me to his opulent mansion in an affluent suburb north of the city core. He had called ahead to make sure his two servants were sent home for the night, so as not to provide fodder for any rumours of his philandering that might find its way back into his religious community. Immediately upon closing the front door he came at me. I was glad I was there willingly because it was clear from his eyes that unwilling he would take me anyway. I stopped him short of touching my skin and told him to go upstairs, asking if I could borrow a long coat from his hall closet so that we might better "play". He went and got me a long dark grey raincoat, which I carried upstairs over my arm. Going into his en suite bathroom, I put the raincoat on over my dress and buttoned it up to the top, so it appeared I was wearing nothing underneath but my stockings and three-inch high heels. Reaching into my bag I pulled out a new pair of dressy black gloves, putting them on and then taking out an opaque plastic bag and a good-sized hunting knife I had purchased the day before, both of which I slipped into the pocket of the coat.

I opened the door to the bathroom and stood there for a moment, watching his beady, greedy little eyes look me up and down from where he stood in the centre of the room, and walked towards him. With one motion I pulled the knife out of my pocket, unsheathed it and stabbed him in the solar plexus, taking care to drag the knife upwards as hard as I could. He didn't have a chance to scream; he only made a strange, long-winded gurgling sound before I ripped the knife out of his chest and he slid to the floor. It took him about ten minutes to die and I squatted beside him and watched the process with interest. Just before he took his last breath I leaned in and whispered, "I told you that you didn't deserve to have a heart," and he gaped at me in horror as he realized what I was about to do.

I put the knife down and took off my gloves, pulled a shower cap out of my pocket and covered my hair, then put the gloves back on. Taking the bloody knife in my gloved hand I proceeded to roughly but accurately stab him in a circle around his heart, cracking through a few ribs and sending spurts of blood up and all over the coat I was wearing. It was much harder than I had anticipated and I made quite a mess as I struggled to open his chest cavity. I was glad I had learned this lesson now and not on some poor defenseless animal I depended on for a meal; I had definitely contaminated the meat. Reaching into his chest, I pulled out his heart, using the knife to saw it loose from the associated arteries and tissue that clung to it. It was warm, almost hot, and still seemed to be beating. I placed the heart on the floor beside his body and stood up, taking the plastic bag out of my pocket, dropping the knife inside and removing the gloves, coat and cap, which also went into the bag. I went back into the bathroom, washed my hands and took a new, clean pair of gloves out of my purse, which I donned without delay. I gave the sink and faucets a quick wipe, gathered my things together, including the plastic bag, did a cursory check to ensure nothing was left behind and sauntered casually downstairs and out of the house.

Lighting a cigarette, I took a leisurely walk for about five blocks, fantasizing about my upcoming survival lessons with Shaun, until I came to an open convenience store. I went inside and asked the clerk if he could please call me a cab and then went back outside to have another smoke while I waited. I took that cab most of the way downtown at which point I got out, hailed another cab, which I took until about a block away from my condo. I walked the rest of the way home and then, over a vodka and tonic and a few cigarettes, I burned the evidence in my fireplace. The plastic bag I washed out thoroughly with pure bleach that I left, inside another plastic bag along with the leftover Chinese food that had been rotting in my fridge for a week, in one of the building's recycling bins.

The media and the public couldn't get enough of it. Over the past week the Reverend Giles' life had been exposed for what it was: a series of moral and criminal acts that included rape, extortion, fraud, political interference and assault. The Tories did everything they could to disassociate themselves from this abhorrent creature, to little avail.

It was simply glorious.

6.

Day five in the woods just northwest of North Bay and I am heading back to the camp site with Shaun at my side, about to demonstrate for the first time that I have learned from his careful instructions and am able to gut and cook the large brown rabbit that I have just killed on our morning hunt with my slingshot. I have been having a great week so far; I suppose I should have guessed it but I'm really quite a talented hunter. I have taken to the slingshot like I've been using one my entire life. I'm not bad with the rifle, either. Fishing, too, is turning out to be very easy, both with a pole and reel and with a self-fashioned spear. Shaun is really very impressed with me.

Base camp, which we constructed together from material in the woods, is a good sized shelter made of branches and covered with pine needles and mulch and really more comfortable than I had ever thought it would be. Like an expert I sit down and start a fire in the fire pit from some dried moss and a stick; soon it is a blazing open flame. Sitting on the rock that has become my seat around the fire, I lay out the rabbit carcass on another rock and with a hatchet I hack off its head and legs at the knees. I cut a slit horizontally across the hide near the back legs. Grabbing the skin, I pull it right off. Then I take a small, sharp knife, pick up the dead rabbit, hold it in my left hand around its chest and insert my knife just below its ribs at a shallow angle, making an incision about three quarters of an inch long, being careful not to insert the knife more than a quarter of an inch, as Shaun tells me that I might contaminate the meat if I were to puncture the entrails. Then, to get the entrails outside the body, I take the rabbit by the back legs with one hand, around the chest with my other and raise it as high as my shoulder, and swing the rabbit downwards that way I would if I were trying to empty something stuck to the bottom of a bucket. I pull and break the bottom of the attached entrails, but to remove the top of the entrails without contaminating the meat I reach up under the ribs and pull out the stomach. I look inside the chest cavity and puncture the diaphragm, which looks like a tight membrane, and then I pull out the heart and lungs. Shaun says I don't have to do this part if I'm cooking the rabbit whole, which we are, but I figure best to learn while I still have an instructor around. Over the fire, I proceed to sauté the rabbit in a frying pan with onions and garlic. It is a delicious meal. Strangely, it doesn't give me a stomachache at all.

That night after Shaun goes to sleep I stay out by the fire and chain-smoke for a while with Gable at my side. He and I have bonded anew this week, dog and owner hunting together, not sitting, staring, judging.

This is the life. He says to me now. *It is better here than in the city.*

"I think so too," I agree. Quite frankly I am surprised I have never spent any time in the wilderness before. Mosquitoes don't seem to bite me; I'm not bothered by insects or shitting in the woods or any of the things my delicate urban comrades complain of. Hunting for food seems to fulfill me in the same way hunting for justice does in the city, and out here I can forget other people even exist. I am surprised to find that in forgetting other people exist, I forget that such a large portion of my own personality does not. What had hitherto been a fantasy of escaping the city and my life there has in the past few days presented itself as a real possibility. Exactly how I will go about extracting myself so that I leave no trace of my existence is going to take some planning, but now I know it can happen.

7.

"Oh for fuck's sake!" I exclaim as I butt out a cigarette in the ashtray beside my laptop, where I have been reading the paper online. Gable walks into the room and looks at me curiously. I have just finished reading yet another "breaking story" about social networking sites such as Facebook or Twitter, the latest of the evil spawn on the world wide web, one more thing for people to distract themselves with so that they can never, ever get anything accomplished ever again.

My frustration at all of this has been amplified since I spent the time in the woods with Shaun and caught a glimpse of the actual depths and capabilities of the human mind when not being rotted from the outside in. The advent of Twitter is what annoys me the most at the moment, a tool that has people crafting short sentences about what's on their mind to post to the world. Like the blogs before it, few people are reading or digesting or learning from this, and those becoming obsessed with broadcasting their every waking inanity are further cutting themselves off from any real thought or progress about anything. All information becomes fragmented and nothing is whole.

Ideas, real ideas, the sorts of ideas that have propelled humanity forward throughout history, need time to develop and be digested. They are borne not of the spectre of brilliant explosion, but through the agitation of an unoccupied mind. In short, the more bored a person is, the better chance they have of focusing their thoughts and activities on creating something innovative and exciting.

Think for a second of the day to day experience of a young teenager or even adult in this age we live in now. Wake up, text your friends, turn on your computer, login to Facebook, update your status with how you feel at the moment (I don't want to go to school/Is it Monday again?/I have a busy week ahead of me/Can't wait til after work and going to the gym/The big game is on tonight/I hope traffic isn't too congested), eat a quick breakfast, go to school or work. School and work is but a mere skeleton of the time and effort put into the same even twenty-five years ago – children go to class and use a fraction of their minds while working on computers, cell phones radiating a future tumour into their bodies while they buzz incessantly all day long, kids sharing undeveloped thoughts and amplifying the cruelty of the childhood experience on a worldwide, public scale. Facebook, Twitter, Messenger, Chat, Blogs, all these things need to constantly reflect where and who we are. Then lunchtime or after school, homework searched out on the Internet from at best, questionable sources, the quality of information degrading by the second, rumour replacing fact, history being re-written at a faster pace than any government revisionist project could ever hope for. Video games sucking up hours of time, where thought is numbed, progress is stunted. Television must still be fit in, not to mention other video entertainment online like searching for and watching pointless and tiresome YouTube videos, Facebook videos, or television network libraries.

And it shows. In a new world order that favours the temporary over the permanent, where everything can be changed or revised or erased, pilfering off of other people's ideas that have been pilfered off of other people's ideas that have been pilfered off of other people's ideas until the quality of everything is degraded. Real analysis and insight is a thing of the past. Everybody is suffering from a self-imposed and highly curable cased of Attention Deficit Disorder, but no one wants to take responsibility for it.

It doesn't matter what industry or what scenario. We have made ourselves stupid while simultaneously convincing ourselves we are brilliant. We brag about the greatness of technology, but the truth is that most of the genius that has gone into most things we utilize today was created long ago by minds that no longer exist; creating eCommerce from a web site, creating Facebook from discussion boards and chat rooms, creating Twitter from all of this, it's like adding a leaf to a tree.

The reason someone like me is both compelled to and able to exist is because no one can pay attention long enough to really give a shit.

8.

Public relations professionals are the new white meat.

They are the perfect mix of corporate and political motherfuckery and hunting them turns me on. I'm talking about the types who work for companies like Hill & Knowlton and are the masterminds behind campaigns such as helping the government convince America that there were weapons of mass destruction in Iraq to convince people that they were justified in going to war and overthrowing the Iraqi government. Or the first Gulf war, the Nurse Nayirah campaign, the "innocent" young refugee who was really the daughter of a Kuwaiti ambassador, who told Americans the completely fake story of Saddam Hussein's troops throwing babies out of incubators in hospitals, a $14million campaign for H&K. The campaign to convince people that high cholesterol is an epidemic that leads to certain death – or any pharmaceutical attempt to sell largely untested drugs for profit over health. Et cetera. Public opinion campaigns for profit and public relations campaigns for cover-up. The more of these assholes who can be wiped off the face of the planet, the better chance we have for survival.

So it was with renewed energy that I go home with Ian McKinley, a hot young executive with the aforementioned Hill & Knowlton, whom I met earlier in the evening at the absolute most pretentious bar I have ever seen in the city. Actually named *Shmooze* (don't mind they spelled it wrong; none of the patrons would notice), it is described thusly: *"Hiding down a side street, Shmooze's interior features cathedral ceilings, chandeliers and hardwood floors. Good-looking patrons in their 20s and 30s sporting designer clothes and attitudes flock to the dance floor, or sit at one of the two bars and order drinks off a menu that includes 12 specialty martinis."* It is the perfect place to go hunting for corrupt, shallow, greedy, societal aberrations that would be better off extinct. I have never had an unsuccessful evening there. Tonight was one of the most successful to date.

When going to this and similar bars, I find it best to go as a platinum blonde with a fake tan, iridescent blue or silver makeup, lip-liner, dressed in something like this tight black low-cut Versace and strappy Gucci sandals winding themselves half way up my leg. Just the sort of woman these up-and-coming executives picture themselves taking to the summerhouse in the Muskokas or the villa in Barcelona, meeting their boss or managing the nanny.

Ian McKinley not only worked at H&K, he was on the "Tell Someone" Gardasil public awareness campaign – a campaign for Merck to sell the "cancer vaccine" Gardasil by convincing people that HPV is an epidemic putting your life in imminent danger and distracting you from the fact that their five year clinical trial was riddled with problems and assured no efficacy of the vaccine. 1,400 deaths per year from a highly treatable form of cancer that takes decades to develop, which may or may not be caused by two strains of the HPV virus does not warrant rushing a product to market and force-feeding it through a hysteria-inducing "awareness" campaign which in many parts of this country and across the world has led to near-mandatory widespread application of the vaccine to children as young as nine years old to young women as old as thirty, for a total profit of $900/person for each three-part vaccination.

I consider Ian's imminent death to be nothing more than one of many that occurred during the clinical trials and were deemed not worth announcing or investigating further. But, after leaving his house an hour later, his broken, lifeless body still bleeding out at the bottom of the stairs where his skull has been cracked open on the imported tile floor, I feel unsatisfied. Moreover, I *feel*. Unlike the day when I missed Paul, I can't place what this feeling is, only that it is equally as strong and as intense as that day now almost a year ago. And like that day, all I want to do is run, which I can't do at the moment as I am wearing 4-inch high heel sandals. What the hell is happening to me?

I light a cigarette, walk another block and then hail a cab. I need to get home. Now. I need to get out of this outfit and this wig and take a hot or cold shower, go for a run, pour bleach into my eyes, anything to distract me from this avalanche of indecipherable emotion. Twenty minutes later finds me back out on the street, this time in athletic-wear, running as fast and hard as I can towards the lakefront path, where I follow it west for nearly forty-five minutes and then turn around and head back home. Nothing is working; nothing is helping.

What's more is, I'm crying. Crying. Me. The tears run freely down my face as I jog along. People out for a late evening stroll or run stare at me with a mixture of concern and curiosity as they pass me by. Tears are mixing with snot and running down over my lips. It's all I can do to keep from running off the boardwalk and right into the lake. Is it guilt, sadness, fear? I cannot tell. Only that it's stronger than anything, anything I've experienced before.

"Please, please make it go away," I whimper as I jog. "Please, please, please…" This isn't working. Nothing is working.

Finally I get back to my building and go upstairs, hiding my tearstained face from the concierge. In the elevator I look at my reflection in the mirrored walls. My eyes are different, vibrant and something is in them, something alive. Is this what emotion looks like? Have I become whole?

I get out of the elevator and walk directly into Beech's arms, who was apparently let upstairs by the concierge and was waiting outside the door to my condo. Directly into his arms, without a word from either of us, lips coming together hard, ripping at each other, tongues wrestling together. He pulls my t-shirt up over my head pushes aside my bra and roughly takes my sweaty, salty nipples into his mouth, sucking hard, pulling, emotion and sensation pulsing through my entire body at the rhythm he is setting, flipping me around so my back is against the wall as he tears down my shorts and panties. I fumble with my keys and finally open the door to the condo and we slide inside, me expertly opening his pants and releasing his cock, his hard cock, drawing it to me, up me, in me, as he pins me against the wall, pounding me, kneading my ass, door still open, elevator still in view.

I feel how much I missed him, how much I want him, how much

I don't want him gone from my life again, hard and unmistakably. I am losing my mind.

9.

The next morning I awaken and discover Beech is gone. There is a note beside the bed that says, "I couldn't stay away, but I'm going to keep on trying. –X". I feel nothing. It is as if last night was a dream. I get up and look in the mirror. My eyes are my own again, impenetrable, unreadable, dead. I go downstairs and put on a pot of coffee, then head down briefly to the lobby to check my mail. I have an invitation from the Tories to another fundraiser, addressed to me, the real me, the one who as far as they knew didn't show up to the last one. I vaguely wonder how they got my address, as I certainly didn't give it to them. I cannot even entertain the thought of going, though; one more evening in a room with those people and I would kill them all. And now, getting so much closer to being able to leave this shit forever, and with Beech so connected to me, I do not want to take the chance of being caught.

I no longer feel like I am going insane, at least not today. There isn't even any measure of sanity anymore. As far as I am concerned, the whole world has gone insane and done it with gusto. Our brains are no longer our own; from my usual vantage point outside of regular society, it is painfully clear that humans have allowed themselves to be convinced that the most normal of function and emotion is a symptom of a disorder or syndrome, and therefore we flock to rid ourselves of normality. The new human prototype, propagated by the pharmaceutical industry's undying quest for profit and various governments' undying quest for control, is truly insane indeed. Though there is no reason in the history of humanity to believe that happiness is a perpetual state, we have convinced ourselves it should be. That in itself is the biggest symptom that we have all lost our minds, this new belief that we not only have the capability, but the right, to be calm and happy and stable at all moments in our life, that pain is an indication of weakness rather than an instigator of growth and change and evolution, and it demonstrates to me as an outsider that the vast majority has willingly released its grip on reality.

Every single person I know who has had children in the past ten years has subsequently been told by doctors, nurses, teachers, or mental health professionals that not only do the normal variety of behaviours displayed by their children fall into any number of categories of psychological "disorders", but that there is no choice other than to drug these small developing minds. Rather than encourage development and take responsibility for the roles of the adult in the child's life, we instead blame the child, or inflict some imaginary disease upon that child and therefore shape the mind with chemicals instead of allowing it evolve naturally. No one seems to ask themselves what is to become of a generation that has had its mind altered by drugs from early childhood until adulthood, how an identity is supposed to be formed when the mind is being controlled by an outside force.

Most of my peers are terrible parents. Driven by some idea of their right to bear children, they are grown, fashioned, induced by experiment even before conception, only to be discarded for a majority of the time in favour of pursuing their own dreams and goals. It is so necessary for them to have babies, but at the same time they are not willing to raise them. A stranger is paid to keep them during the day, video games and television nurture them in the evenings; any behaviour outside of perfect calm and happiness is seen as abnormal. Their children have ADHD, they're not reacting perfectly normally against lack or nurture, lack of nature, lack of exercise, lack of sleep, processed food, divorce, abuse, etc., etc.

And if it can't be cured by drugs, then it will be cured by God. True insanity is to be found in the swelling of the fundamentalist religious movement, no matter what the religion. Logic is discarded in favour of religious fervour. Bizarre, tedious religious language has crept into everyday life; people I have known from childhood who were raised in perfectly normal homes by perfectly normal parents have allowed themselves to get sucked into a dangerous group psychology wherein speaking to non-existent spirits and giving up one's mental and motor skills to the temporary thrill of a hysterical herd mentality is redefining the very term "normal". Religious texts that were written mainly to provide some comfort to humans coping with the reality of our painful, dangerous existence on this planet have been manipulated and reinterpreted to allow people to live their lives inside a magical fairytale more stunted and immature than anything conceived of by a child.

Gone is any attempt to achieve peace of mind, tolerance, compassion, wisdom, or empathy; instead we strive to devolve from the moment our personal evolutions become apparent. Feeling the presence or hearing the voice of a spirit you know beyond any shadow of a doubt is the historical figure of Jesus Christ is insane. Demanding corporal punishment because someone has spoken ill of or defaced the graven image of a deity you have been taught is real, so that you can continue worshiping something that asks only that you are kind is insane. Not knowing or wanting to know that what is happening is an unnatural fantasy arising around natural psychological phenomena and is a further indication of your insanity. Am I offending you? Tough shit, because quite frankly you are offending me.

Who are we to say that the elephants are going mad? That is rather the pot calling the kettle black. I posit we are the society that is willfully, excitedly losing our minds. We have *chosen* our insanity and that is the most insane thing of all. I posit instead that the elephants are *getting* mad, sick to death of watching us destroy ourselves, destroy them, destroy everything. They are sick to death of having to put up with the human race, one that makes everything and everyone bow to it, one that treats itself and everyone else with unnecessary and abject cruelty, one that chooses – *chooses!* – to do so to the detriment of the entire planet and everything on it.

I am like the elephants. I am not going mad. I'm just sick of living in a world where everyone else is.

10.

Today I am going to visit Renee; I have barely seen her since she had her baby four months ago. I am not particularly looking forward to the visit, to feigning the necessary fawning, to whatever conversation we must muster together that I am sure to be wholly disinterested in.

It is a gorgeous autumn afternoon, still warm enough to walk through the city bare-legged, so I decide to delay my arrival by walking the five or so kilometres to Renee's apartment above her studio on Markham St. I blind myself to the throngs of people around me: the shiny city-folk and the fascinated tourists. I instead focus on the architecture of the city, the living history that is slowly but surely being decimated by modern renovations of much lesser quality. All too soon, I find myself approaching Renee's doorstep. Setting my mouth in a straight line and preparing for the theatrics to come, I go inside and up the stairs.

"It's so good to see you!" she exclaims as she opens the door, and for a moment I forget that I have been so fed up with her for so long. She seems, almost, like the girl I knew and woman I admired. She has an easel with an unfinished painting of the child set up in the spacious living room, and the subject of the painting is sitting in person in a detachable baby-carrier/car seat on the floor next to it.

"So good to see you too," I say to her. I accept a cup of tea and resign myself to the fact that I will not be allowed to smoke in the apartment with the baby around. I dig around in my bag for a piece of nicotine gum, locate one and pop it into my mouth. The child and I stare at each other.

What am I doing here? it asks me with its eyes. I shake my head. I don't think it would like my answer.

"So how have you been?" I ask when she returns with the tea.

"Oh, all right, I suppose," Renee says, immediately adopting a self-piteous tone of voice that sets me on edge. "It's been hard coping with the baby. Jeffrey is at work so much. I barely ever see him. I feel like all I do is play with this infant." She shoots the child a rather scornful look. The child's eyes say, *I know what that means. Why do you hate me so much?* Renee doesn't get it.

I drink my tea and watch the child listen and comprehend, if not the words, then the feeling behind the words, as Renee complains like all tired new mothers do about the trials and tribulations of motherhood, simultaneously casting themselves as both persecuted and superior, disdainful of those who do not have children, convinced a childless person simply cannot understand *just how much* the new mother suffers and triumphs. I know these speeches by heart.

"Thank goodness I have Jack," she says finally.

"Jack? You mean Jeffrey?" I honestly thought it was a slip of the tongue. As Renee looks away, however, and then back at me, the truth of the situation hits me with sudden certainty. "You're not... seeing him again are you?"

Looking down, she answers, "What do you mean by seeing him?"

"Holy fuck, Renee, who do you think you're kidding? If you weren't still having sex with that motherfucker you'd have said so right off, not try to dance around the truth. How long has this been going on, or did it ever end?"

"I don't know!" she says, starting to cry. "You don't understand! I just can't stay away from him! He's married now too and he's just not happy, and neither am I, and we're just so drawn to each other, we can't resist."

"Oh try a little restraint," I shoot at her, looking at the child. *I've seen it*, it says. I look back at Renee. "Do you take the child with you?" I ask, already knowing.

"What am I supposed to do?" she wails.

Something inside me, that thing that is so hollow, becomes even moreso. The last shred of respect I had for Renee is gone. I can see the future of that child, that little child who sees and understands, dealing with the memories Renee has carelessly already put in its head. I see the behavioural issues, the eventual medications, the hardening of the spirit, the confusion, the pain, the loneliness. I can see it all, and worst of all I can see that it's completely unnecessary. I can see that the child sees it as well. I hope wildly that Jeffrey will find out about the affair and take the child away from Renee.

"You have to tell Jeffrey," I tell her.

"I can't! What if he leaves me? What if he hates me?"

"If you don't tell him, I will. I will also tell Jack's wife. You have a week."

She stares at me and a rare flash of anger crosses her face. It doesn't become her. "This is none of you business!" she hurls at me.

"Of course it's not, I never said it was. But it *is* Jeffrey's business." I am deadly calm.

"You fucking bitch!" she jumps up and screams. The child starts to whimper and cry.

I walk across the room and grab Renee by the shoulder and force her to sit down. I bring my face very close to hers and whisper, "Now you listen to me, Renee. You get a grip on yourself and grow up. You have the ability to do the right thing, to not fuck up this child with your stupid issues, to be responsible. I am not going to let you ruin this kid. I'll be watching you, believe me."

"Get out of here," she hissed, her eyes narrowed down to slits. The baby wails. "Get out of here, you and your ignorant threats and your moral superiority. All you do is lecture everyone else, judge everyone else, but what of your life? Who the hell do you think you are? Stay away from me and my family."

"You'd better hope I do," I say archly. I get up, walk over to the child and touch its cheek. It immediately, if temporarily, stops crying. I turn and leave.

Moral superiority! I laugh as I walk down the street.

11.

Sitting in the hot tub the next evening with Beech, I relay the events at Renee's to him. I am not looking for opinion or approval, but am rather relieved that I have something normal to talk about with someone.

"It's a complicated issue," Beech agrees. "As a cop, I see it all the time; there aren't many people you come across on the beat or during an investigation who are what you might call 'exemplary parents'. Certainly most of them should have thought twice before they decided to add another messed up soul to the world, but I'm pretty sure most of them didn't even think once about it. But that's the foundation of the human race, isn't it? Surviving against all odds? Having irresponsible parents like you have described your friend Renee as doesn't guarantee her kid will be screwed up. Parents have done a lot worse to their children than bring them along while they get a little extramarital something on the side. And parents have been as close as a person could get to perfect and turned out serial killers. Not everything is a product of your environment."

"You're probably right," I say agreeably, reaching over the edge of the tub for my cigarettes, offering him one, which he takes. I pass him the lighter after I've lit mine. My parents were pretty much perfect. They would be horrified to find out who I am and what I've done. So would Beech. He thinks I went a little gangbusters and blew up a boat with a bunch of people on it he could do without in this world; and he comforts himself by not facing the reality of that, by saying he only suspects and has no evidence, will likely never have any evidence and that it is wrong of him to project that suspicion onto me, who he hopes is truly an innocent person.

Lately I've been wishing pretty consistently that I *were* an innocent person. In between kills I can even convince myself that I am, that everything I've done is nothing more than an elaborate fantasy, at worst a temporary psychotic break. For the first time in my life I wish I could feel because I would like very much to know what it's like to fall in love with Gerald Beech, to live a normal life with him, to get a house, maybe even spit out a few kids. I can imagine how that feels, but inside nothing is happening.

I glance down to the end of the patio where Gable is sitting; patiently waiting for us to finish and come inside, with his eyes telling me he forgives me. I don't want him to forgive me. I don't *need* him to forgive me. I turn away from him and put out my cigarette, moving across the tub and crawling up onto Beech's lap, which is immediately eager and willing beneath me.

We have given up the pretense that we had been keeping for a while that this was a temporary thing we have embarked upon. There was no point denying the magnetic force that not only continued to draw us together, but grew stronger with each encounter. Though I'm sure Beech would have been game, I have been making him keep his distance insofar as not allowing us to become a daily habit; sometimes more than a week goes by and we would not see each other. We rarely speak on the phone. We do not exchange romantic niceties. There is no outward display of emotion. We just can't stay apart, keep our bodies away from each other, our hands off each other, our skin disconnected. I don't know how Beech really feels about me in his infinite and enviable capacity for feeling, because he is wise enough to never cross that line with me. It is, overall, a situation I could live with indefinitely, or so I think now.

I think about all of this sitting in my armchair, smoking a cigarette, body still tingling from Beech's touch, even though an hour has passed already since he has left. Gable comes padding quietly into the room and sits across from me with his big eyes.

I forgive you, he says. *You want to change and you can't. I forgive you now for what you've done. But you have to go away. We will go away, we will leave it all behind; you have to do this for Beech, for yourself. He's going to catch you and you will destroy him by forcing him to destroy you. Maybe you don't care, but you know this is true and you know you have a choice.*

"Shut up shut up shut up!!" I scream so suddenly I surprise myself. A whirlpool is churning inside my chest and stomach, threatening to drown me from the inside out. "I can't take your fucking judgment anymore!" I scream at Gable. "That's *IT*, it's *OVER!*" I jump and run upstairs to the bathroom and open the cabinet, where I have a bottle of chloroform. I grab it and a dust rag, run back downstairs, grab Gable by the collar and drag him into his kennel. He starts whimpering, knowing something is wrong, terribly wrong, that we're both in danger. I go to the kitchen and get five oversized garbage bags and some duct tape and proceed to seal off Gable's kennel. Before I drop the last flap I douse the rag in the chloroform and put it and the open bottle inside.

He howls a few times then whimpers for about 15 minutes and is then silent. I smoke a cigarette, tears streaming down my face. I smoke another.

"Fuck it, FUCK IT!" I yell with another burst of movement; I run over to the kennel and rip off the plastic, open the kennel door, put the cap back on the chloroform bottle and drag a groggy but conscious Gable out into the air. He licks my hand weakly. I am crying uncontrollably, wracked by the first attack of conscience I can ever remember having. "I'm so sorry, Gable, I'm so sorry," I sob, sitting on the floor beside him and hugging him around his neck. "I do want you to forgive me, I do, please do. You're right, you're right, we'll go away from here, just you and me, we'll get away, we'll forget everything that's happened. I promise."

I lay there with him for another hour. Minute by minute the surge of emotion I had felt recedes, until it has left me altogether and I once again feel cold and hollow. By early evening Gable is evening walking around, eating some food. I am sitting by the window staring at the lake, at the ever-present shadow, at my trophy, my reminder. Gable walks over and puts his head in my lap; I stroke his forehead.

"I do promise we'll leave, Gable, I'm planning for it and I'll plan for it more seriously now. But in the meantime…" I trail off, a smile traveling slowly across my face as I look down at him.

I felt certain you'd say that, he says to me. *Go on, go upstairs and get ready. Have yourself a little fun while you still can. This city is still full of assholes.*

12.

Liberals prefer brunettes. Over the course of this evening, one of the main things I've noticed is that women with darker hair command an immediate respect that blondes do not. The blondes are seen more as playthings, as symbols of beauty, as an attractive lure for both the men present and the electorate at large. But brunettes project an air of sophistication, of education, that women with other colours of hair do not. How boring it is to realize that in this room full of academics, lawyers and the corporate elite, such a basic psychology of stereotype abounds.

As with my foray into the right side of politics, I am as immediately and thoroughly disillusioned by the left. This fundraising event drips with elitism. The venue is one of the most expensive and exclusive clubs in the city. The guests talk to each other in small circles, champagne or martini in hand, speaking in controlled tones about their own successes, or about political ideas theorized by whichever published analytical mind is in current fashion. Their opponents, if referred to at all, are snottily discarded with a pretentious laugh and derisive words of dripping disdain. The electorate... well, they're never mentioned at all.

This group is much more colourful than the one I encountered at the Tory event. Samplings from nearly every culture is found here; unlike the Tories, the Liberals don't identify race or creed when they think of "their own"; they care only that whatever group you belong to, it is affluent, powerful and superior to the tiresome rubes to whom they pay public lip service. The Old Boys' Club persona is tangible here. Distinguished silver-haired pillars of society tap expensive cigars and drawl with Bostonian eloquence as their wives, well-kept, bejeweled duchesses, listen on intently, contributing with nearly, but not quite, as much confidence and knowledge as their male counterparts.

Whereas the group of Tories I met have clawed their way to the top in the past couple of generations, the Liberals have been born into it, or at least wanted any onlookers to believe they have. Politics is the new money versus the old money, but always about the money, the power and all the benefits that go along with it. In these circles, feudalism is not dead; they've just changed its name and convinced the huddled masses that they have a voice, a choice and a very slim chance to join them.

I walk into the room alone, greeted by the approving looks of the male guests, ignored or stared at by the females. I see immediately a few of the polished public faces of the party, one such elected member who quickly finds his way over to introduce himself in a tone of voice that demonstrates he clearly believes he needs no introduction. His wife, across the room, eyes me with pure malice and so she should; within a few moments it becomes clear this politician has every intention of getting me alone and fucking my brains out. I let him believe it; not only am I in disguise, but I know already that these people won't remember a name or a face fifteen minutes after it's left their line of sight. Soon he is joined by another face I recognize, a politician famous for his apparent alcoholism, a condition that upon meeting him in person I decide is more than just "apparent". This man coos and dotes on me like a would-be sugar daddy and even manages to slip his hand down and cup my ass like a pro while talking to me.

I make my way around the room. Lawyer, lawyer, lawyer, doctor, CEO, lawyer, CFO, doctor, real estate, philanthropist, lawyer, lawyer, doctor, philanthropist, professor, journalist, lawyer, author, lawyer, lawyer, lawyer. Shaking endless limp, soft-skinned, well-manicured hands. Looking amused while man after man tries his luck at laying the groundwork for seduction; truly amused at the number of short, young, eager little would-be politicians who try as well. The women, ignoring, belittling, or outright insulting me whenever the opportunity arises, then going off to try and get the attention of whomever they have personally deemed has the most to offer them and their future. It's a schmooze-fest that promises to outdo any of the sorts that I experienced in the corporate world, the type of event where deals and careers are made and unmade. There was a shocking lack of conversation or interest in society, policy, or the populace. The collective chips on the shoulders of those in this room would have weighed more than the Parliament Buildings.

"The Tories are still refusing to intervene on behalf of Canadians abroad who are in prisons and facing torture or death. We need to start a campaign to bring them back; that will bring a positive spotlight onto us and will also bring a lot of people to a fundraiser to earn money for the party," says one party operative in a conversation I stumble into.

"How does one go about bringing someone back from that sort of situation?" I ask, apparently innocently, because I get a bunch of condescending laughs.

"Oh, it's pretty simple. Any of us could basically go down and participate in a bribe, money for dropping the charges, then deliver them safely to the Canadian embassy to return home," the man tells me patiently.

"Ah, yes, I see," I answer. "It is actually simple to release our people from these foreign prisons, simpler for the Liberals than the Tories since the Tories are officially the government, but it is more beneficial to the party to use this to sway public opinion in your favour. Smart move," I add agreeably, thinking of how this man is a lawyer, you know, those people who pledge their life to justice, liberty and so on.

"Exactly. We always have to be thinking about the next election," he says. "Not to say that the government couldn't issue the bribe to free them either; they simply can't let the public know. I don't remember seeing you here before; what's your name again?"

But I am already moving on looking for an outside door so I can go and have a cigarette. *Why can you smoke cigars in here but not cigarettes?* I ask myself. I pick up another vodka and tonic from the bar on the way past it and listen to another lawyer, this one a young short little elfin lawyer with a napoleon complex, going on about Israel, about how six Israeli deaths by suicide bombers is more heinous than dozens or hundreds of Palestinian deaths by the military because Palestine harbours terrorists. I am reminded of a certain but oft forgotten bit of history as I slide quickly past him and locate a door, where outside I can see several party guests puffing happily away on their smokes. I pull my white fox stole tighter around my shoulders and step outside to join them.

"... the key is to keep the media on the story about the Tory MP's racist comments," one woman is saying to another short man. "So long as the multi-cultural minorities can keep it in their minds that the Tories are all racist, their votes will come to us. We have all our operatives on the comment boards to create the 'public outrage'."

I actually agree with the first part; many of the Tories I've met are racist, or at least exclusionary enough to come across that way. "What comments are you referring to?" I ask, not having heard anything on the topic recently.

The woman laughs. "Actually, they were comments referring to an article written about someone else, but taken out of context we have a very real quote we're running, and trying to defend themselves against it will only dig their hole deeper."

I turn away.

Across the patio I see the party leader himself, and am surprised to see him in a tête-à-tête with the very man who had worked very hard to ensure this particular leader never came to power. That villainous bastard, the one who smeared for the sake of smearing, who I knew had ruined more reputations than whole political parties put together, was the one I had been looking for; he was the culmination of all the dirty goings-on in politics that reviled me. I made my way over and introduced myself using my evening alias, and was prepared to give it my all to ensure I could get this man away from his wife and somewhere secluded whereupon I could take out my growing wrath upon him. Within a few minutes, however, I realized that if he slept with his wife at all it was the only woman he ever slept with; this man was clearly the sort of closet-case homosexual who would burn one of his brethren at the stake before admitting his sexual orientation, a self-loathing gay who is always on top and prefers not to admit to his many restroom escapades.

I decide I've had enough of this event and with politics in general. Over the course of the evening a fire has started burning deep inside me that has already over-shadowed the rage and disgust I had experienced with any other party, group, or organization that had compelled me to kill. There weren't enough graves for what I was planning to do.

I left the patio and walked back through the bar, dropping off my glass. A middle-aged gentleman whom I had met early approached me, scotch in hand, words slurring either from the alcohol or the silver spoon lodged in his mouth, reaching out to brush my breast and grab my ass and tell me how spectacular I am. A lawyer, quite famous in his own right for the defense of an equally famous corporate giant who had swindled thousands of innocent investors out of their life savings and managed to get off scot-free. I told him I was about to leave.

"Care to join me for a night cap," he asked me.

"But of course," I answered, holding my gloved hand out to him.

13.

I have very few memories of the past month, just glimpses, really. It's been a whirlwind, day indistinguishable from night, weekday from weekend; I don't know if I've slept or eaten and I don't know for how long I have or haven't. The lawyer from the Liberal event, yes, I remember him, locked in his walk-in freezer with the broken safety release handle; that is the last clear event I can remember that I'm sure is real. The rest, well, I hope it can't all be true because if it is surely I've made the terrible mistake Beech has always suspected I would and he is on my tail. I know everywhere I've looked it seems all I can see are disingenuous, corrupt, greedy bastards, leaving a trail of destroyed innocent lives in their wake as they plough to their own personal dreams of wealth, power and success. Rapists, extortionists, men who abused their corporate employees, their home employees, their wives, their children, their friends, their communities, just to get what they want or hide what they can't face. Countless nights in countless disguises hunting them down and taking them out.

I have woken up this morning feeling as though the past four weeks was just a dream; and maybe most of it was, but the time has definitely passed. The computer and my cell confirm the date. There are eight messages on my voicemail from Beech. None sound too concerned, just disappointed that he hasn't been able to connect with me and that I haven't contacted him.

Before deciding I must call Beech, if only to find out if anything has happened for which I am the suspect, even if only to him, I check the Sun online and its archives for the past month; they're the ones that carry the kind of news I'm looking for. There is the story of the Liberal lawyer, there, which was front-page news. Two more party operatives who disappeared and for whom foul play is not suspected at the present time; there are no pictures of them and their names don't ring a bell. They could just as well have been running from their own crimes than have fallen prey to me. CEO of an advertising firm died of a Viagra overdose – that one sounds familiar. Another executive who OD'd on coke also sounds familiar; I think I can picture him frothing and convulsing on the floor. Another who hung himself, another who drowned in his indoor swimming pool. One who got drunk and passed out in his car in the garage with the motor running; I feel certain I am behind that one since I used to work with the man and have despised him for going on a decade – he was in fact supposed to be on the boat but didn't make it. A bizarre case of a billionaire local movie producer who accidentally locked himself in the room with his illegal pet panther, who proceeded to break its restraints and devour him; even that one sounds familiar to me though I can't recall for a moment any details surrounding it. So far nothing that seems to stand out as outright murder or anything that could be tied back to me.

A quick phone call to Beech seems to put him at ease, and me as well as I get no indication from the quality or content of our conversation that he is following any case that might have set off alarm bells to him insofar as I am concerned. Just to make sure, I cover my phone number and telephone Renee and hang up when I hear her voice pick up on the other end of the line. I breathe a short sigh of relief and light a cigarette. I have never lost time or memory before like that. It can't be a good sign. The pressure to get out of town like I promised Gable is growing greater by the moment. It's time to really start planning.

Good for you, Gable says, staring at me from the couch beside me, his head level to mine. *It's time for us to go. You must have killed close to forty-five people now, and your luck can't hold out forever.*

"Do you think it's been that many?" I ask him, experiencing a spark of interest at the prospect. That's a pretty impressive number for any serial killer to have under their belt.

Don't start getting cocky, Gable says. *And yes, I think it's been at least that many. You're pushing your luck. You're out of control. If you have another month-long blackout, you're going to wake up in prison.*

"I know you're right," I say out loud.

14.

I have just left the bank, ending a series of transactions that has left me with what I am fairly certain is an untraceable briefcase full of cash. Over the past few weeks I have liquidated some assets and cashed out a number of the investments Paul has left me, which I then laundered through a numbered bank account out of Barbados. This very morning I have met with a stereotypical hoodlum introduced to me by one of Shaun's punk-assed friends in an even more stereotypical back alley and have obtained what looks to me as and what I am assured is a series of perfectly forged identity documents of what will be my most final alias ever, including a birth certificate, driver's license, social insurance number, health card, three credit cards with perfect credit, a passport, five years of perfectly normal tax returns and a university diploma. At the bank today I had opened a new account under my new name and transferred into it all the funds I had run through the offshore accounts. My new identity is very well off. If I wanted to, I could disappear right now, but I still have some planning and training to do and some unfinished business to take care of.

I get into my car and start the long drive back to the city; I plan to be there by nightfall. You can stop hoping, because I am not going to mention in this memoir where it is I drove to to set up my new bank account. It is on purpose that I don't even say what time it is right now. When I disappear, I intend to disappear completely.

15.

The next day I take a drive past the twin Victorians. I see Duncan's car parked out on the road so I pull up behind it, park, lock the car and go inside. He is sitting at his desk in the little office just inside the main entrance and he looks up and smiles when he sees me.

"How are you?" He asks with a broad grin.

"I'm doing pretty well," I tell him. "How are you? How are things going here?"

"Fantastic, fantastic," Duncan says. "This project just keeps getting better every day. We are now on our sixtieth success story of tenants who have come in wanting to get themselves off the streets permanently and have managed to transition out of here and keep themselves off the streets for more than six months. Out of seventy-five, that is an excellent rate of success."

I am actually thrilled. This may very well be the only good thing I've ever done in my life, the only idea I have had that has actually worked out for the betterment of mankind without involving a criminal act to achieve it. The wall in the front hallway is peppered with various plaques and award certificates the project has won over the past year.

The building is in terrific shape. In the living room across the hallway I can see five or six perfectly healthy and clean-looking individuals sitting around watching a movie on an average-sized high definition television. Out of the kitchen comes the smell of some sort of delicious stew.

"Do you mind walking me around the place?" I ask. I haven't been here in nearly six months and I haven't gotten a call or email from Duncan in several weeks.

"No problem at all!" Duncan says enthusiastically, and we take about a half an hour to go through most rooms of each of the neighbouring houses. In the backyard of the main house I see they have built a partially covered patio that has a very large barbecue range under it. In the other yard there is a medium-sized aboveground swimming pool. I can't see the lawn or garden under the snow, but Duncan assures me there is a well-kept rose garden under there and that they have already excavated a section of lawn for a rather large vegetable garden which they will plant come spring.

"This is fantastic," I tell Duncan with a carefully crafted warmness in my voice. "I am truly impressed with the work you have done around here."

"Well, I couldn't have done it alone, and don't you forget for a second that none of this would be here at all if it had not been for both your vision and your money."

"So there haven't been any problems at all?" I ask. The people in social services had doused me with dire warnings about how homeless people, as pathetic as they are, are unlikely to really want to take the time or effort to change their lives and start over. They claimed an 85% failure rate for those who tried to get themselves off the street, get employment, get off drugs or alcohol, what have you. I had gone into this project with no viable research under my belt and no conclusive study to prove that my theory could work. Only Duncan had believed in this at first, and even the awards we had won had more to do with optics on the part of local groups and politicians than it did on proving there had been any real success, however fleeting that success might even be.

"Well, there has of course been the odd problem; hope as I would, nothing ever runs completely smoothly, but the sorts of issues we were warned we'd run into haven't ever really occurred," Duncan tells me. "We haven't had any noteworthy acts of violence, no one has stolen from any of the other tenants and people have respected each other's space and privacy, which I think is a testament to your original idea of building so many small but private rooms rather than have people share space with each other. It's a lot easier for someone to get their act together when they can go through the painful parts without someone watching or listening, and no one has complained that a room just big enough for a cot, a dresser and a closet is too small. A group of ladies in the first wave of tenants started this sort of private used clothing shop out of the basement of the house next door, which not only shows initiative on their parts, but ensures everyone has access to clean clothing in good shape, and also brings in extra income for the project. One of those women has since left and gotten a job as an assistant to a reputable tailor, and she comes by once a week and spends a few hours mending the tenants clothes who need it.

"Two of the paid kitchen positions have been reliably handled by ex-tenants, one from the first wave and one from the second. The other employee from the first wave has since moved on and gotten a paying job at a real restaurant. The two unpaid positions have been staffed by tenants, and I believe we're on our fifth and sixth now; all but one of the others have used the experience to get work elsewhere. Same goes for the cleaning staff; we've retained one of the first wave for the paid supervisor position and all the others have gotten jobs as cleaners, both residential and corporate. Joe – I don't know if you remember him from the first wave – is now a window cleaner and works mainly on skyscrapers on Bay St. Exactly ten ex-tenants have gotten jobs as couriers; you'd be surprised how much it prepares you for those jobs when you're used to surviving through the worst of what both the elements and the people in the city can throw at you. A dozen or more people have gone back to school, several have gotten municipal jobs and out of that a couple are truly impressive. I have the paperwork detailing all of their progress if you'd like to see it."

"Maybe you could just send me a copy for my records sometime over the next couple of weeks," I say. "Well, this is really great, Duncan." We're back at his office now and we go in and sit down. "Now, I'd like to talk about making you a true partner in this, Duncan, to have controlling interest in this project equal to my own, just in case I end up traveling for an extended period of time, or worse, am no longer around at all."

His face flushes with delight.

16.

I am at Beech's apartment, a small but beautiful old walkup just northwest of the city core in a modest blue-collar neighbourhood. I am standing at the bar in his kitchen, watching him expertly prepare a spaghetti dinner for me. He cuts his vegetables like a pro and I admit it is more than turning me on to watch him wield his knife like that. Maybe later I will entice him to handcuff me to the bed and engage in a little hardcore rape role-play. I'm so rarely the victim, after all. Just to see if it's possible, I decide to suggest it right now. When I am through describing in a husky yet nonchalant tone of voice exactly what I want him to do to me from top to bottom, start to finish, he has ceased to chop vegetables and instead turns around with the look of a wild animal in his eye and crosses the kitchen, knife still in hand, pushes me roughly back against the wall, rubs my neck gently but with a hint of menace using the side of the knife and jams his tongue into my mouth. I gasp in both pleasure and surprise.

"Is that what you want, bitch?" he growls at me.

"Yes," I gasp.

Turning it off like a switch, he backs up, smiles at me slyly and goes back to the counter where he resumes preparing dinner, saying cheerily, "Just wanted to make sure I got the idea of what you were describing."

"You beautiful bastard," I tell him, making my way to a stool on suddenly wobbly legs.

Within the hour, we are seated at the dining room table, amidst wine and candles and a delicious meal. Beech is looking particularly sexy, his face flickering with shadows around his perfectly cut features, his masculinity heightened by his chivalry. I take a sip of wine and tell him so.

"If you think I'm tearing myself away from this delicious meal to satisfy your horniness, you can think again," he says, winking at me. "If you want to play the victim then we'll do what *I* say. *I'm* in control now."

Again I gasp involuntarily. This is going to be a fantastic night. But I dutifully say no more about it and try as I may to contain myself.

"It's about time I felt in control," he goes on, his face getting suddenly serious. "I'm at the point now where I have to officially admit the boat explosion has become a cold case. It's the first one I've ever had go unsolved." He pauses and stares at me with a penetrating gaze. I wish I could read his mind. I take another sip of wine. "But it's also the first case I've ever had that I've come to the point of *wanting* it to go unsolved. Whoever did it did a whole lot of people a whole lot of favours. The people who were on this boat were a sorry bunch. Functional psychopaths, ever last one of them. Collectively they have committed more crimes they haven't been charged with than I have charged anyone with in going on twenty years on the job. White collar crimes, where they would end up at cushy prisons with tennis courts and stables that serve mostly only to put a group of them together and have one long wine and cheese party. Other crimes, where it would be hard to get the victim to even press charges much less convict them. Crimes one would be hard-pressed to get enough evidence to even come up with a suitable charge, like emotionally abusing people to the point of suicide, ruining peoples' reputations, having affairs, buying their unqualified children's way into schools to the detriment of a student who has earned it but isn't rich enough, bullying and cheating and stealing and making everyone but themselves miserable."

Oh, you're preaching to the choir, honey, I think to myself.

"I mean, learning what I have learned about this group over the past year has seriously made me fantasize about going on my own rampage through the industry," he continued. "I find myself wishing the boat was bigger! How the hell did you put up with these whelps for so long?"

"I hated it," I said. "That's why I took the opportunity when I had it and got the hell out of the industry." I take another sip of wine and light a cigarette. That meal was so good I could have licked the plate clean. I'll lick him clean instead.

"Good for you," he said. He gives me a funny look. I wonder what expression I got wrong. Could this man read my mind? "Because all it would take is someone with an over-developed sense of justice and a total lack of conscience to kill people like this based on the reasons I just listed."

I freeze. I know he sees it. I am clearly uncomfortable. I've let him get to know me too well. I butt out my smoke and stand to offer to clear the table for him. He stops me.

"No way," he tells me with a smile, flicking me lightly on the tip of my nose, "I told you I was taking care of dinner and so I am. You sit your beautiful ass down there and have some more wine, or I'm going to make you," he winks. I think I am shaking a little both from fear and desire.

He returns a couple of minutes later with two fancy bowls of frozen yogurt topped with fresh mint. While we eat I amuse myself by running my toe up and down his leg beneath the table, getting him distracted, getting me going. As soon as I'm done the dessert and move to light a cigarette, he reaches across the table and grabs my wrist: hard. His eyes have gone dark and dangerous.

"I think you've had quite enough for the moment," he snaps at me. "Get up."

I get up. He lets go of my wrist and pushes me back hard enough for me to lose my balance and land indelicately on the floor, bruising my hip a little and turning me on even more. I can tell he likes this, in a way he probably never thought he would or even could. Everybody's got a dark side. To antagonize him I give him a slow smile and say, "Is that all you've got? You'll never break me."

"Oh, I'll break you to fucking bits," he says, kicking me a little, sending another thrill through my body. I turn on my hands and knees and pretend like I'm trying to get away from him, ripping a hole in the knee of my stocking and causing my skirt to start riding up my thighs. He chases me, grabbing the back of my skirt and pulling me back, but I wriggle out of his grasp. By now my stockings, garter and thong are clearly exposed. As I near the door of the bedroom, I hear him abruptly stand up and walk away. Panting, I turn around and my eyes grow wide as I see he has come back with the knife.

"Turn around," he says, "and stay down." He puts the tip of the knife under my chin and pulls up just a big so I can feel the sharpness of the point. With his other hand he undoes his pants and releases himself. "Suck it." He tells me. I do what he says and think I'm going to explode as he moans loudly and shoves my head hard against him so I can barely breathe. Suddenly he grabs the back of my hair and rips my head away, pulling me to my feet and cutting open my blouse and then my bra with abandon. He bends my arms behind my back so hard I think they're going to be pulled out of their sockets and bends to bite and suck on my breasts. I'm now groaning loudly and I want him more than I have ever wanted anyone. He pushes me back into the bedroom and onto the bed, where he rips off my skirt, rips my stockings to shreds and then merely pushes my underwear to the side before climbing on top of me and thrusting himself cruelly into me. "That's what you want," he says to me. "That's what you need. You take it, bitch, you take it all." I bite down hard on his shoulder and he starts pounding me even harder. By that time I'm literally screaming my head off, and he jams three fingers into my mouth that I am helpless to do anything but suck, which just propels him further. He starts making those low, guttural sounds he makes as he gets close to coming, and I myself am already well past my second orgasm and onto my third. Together we begin moving in perfect rhythm, and then he flips me over and takes me from behind. That's the last straw for both of us. As he pushes my face down into the pillow and slaps my ass, we come together.

17.

I am in an undisclosed location, an undisclosed distance from the city. Maybe it's a different province altogether, maybe it's a different country. Maybe it's a different planet or even universe for all you are ever going to know.

The important thing is that I am standing in the centre of what will someday soon be my new home, my new world, my new life. It could be ten acres, could be a hundred acres, could be a thousand. It could be swampland or mountain or rock or waterfront; could be cold or warm, temperate or tropical. It could be plain or forest, high elevation or low elevation. My description of this place could be entirely within my imagination, could be slightly exaggerated, or could be the straight-out truth. The point is, when I am ready and I finally come here, I will be free and you will never find me.

I have been on the road for over two weeks, partially because I was looking for the perfect location in which to start my future, and partly to throw off the trail of anyone who may at some distant time be reading this memoir and think they are able to investigate my schedule, find out how long I've been gone and when and from that information attempt to track down my coordinates. I am the closest I have ever been to hopeful, or happy, or satisfied, looking at where I will live. The house and all its interesting nooks and crannies delight me. The area underground – part of the building or detached from it? – Sorry, I can't tell you – where I will be able to store food, grow mushrooms, avoid heavy storms, perhaps even a war. There is an attic, yes, where I will put a spinning wheel and learn to make my own wool and thread and clothing, because I do not intend to enter society ever again after the first six months or so of settling in. There is the capacity for getting off the grid entirely, though I have not yet decided whether or not I will power myself through wind, or solar, or geo-thermal, or simply give up energy altogether and live as a pioneer might have done, by the sweat of my brow and off the lay of the land. Inside the house there is a library with built-in shelves on the walls, enough space to ensure I could read every day for the rest of my life and not want for material. I wish I could describe the details of the kitchen to you, but they are so unique and delightful it would be a tell. All I can say is that it is equipped for living off the grid and living well. Ah yes, of course, there is a well, and it is purported to be free of chance of contamination or running dry for the next fifty years at least, at which point I am sure to be dead anyway.

You won't find me by aerial search and even by high-powered satellite it will be nothing but a maze to track me down.

When and if I have to enter society for any reason, I am already fully confident that my new identity is rock solid. I will respond to the next census. I will not raise any red flags. And if I feel the need to kill, I will hunt. There are both large and small game around here, I will have by then purchased two horses, I will be as wild as a renegade warrior and master of my land.

But for now, there is much on my mind and the isolation of being left here in this new place for even these first few hours has made my thoughts busy and sore and fraught with all I need still accomplish before I disappear. There are still things I do not know how to do. The aforementioned spinning, for instance. Or learning to farm the animals I would need to make such an activity possible. How does one care for sheep? What about goats? Or chickens – how do you get the feathers out? How do I milk an animal? How do I make leather? How do I smoke meat and fully prepare for winter? How do I know how much wood I will need to burn comfortably for the entire cold season, how do I cut it myself and how long does it need to dry before it is suitable for burning? How do I make candles? Will I have to bite the proverbial bullet and go into a nearby town or city, succumb to my ultimate ineptitude and purchase what I need, or will I really be able to do it myself? It seems to me that a human being who is smart enough and capable enough to kill as many people as I have while simultaneously hiding my personality defects from those around me and participating in what up to this past year has been a successful career, should be smart and capable enough to take care of themselves in the wilderness. But you never know; I may just accidentally eat a poisonous berry the first week I arrive. I may choke on a fish or chicken bone and be unable to save myself. I may drive myself insane or to suicide as my mind has too much time to reflect on all I have done, as paranoia consumes me and I am left sitting on my front porch with a shotgun waiting for what I feel is the inevitable arrival of law enforcement, unable to eat or sleep, eventually starving to death in my madness.

I will not have a television, computer, Internet connection, video game, PDA, or any other semblance of modern life with me when I finally arrive. If I have any chance at successfully extracting myself from my past, I must sever all ties completely and fully. My family will not know where I went; whatever pain caused to them by the mystery of my disappearance and eventual assumed death is only a fraction of what would have been caused them by my arrest, the public disclosure of my crimes, the trial, the conviction and the lifelong incarceration. I feel no particular allegiance to them anyway and will not miss them. If I were to have any connection to the outside world, it would result in me realizing that my work there is not done, that it exists with the same amount of injustice, if not more, that I could hunt motherfuckers til the end of time and barely make a dent in their insidious manifestation of this planet.

So here I sit, smoking a cigarette on the hood of my car, the rental I drove here from the city, the only time any connection with my real identity will be on this property, Gable warm and sleeping on the backseat, and I breathe in the crisp, cold winter air, listen to the musical silence around me, then close my eyes.

Soon, I say to myself.

18.

And holy Christ, it can't come soon enough. I have been back in the city less than a day and that feeling of peace I had fleetingly experienced at my eventual new home has evaporated as if part of a dream. I can hear the city in a way I never could before, a deep, low-decibel throbbing that reaches into whatever soul I have and twists it in its relentless grasp until I want to scream, to kill, to destroy.

I turn on my computer and watch as several weeks of emails pile in. Of the 383 emails that arrive in my inbox, only 75 of them are actual emails I need to read for one reason or another. A sampling of the others, a constant flow of spam, electronic garbage, a maddening waterfall of virtual junk, misspelled abominations of English meant to entice half-wits into opening them and launching whatever attached spyware, virus, or scam is attached. Some of it is meant to lure the weak, stupid, corrupt, or desperate into purchasing inferior, stolen, dangerous, or fake products. These spammers get your email address because the people you pay to keep your confidential information confidential in turn sell lists to these spam warehouses, or let in hackers through their inferior security systems. This is a small, small sampling of the spam my email account has received in the last three days of my 24-day trip:

Man looking Foor a Hose Spreads Fire on Flaming Hay Wagon
Get a degree with no problems.
Try to shop in our cheap and reliable drugstore.
Pay less for luxury and qualitative watches.
Bachelors, Masters or Doctorate degree.

Do you want some party?
Fantastic deals on all men's health products.
Cheap designer watches could be worn for years.
Solution for people who can't afford a classy watch.
Get University Dip1oma/Degree/MBA the Easy Way, No study/class, at Cheap Price!!
Review: our top market performers.
Your ticket to a new Slim and Vibrant life, Acai berry
Our medicine will remind you that you are still a man.
TAKING A WOMAN TO BED ...
Best software, best prices.
Your male friend will look great even in loose jeans.
You are sure to be satisfied with our medicine.
Your account has been broken into. Verify your password.
I am a lonely girl looking for your company.
Women don't care about your money as long as your trunk is long and hard.
Dear colleagues. – HUGE discounts, Pharmacy
What's with the last task?
Having a big penis is the most important of all male qualities.
Plaetze frei
We offer the hottest deals on the best medicine.
EnlargementPenis Pills & HarderErections & BiggerPenis at cheap price
The World's Coolest Bridges
Warning on IP activity
We will call you back.
Fast, cheap and reliable shipping of your drugs.
Einkaufer gesucht
Discount invitation 444982367
Get the Job fast this one.

Hundreds Pose Nude on Siwss Glacier
Production puzzle
Arbeit zu vergeben
Please respond, you have inherited fortune
We deliver timepieces worldwide in no time!
You best-choice
Hey, join our team
Work from home, make mega $$$
Now you can afford as many Viagra tabs as you need.
Selection for honorees
Embarrassed of a locker room issue? Then add some inches to him.
We offer watches at very seductive prices.
Start your weight loss journey immediately
Promising SmallCap Advice
FDA-Approved PrescriptionDrugs withoutPrescription need
Your bed is empty? Maybe you should enlarge your little friend.
Failure notice
Gear up for summer with eBay.ca
Even CEOs consult us.
More inches in your pants, less steps to success.
Add dr. to your name
Our medicine will remind you that you are still a man
Let's have a conversation
Greatest WallStreet fraud
Our medicine will help you bring your passionate nights back
Acai Diet will burn your unwanted fat, Endorsed by Oprah
Fast and easy way to enlarge your penis, no risks and no surgeries.
Elegant watches for men and women
Super savings $1.20 forViagra, $1.87 for Cializ

No more books for MBA
She is bound to lose her mind over your great size.
Give Santa the sack – he's noot the real thing
Idnian women take 500-year-old hunt to city streets
5 Areas to Stimulate and Send Her To Orgasm Heavenn
more work would be good
Cow Takes Dip in Swwimming Pool
Female Orgasm Tricks – See How Easily You Can Hit HHer
G Spot Every Time
5 Top Lovee Making Tips
Expand your manliness spire
In 2 days, I'll sue you
Forgot keys, forgot phone
Infection attacks! Fight back!
Waht Did Shakespeare look like as a Kid?
Our tasks's details
Hello – Brand items and dirty cheap price
Her beaver needs more times a night
Wait for me
Join me this Saturday
Reply right after reading
My mail stolen and changed
Let's talk about happiness
Partisan
SALE 80% OFF on Pfizer
Wine 'allows guilt-mfree gluttony'
Send me code
I know how it feels being fat – so start losing weight today!
Your fan writes
We care about your body
Where were you yesterday?

Become woman's ido
Hey boy, howdy?

Come to our room
Videos of explosions
Join me at party later
Your beast will get deeper in
Gave you wrong number
Confirm delivery
Get real rod for doing her
Dpulicating sms message
She'll whisper: "You're the best!"
We got questions for you
Your last forum posts
I left note on table
You won'f fail this time
Lovingkindness Desire will literally circulate in your wang.
Violone hysterical
Truth about Britney Spears.
Help to recognize him
High quality drugs.
Your vacation date
Expiring order
Loudspeaker Karadoke Scares Conn. Teacher
Resend your number plz
Where will we meet?
Britney naked
Jokes aside, answer
Please buy from us
Soke Give her real aggressive drilling confiscation minauderie
hysterical unhandy
Johansson without underpants!

30 gays killedo n party
Your girl's pic?
Got high in club?
Having pack in this pocket means having success with four or
even more girls a night
Why are you not in MSN?
See for yourself
Your car's photo?
Feel as if you are walking on a frying pan? Dermatophyte can
be stopped!
Become superman
I told you about Obama!
Corporate training next week
Disney giving brides-to-be a chance to dress like princesses
College photos
Tired of physical exercises? Here is a way out!
Ready to serve you.
You are welcomed at party
Don't be a fool!
Oops. I did it again.
The whole Net laughs on this
Epicureanism Say STOP to rod weakness rollicker outright
Wanna try? No problem in raising wang
Have Mary already told u?
Your money transfer
Second Swine Flu attack
Deep, Hot sex – A Deep Penetration of position
Pirate files on your IP
Naked Riahana
Prawns are plentiful and cheap
Nothing heals better!

33 Things that Just Might Improve Your sex Life

3 Not-So-Common Ways to Your Wife in ththe Mood More Often

Let's go to park

Private vid of J Lo

Remember summer days?

It's your enemy writing

Bum kicked Condolesa

Woman with artificial butt

And the Dong with a luminous nose

There was a crooked man, and he walked a crooked mile. The Pobble has no toes

Don't desperate enhance designer

Configures horrify

Claustrophobic quietly – axiomatizations radius befriend

Your car in trouble

CONGRATULATIONS! CONGRATULATIONS! CONGRATULATIONS!

How crysis affects you

Is that you? Found u by surname

The Advantages Of Getting Prepared oFr sex

Turn your outsider to leader

Aphrodisiac Recipes to Inspire Intimtae Desires

Make your banana huge

Your naked video on tube

A CRY FOR HELP – Dear Respectful, I need you.

I double dare you. Answer!

Make her explode with Erotic Fire!

And the list goes on and on; scrolling through my inbox is like hearing a silent scream build up in my head and continue, unabated, until all of it is gone. This is not even counting the spam that is filtered and caught by my email client and immediately deleted or removed to Junk Mail. Taking the time to delete all of this takes up nearly the next two hours of my day. The entire time I am becoming more and more disgusted.

And this is how it affects me, someone who has a very high capacity for not giving a shit about anything. A colleague of mine lives next door to a sixty-year old woman who gave up $50,000 of her life savings, which was pretty much all of her life savings, because she received an email on a computer she can barely use and understands even less, that told her she inherited money from a non-existent person in Somalia, who as coincidence would have it shared her mother's maiden name and claimed to be located in a village not far from where her mother was born. It didn't occur to her that someone could have gotten her email address from her Internet Service Provider.

I would love, just love, to have the opportunity to run into just one person who runs one of these spam warehouses for a living. I would love, just love, to wipe him or her off the face of the planet. Yes, I'd made *them* explode with erotic fire.

19.

The breakdown of the elephant society began when humans started to infringe upon their herds, whether through urbanization destroying the wilderness, or poachers killing them for their tusks or meat. Herds are led by a matriarch, who is traditionally the oldest and most experienced female in the family lineage. When she dies, she is replaced by the next oldest and most experienced. Baby elephants stay close to their mother's side for many years and are influenced deeply by everything that the mother experiences. Love of matriarch goes beyond love of self; so if the mother is in trouble or is attacked or sick or goes insane, the rest of the herd is more likely to put themselves in danger attempting to help or revive her and therefore die along with her, not necessarily in defense of her, but because they are confused when the unit breaks down and do not seek self-preservation above the herd. The female is of utmost importance in the elephant's society; only elephant and human females live for a long time after they cease to reproduce, which is a great indication of their necessity.

Male elephants, left to their own devices, are independent creatures, which stay close to the females of the herd who have helped raise them for a long adolescence. Disruptions in this experience leads directly to disruptions in their behaviour. When fully grown, they tend to lead self-involved lives independently or in separate bachelor herds, joining with the females only for ancestral pilgrimages and to mate and breed. Size and wisdom are highly revered and so it is the largest and most mature of the male elephant that has earned itself the first right to mate.

When elephant herds become persecuted or start to break down, lose their traditional matriarchs, or face threat from man or environment, they start to assemble in larger and larger herds. Instead of the traditional herd made up of 9-28 elephants in two to three family units, elephants under duress will begin to aggregate in herds numbering upwards of 200 and as high as 1000 animals, made up mostly of young elephants and with a marked number of big male bulls.

Like elephant society, the human world is best led by a female benevolent dictator and when such a thing is not present, whether in a family, a city, a corporation, a country, or a world, it is only a matter of time before all hell breaks loose. How long that hell lasts is entirely dependent on how long it takes for the society to self-destruct.

20.

It is a week before Christmas and I am downtown, in Kensington Market, looking for some gifts to send to my family, specifically my nieces and nephews, who I will not be going to visit this year, much like the past five years, this time citing a non-existent scheduling conflict with an event at the twin Victorians – an event I was invited to, but am declining to attend. It is twilight, and the streets are sparkling with newly fallen snow.

Upon leaving a basement shop with a bag of handcrafted, retro dresses for the teens, I am less than impressed to run headlong into Renee, with Jack and child in tow. I have not seen her since that last day at her apartment and was not looking forward to ever seeing her again. Through my constant scanning of the obituaries, I had about a month ago discovered that Jack's wife, Janet, had succumbed quickly and painfully to pancreatic cancer, living only four weeks after her diagnosis. Though I had never met her, I learned through the obituary that she had been the sister of a woman I had worked closely with several years previous, Jenna Hickey, and under cover of sympathy I had called her to offer my condolences.

"Thank you so much for calling," Jenna had said, a shadow of tears haunting her voice. "Janet and I were so close. If it wasn't for that bastard husband of hers, I know she would still be alive."

"I'm sorry, Jenna," I said into the telephone, "I thought I'd read she died of cancer. Did her husband have something to do with that?"

"As far as I'm concerned, he is the reason she got it," Jenna spat out bitterly. "I know in my heart that her body gave her a disease that would get her out of that marriage and that life as quickly as possible. He was a crazy man! She never should have married him, the schizophrenic asshole. She just felt so sorry for him. She was on the board at the Schizophrenia Society and believed so strongly that people with that disease could live perfectly normal lives if they were properly medicated. Jack was like the champion of their cause a few years ago; he was so far gone and emerged from a program at the Centre for Mental Health and Addictions as an entirely new person. He was their poster boy. Janet fell madly in love with him before he even got through treatment. I warned her from the start. They got married just over a year ago and it's been hell for her. She just wouldn't admit it and leave him because she thought she could fix him, because she didn't want to admit she was wrong. It ate her alive. That's why she got the cancer."

"It's a terrible thing when people with problems like that go off their medication," I said gently. "Schizophrenia has destroyed so many lives." "It wasn't the schizophrenia, it was *him*," Jenna ascertained. "As far as I know, he never did go off his medication. What he did was lie to her, cheat on her, abuse her emotionally and physically and basically beat her down to nothing. He promised her children, but wouldn't even try. Last year I saw him out with this woman, this little blonde artist thing. I followed her one day and saw where she lived, some artist's studio in Mirvish Village, I understand her father was some sort of author in the 70s, though I'm not sure I've read any of his books. I put out an APB on her with my friends and found out that she and Jack were seeing each other on a regular basis. Then I find out the bitch has a kid! I'm sure it's his even though I know now that she's married too; I mean, who would have their husband's child but be seeing someone else before, during and after the pregnancy? Finally I decided to hire a private dick and get proof of it to show Janet. He got a whole book full of photos of them; these two didn't do a thing to try to hide their relationship. They almost all had the kid in them too. On top of it, half of it was proof that Jack was having the little tramp over to his house, to have sex in Janet's bed, while she was off helping people with mental diseases cope with the disasters of their life, he was at home with another woman creating a disaster of hers!"

"Holy shit," I said.

"Holy shit is right," Jenna went on. "I showed the pictures to her about three months ago. At first she wouldn't believe me, but then she got mad enough to confront Jack with it. And what does he do? He slaps the shit out of her and tells her to mind her own business. He tells her the kid isn't his and she's lucky to have him at all. And then he breaks down in a typical male pile of remorse and begs her forgiveness, blames it on the mental disease, says the woman is no one and means nothing to him and never did and never will, that he will leave her right away, just give him some time to break it off because the woman is psychotic and likely to do something insane. But he doesn't break it off, he never does, he still hasn't, and she kept trying to believe him, kept trying to forgive him… and then she got sick and died. I'd kill the bastard myself if I had the guts. The only satisfaction I was able to get is that I also sent the photos to that bitch's husband. I hear he left her."

I should have killed Jack years ago, I think to myself as I express surprise and disbelief to Jenna. "I'm so sorry this happened, Jenna."

"Me too. It will be all I can do if I can keep from strangling him at the funeral. Can you be there? I could use the support," she queried.

"I wish I could," I said, "But I'm going to be out of town for the next few weeks. Let's get together when we get back though, if you're not in prison." Jenna laughs a little, thankful the minor distraction from her grief.

"Well, I'm really glad you called," she said.

"And don't you worry," I told her. "One of these days, Jack will get his."

I am thinking about this as I come face to face with Renee and the bastard himself. Renee passes as if she does not see me, but Jack greets me with a sneer; clearly Renee has conveyed to him our falling out, though what she may have said I cannot fathom. No doubt Renee assumes that I am the one who sent Jeffrey the photo evidence of her affair; after all, I did threaten to tell him. I had gotten distracted with my own life and never bothered. If I'm going to do something for the sake of justice, I am really going to do it.

I look at the child in the stroller; it looks back with eyes that show it has already seen too much. As I picture the years it has ahead of it, with Jack in its life, with the poison of his and Renee's relationship bleeding into its small soul, I make up my mind.

Not that I needed much more of a reason.

21.

About a week after Christmas I get my opportunity. There is a strange, unseasonable melt and all the snow that had built up before and over the holidays disappeared in a matter of a couple of days. During my promised coffee visit with Jenna, I learned that the private investigator had discovered that whenever possible, Jack had once again taken up his long-standing jogging route of running along the waterfront west to Humber Bay Park, down to the lighthouse, and back again. He always goes at the same time, just after 7pm, regardless of how cold it is. And at this time of year it is also nearly pitch black.

I start haunting the lighthouse in the evenings. It doesn't take long for me to find him. The second day I am there, I see him approaching, his long thirty-something-mullet-rock-star hair half-covered by a black toque. I stay in the shadows near the rocks where I know he always stops to rest for a few minutes before starting out on the return trip. When he gets within a few feet of me and stops, bending over and holding his knees, catching his breath, I step out. A cursory glance around assures me no one else is anywhere nearby. Some music floats over to us in the night air from the nearby marina and club.

"Hello Jack," I say, appearing as though from nowhere.

Jack nearly jumps out of his skin, drawing his hands up into fists in an involuntary reaction. He recognizes me. "Holy shit, you scared the living hell out of me."

"I'd like to scare the living everything out of you," I respond.

"What the hell are you doing here?" he demands.

I ignore his question and gesture towards the nearest rock. "Let's sit down and talk for a bit, Jack." I pull a bottle of Jack Daniels, his favourite, out of my bag and offer it to him. "Come on, let's have a drink."

He takes the bottle almost gratefully and follows me to the rock, and we sit in silence for a minute, looking at the lake, waves crashing at the shore, dark and menacing in the mild winter night. The light from the nearby lamp is dim at best.

"I suppose you want me to talk to Renee for you," he says, finally, "and convince her to forgive you for what you did."

"And just what is it I did, Jack?" I ask.

"As if you don't know," he sneers. "You ruined her life, you jealous bitch. You've always been jealous of her. First you tried to break us up, then when you couldn't you convinced her to commit me when you knew nothing was wrong with me, and then you ruined her marriage."

"How did I ruin her marriage?"

"Uh, by sending photos of her and me to her husband, you moron?" Wow, this guy really is an ass.

I smile at him. "I didn't do that, Jack."

"Oh yeah? Then who did?" He takes another swig out of the bottle.

I light a cigarette. "Your wife's sister, Jenna, did it."

"Jenna?" he laughs to himself and shakes his head. "I guess I should have known, eh? She was always sticking her big nose in where it didn't belong."

"Didn't belong, eh?" Really, should have killed him years ago. "She thinks you killed her sister."

"I *should* have killed her," Jack says. "Stupid bitch wouldn't stop bugging me, nagging me. *Where are you going? When will you be back? Who were you with? Why can't we have kids? Why don't you talk to me? Are you off your medication?*" he mimics. "I think I might have finally snapped and beaten her to death one of those days, but luckily the cancer came first, like an answer to my prayers."

It's funny. Schizophrenia has been such a diagnosed characteristic of Jack's personality for so long I had never really noticed that he was just an asshole in his own right. I wonder vaguely what was wrong with Renee that she would be so attracted to someone like that. I suddenly realize there is no point in trying to make Jack understand that he is the one who ruined Renee's marriage, both of them together. There is no point in reminding him of the threat I had made to him so long ago. Both of them together killed Janet and they don't care. Both of them have been working together to ruin that child's life and they don't care. He is responsible. She is responsible. And I am about to be responsible for making it end.

I beckon for the bottle, which he hands to me, now only about halfway full, and stand up. Lifting it high over my head, I bring it down with a satisfying thud onto the back of his skull, at the last second plucking the toque off of his head so it would not cushion the blow. The bottle is still full enough that it doesn't break. I raise my arm and bring it down again. It still does not break, but Jack, if not dead, is certainly no longer conscious. Nonchalantly I put my foot against his back and push him off the edge of the rock, where he falls into the churning water below. I toss the bottle in after him, turn and walk away.

22.

Beech and I are lying together in a tangle of sheets in my bed, smoking a cigarette. His head lies on my breast and my free hand is playing with his hair. All the lights are on and we have just finished putting on a fantastic show for whoever may have been watching. I lightly indulge in my most frequent fantasy of late; I imagine I can erase the past and actually participate in a future with him. But it is not to be. Over the course of the winter I have learned that even if there is no chance of me continuing to kill, even if there is no chance of my ever being discovered for the crimes I have committed, I simply cannot love, and love is something Beech needs. I am fond of him, fonder than I have been of any other human being, fondness that rivals what I feel for Gable, who also shares the bed with us as we lounge. There are too many holes in my personality, in my soul, for me to ever really care, to ever act out love in such a way as to be convincing, to ever satisfy either of us in what would only be a charade.

The only reason this highly satisfying relationship has gone on as long as it has is because I have managed to keep it aloof, to never let us get too close, to never get over that feeling of newness and discovery, and even so I can tell that Beech's patience for it is growing thin. He wants to get serious. There are words on his lips on a regular basis that he aches to say but fears the consequences of. He wants to tell me he loves me. He wants to tell me he dreams of us seeing each other every day, of an end to the sometimes month or more breaks we have, to solve the mystery he sees in me, to truly know me. It's written all over his face, his beautiful, haunted, manly, passionate face. Sometimes I wish I could give in. I have imagined time and again what would happen if I were to simply pour out the truth of my existence to him, but that scenario always realistically ends with me being led to the precinct in handcuffs, never to taste freedom again.

23.

Renee is knocking at my door. The concierge called up and told me she was here and I told him to let her in. By the quality of her knock I sense that she is upset. I'm not really in the mood for a confrontation. Jack was my last kill, I promised myself, and in the two weeks that have passed I feel as though I have gone into a sort of withdrawal. I am afraid if pushed to any extent I will unleash myself upon anyone, and Renee as she has become to me is far from an exception.

I have been sitting at my computer researching how to build a smokehouse and smoke my own meat. It doesn't seem as though it will be that difficult to do and I can easily get my hands on the equipment needed to do so. In fact, I can order much of what I need over the Internet but I don't want to leave any sort of a trail. I'll have to do it later with cash.

Gable barks as the knocking becomes more and more insistent, so I get up and go to the door and open it. Renee is standing there, tearstained and distraught. She rushes in the door and throws her arms around me. I recoil slightly but let her do it. I suppose, in a way, I have missed my old friend.

"Jack's dead," she sobs into my shoulder. "He's dead!"

I had seen the article in the paper about his being reported missing and had assumed the story this morning about the discovery of the body of an unidentified man in Lake Ontario was likely him, but was not totally sure as the body had somehow found its way across the harbour and lodged itself on the outreaches of Ward Island, moments away from being swept out into the vastness of the lake and likely being lost forever.

"Dead?" I say, feigning surprise. "What happened to him? I read the article about him missing, but assumed he'd just gone on a bender."

"He drowned," she wailed. "He went jogging one night a couple of weeks ago and apparently got drunk and fell into the water at Humber Bay Park. He told me he had quit drinking! Why did this happen? I loved him so much!"

"Where is your child?" I asked her.

"He's with Jeffrey," Renee said, wiping her eyes. "I can't bear to even look at him right now. I'm a terrible mother. I really am. I thought I would be good at it, I thought I would, but I'm not. I don't care right now if I never see him again."

I say nothing and stare at her dully.

"No offense, Renee, but what do you want me to say?" I ask, finally. "Are you expecting me to be sympathetic? Because quite frankly, I'm glad he's gone." It feels good to tell the truth. I know I'm running the risk of pissing her off by saying so and I know by doing that I'm risking her own safety in the mood I'm currently in, but I find I can't help myself. No one ever said I couldn't hold a grudge.

Renee blinks back a new onslaught of tears. "Well, you knew him too," she wheedles. "I thought you'd feel something for him."

I feel like lecturing and slapping her, but I know there's no point in doing either. I feel like reminding her that she just finished telling me she doesn't care if she ever sees her child again, that she cares nothing for the destruction of her own marriage and yet wants attention for the fact that her abusive lover, a man who has caused her little but suffering for well over a decade, a man who she knows watched his own wife die in anguish and pain, while she, Renee stood by and watched as well...

that she would sit back and let the people around them go through the confusion and hurt of betrayal and yet still come here feeling justified that the protagonist in the story is *her*. It's just too pointless to say. But I also can't pretend that I give a shit; that is something I find hard enough to do at the best of times.

"Well, I don't," I say cruelly. "And I don't feel particularly much about you, either. I let you in here because I thought you might have changed, changed back to the sort of person you used to be, the sort of person I admired, but all you're doing is proving what I saw in you the last time we spoke. You don't see any of the things you've done or any of the mistakes you made, you can't admit how you've willingly destroyed those around you and it's not because you're not capable of feeling, but it's because you've drowned your morality in the worst kind of emotion: self-pity. It's disgusting."

She stands, takes two wobbly steps towards me and collapses on the floor.

Fucking drama queen, I think to myself as I walk back to my computer and resume my research. Gable goes up to her and starts sniffing at her. After a few minutes of realizing she is not getting the attention she wants – or maybe she really did pass out, I'm really beyond curiosity on this one – she starts to stir and slowly drags herself up.

"Do you have anything to drink?" she asks in a small voice.

"Sure, what do you want," I say off-handedly.

"Anything strong. Please. I'm sorry. I'm so sorry," she starts to cry again. This time, though, I think she means it. I get up and get her a vodka and tonic. I offer her a cigarette. She accepts.

For an hour or more she sits and cries and confesses. I'm right, she tells me, like I ever cared to prove to her that I was right or wrong about this or anything else. I'm right and she's been such a terrible person. She's let herself be blinded by the force of her love for Jack, blinded to the point that she could see nothing around her any longer. She wonders if I will ever forgive her, she appreciates what I tried to do to steer her straight, she hopes she might find a way to get back together with Jeffrey, to rebuild what she has destroyed with him, to rediscover her love for him. She wishes to waste no more time and vows to apply her whole person to making sure she is a nurturing, sympathetic, kind, insightful, compassionate mother to her poor little neglected child. And on and on she goes. I smoke and listen.

And that is the difference between her and me. Words she has uttered, forgive, appreciate, hope, rebuild, rediscover, love, nurture, sympathy, kindness, insight, compassion, these are words that are part of her birthright because she was so lucky to have developed with a whole soul, a complete psyche, a conscience. I have none of this.

Finally I can take no more and I brandish her back out into the world intact with all her human gifts, and then I return to my desk to further plan how to make my escape from this whole fucked up place.

24.

I am on the way out the door to pick up the cube truck I have rented under my new identity to move some equipment and furniture I have purchased up to my new house. Just before I leave, the phone rings, my home phone, which means either family or Beech. Since I'm going to be gone for a while I figure I had better answer it, in case it is Beech. Gable waits patiently for me by the door.

It turns out to be my father. I'm not really in the mood to have a conversation with him right now, but then again, this may be the last time I ever talk to him and for his own sake, I should probably participate to the best of my ability; my father rarely calls me.

"I had a dream about you last night and it really frightened me," he says.

"What was it?" I ask, trying to sound as though I am interested.

"Well, it was very complicated and I don't remember most of the details, except that you always seemed to be wearing a wig, a different wig, throughout the whole dream. I don't know if there was a war or epidemic or what, but people seemed to be dying everywhere, and you were being blamed for it. In order to avoid persecution by the mobs, you went into hiding and I never saw you again. I felt I just needed to call to see if you are all right."

I stand, frozen. That is a pretty uncanny dream. I don't like the idea of some cosmic force giving up my cover, to a judge of all people! Out loud I say, "I'm fine, Dad. Nothing's wrong whatsoever. I'm just on my way out the door to the airport; I have to catch a flight to California and meet with some people about a business deal I'm putting together."

"Sorry, I will let you go," my father says, sounding disappointed.

"No, it's okay," I relent, "I have a few minutes to chat." So we talk for a while about mundane things, I listen about some cases he has overseen, small town petty issues, one interesting murder. Finally he seems satisfied and suggests he let me go so I can make it to the airport. I conjure up the warmest tone of voice I have and tell him I love him. He's a good man after all and deserves to hear that from a daughter he clearly loves very much. Then I hang up.

"Come on, Gable," I say and grab the few bags I had dropped near the door when the phone rang. He obediently trots after me.

I'm going to miss your father, he says.

After picking up the truck I go and pick up the various items I had purchased over the past few weeks, all of which are being stored at a storage unit down by the Distillery District. I am lucky to come across a man at the facility who helps me load it into the truck. I think I could have done it all myself; I better be able to as I have to get all this shit out of the truck and into the house eventually. Of everything I bought, my two favourite items are the Amish butter churn and the spinning wheel.

For the past month I have been teaching myself to knit. I hate it, but it does pass the time. It's just extremely hard to knit with any success when you have to keep stopping to smoke. So far I have made a hat and mittens, and am halfway done a sweater. Next I will make an afghan.

Into the truck goes the bed, a leather armchair almost exactly like the one in my condo, my favourite chair. Rolled up carpets, and a ton of books. Books I've purchased and organized carefully, as they will instruct me on everything from how to use the churn and make my butter, to how manage the chicken coop, to how to grow and cure my own tobacco. There are boxes after boxes of tools. A hundred cartons of cigarettes. A whole cabinet of interesting weapons, including a 12-guage and pump shotgun, and my newest acquisition, a Horton Legacy Crossbow. Camping and survival supplies, including a small hospital's worth of first aid. Batteries, four different generators, two of them solar powered, one an interesting mix of the two – solar until it needs it then kicks in with gas. A box full of rolled up solar panels. An electric and solar water distiller. Seeds upon seeds upon seeds, freeze-dried and kept in a specially insulated container. And endless supplies of dry dog food, canned dog food, dog blankets, dog bones, dog toys, whatever the dog might need. Enough candles to last me for nearly a decade. Enough matches to light each one a hundred times. Glasses, dishes, cutlery, pots, pans, trays, towels, spices, grills, jars for canning, everything my kitchen could need. A wine kit, and a few crates of empty bottles. A coal barbecue and many boxes of coal. My camera and all the equipment needed to set up a new darkroom. Clothes, jackets, boots, shoes, pillows, blankets, towels. Desk, table, chairs, lamps (with LED bulbs that take almost no power and will last longer than I probably will), a couch, an old Victrola, a box of records, a windup radio, windup lamp and a variety of bins and baskets.

I try not to bring anything too modern, not to torture myself, but to not remind myself of the world I have left behind. There's no point in having wireless technology if I don't want a satellite ping giving away my location; and there's no point having something like a laptop or mp3 player or phone or anything else if I don't want to have wireless. I want to be able to survive without electricity, without power, if I have to, though I hope to offset the smallest of my needs by generating my own. I can run a few lamps for a few days off the one generator that charges by solar, which is great because it doesn't really make any noise and is safe to bring inside when it is fully charged. The other two generators are for power tools and/or any other emergency. They are gas fueled, a fair supply of which I plan to pick up when I am closer to my destination. The most modern piece of equipment I have is a medium-sized deep freezer, which will be run by the duel solar/gas generator.

Four days from now I have an appointment with a man from two towns over from my new place, who is going to come and help me build a smokehouse on my property. That is the thing I think I am most looking forward to in this whole experience; hunting for my meat and then smoking and salting it so I can store it for longer and make a larger variety of food for myself. I can also use the smokehouse to cure some of my tobacco and the ashes will be used (along with a Gable's shit) to assist me in the exciting and disgusting process of making my own leather.

Two weeks from now, the house and the property should be fully stocked. After spending a bit of time there it is my hope that I will figure out whatever I might have missed in my preparations. Then I will leave the place until whichever time it strikes me that it is time for me to finally disappear.

When I make that final trip, I'll be doing it on foot and all I'll have with me is my rucksack and some camping supplies. I plan on leaving no final trail. The journey will be hard and might kill me, but I will have finally and completely, disappeared.

25.

I know it is the last day the moment I wake up. It's before dawn and Beech is sleeping soundly beside me. I don't know why it is today or what makes this day different, but I know it in my gut. I had suspected it to be so, which is why I brought my supplies. Gable is sitting near the door, looking at me, as if to say, *I'm ready when you are, I'll just get my things together.* Good dog. These days his "things" pretty much include his new companion, Stella, a gorgeous, dark-faced German Shepherd about a year and a half old that I picked up last month from a shelter. She and Gable instantly became best friends, lovers, companions, and it was my hope that Stella would keep us well supplied with new generations of shepherds for the new house. After all Gable couldn't live forever.

I am at Beech's cottage, about five hours north of the city. I knew as soon as I accepted his invitation to go on this trip, a week ago, that there was a good chance I might never come back. The distance covered in his car was a pretty good launching pad for my on-foot journey, albeit in slightly the wrong direction; at least I don't have to walk out of the city proper, which in itself would take a couple of days and stick me in urban wasteland. And because I plan to leave this memoir behind, I figure Beech is going to instigate a pretty big search for me, to find me, catch me, imprison me. Yes, Beech, I realize what you're going to do and yet I'm still leaving this behind. Not because I want to get caught, but because I want to prove to myself I won't, because after all I've done it's all right that I want people to know they let a monster live within their midst and were utterly unaware of it. And I want to believe that you care about me enough to give me a bit of a head start, at least.

I slip out of bed and pad silently across the floor and grab my robe. I go down the hallway and into the bathroom and step into what will likely be my last shower for some time, until I arrive at the house, if I am lucky enough to get there at all.

I get dressed, go to the kitchen and raid the fridge, eating a good breakfast (I don't cook anything so as not to wake up Beech with the odor). I go to the corner where my rucksack is, complete with the little solar paneled knapsack attached to the front of it, allowing me to power some lights on my journey and a little one-burner stove I have in case I don't think it's safe to start a fire and yet still need to cook food or boil water. My small tent – a Nemo Morpho AR, that has no poles and is instead held up by pumpable "air beams" – is safely packed away. Dry and canned foods have been already prepared and packed before I even came here, but I add some fresh food, bread, cheese, meat, to the supply. Water, and this great little non-electric water distiller in case I can't find water safe enough to drink even with a filter. Food for Gable and Stella in case nothing else can be found. Vitamins, change of clothes, soap, knife, gun, collapsible fishing pole; I think I have everything I need.

I find I'm actually glad I'm leaving. It's been a long winter and an even longer spring as I waited for the perfect time to make my escape. I managed to stay true to my word and I didn't kill another person after Jack. But if I had stayed another second in that noisy, smelly, cesspool of corruption and greed and materialism, I think I would have gone on the bender to end all benders.

The twin Victorians have been safely under the full control of Duncan and his board of directors for some time now. My investments have all been cashed out and are in various offshore accounts; many of my assets have been liquidated and added to those accounts. I didn't bother to do anything to shut down the condo or cancel any subscriptions or services, both so as not to alert anyone of my leaving and because I simply don't care.

It has been a fitting farewell here this week. Beech and I have spent a quiet few days, barely speaking, but sharing a surprising amount of affection with each other, canoeing, hiking, cooking, drinking, smoking, fucking. On our long hikes I was able to get a pretty good idea of the lay of the land and plan my escape route. The busy highway is only a few miles away and from there I can easily hitchhike in any direction if I want to help out my journey at all. But my plan is to stay under the radar at all costs, so it is unlikely I will choose that option unless it is absolutely necessary.

Last night, our final night together, we spent cozily intertwined in bed after our last bout of mind-blowing sex. A huge fire was roaring in the fireplace and we had a bowl of popcorn between us as we stared off into space consumed by our own thoughts. After lying comfortably together for nearly an hour, Beech stirred and put the bowl aside and gathered me into his strong arms, putting my head against his sweet-smelling chest.

"I love you," he whispered. "Madly, completely, more than any woman I've ever known, more than I have ever wanted to love anyone."

I was silent in surprise. Not so much that he had uttered the words - I had been expecting him to do so for some time - but because they immediately created in me such a mountain of feeling, more than I had experienced any of the other times I had been aware of an onslaught of emotion. Quite suddenly, not knowing how I knew, not understanding how to describe it, I was certain of one thing and only one thing: I loved him too. I wanted to stay here with him forever. I was suddenly lost in a kaleidoscope of emotion, hope, love, fear, wanting, imagining the unimaginable, like telling him everything and him understanding and us living out our days together. But I knew this was impossible. I knew that like every other bout of emotions I'd ever had this would quickly pass and I would soon enough be back to myself: hollow, cold, unfeeling, impenetrable. Only this time I didn't want for that to happen. This time I wanted to keep experiencing these feelings. This time I wanted things to be different. I started to cry, for the first time aware of that human trait I hated most manifesting itself in me. Self-pity.

Beech held me tightly while I sobbed against him, soaking his chest hair and wracked with a sort of pain I had hitherto left unknown. *Why?* I was thinking. *Why me? Why should it be that I spent my whole life the way I am, done the things I have done, tried to keep this world that did not want me safe, and those who did not deserve to live from doing more damage to it and those around them? Why did the universe wait until now to show me that I could be human after all, that from this point forward if I so chose to I could be* good *and understand what that meant in my heart and not just with the mechanical intellectualization of understanding the definition of the words? Why should I be so cursed? For it is true, I am a monster, I am worse than a monster and there is nothing left for me but to be punished; whether by the law or by removing myself and condemning myself to live out the rest of my life in solitude.* I was now aware of a palpable, illogical fear, fear of my future, fear of my past, fear of myself. I sobbed even louder, even harder.

"Sshh, darling, it's okay," Beech cooed in my ear and I found myself actually *appreciating* it. "I'll take care of you, I'll take care of you. Whatever it is that's bothering you, whatever it is that you've done, don't you worry, I'm never going to let anything happen to you."

"You don't know what I've done," I slobbered out through my tears. "If you knew what I've done you wouldn't love me at all."

"It doesn't matter," he said again, gently, squeezing me tighter. "I've always known there was something, I've known that if I looked into it enough I'd figure out what it is, but I never have. Don't you understand? I've loved you since the beginning. You're different, you're amazing and I want you."

I positively blubbered, broken-hearted at the internal laughter mocking the wild hope running through me at the insane and utterly impossible possibility that he might continue to love me if he knew, and that I might be at all equipped to live the sort of life with him I now wanted more than I have ever wanted anything before.

Gable looked up at me from the foot of the bed. *Get out of here! Get out of here now!! What are you, a fucking Harlequin novel?* I could hear his voice, my voice, the voice of God, all the voices in my head. Things were turning around in my mind too fast to follow them anymore. Pushing against Beech, I struggled to get up, away, but he held me closer, tighter, until we were wrestling with each other, me hitting him, hard, him surprised and trying to pin me down, me losing all control and going for his throat, him flipping me onto my stomach and keeping me in place with a knee firmly and painfully planted in my back. We were both panting. I was still snarling at him.

"What the fuck? What the fuck is going on?" Beech was demanding. "You calm down, *right now!*"

"I can't!" I wailed. "I can't! I can't take this!" I was having an all-out breakdown. I couldn't gather myself together while these – *feelings* – were still invading my mind and body. "Just kill me," I begged him, struggling against his grip. "Just put me out of my fucking misery." They were the only coherent words I could string together.

"Hey," Beech said. "Hey, it's okay."

Gable had jumped off the bed during the fight and was now standing at the side of the bed, looking at me, at us, with his big eyes. I stared back at the blurred little beast, as tears still filled my eyes.

He's right, it's okay, Gable said. *You have to calm down or else he is going to tie you up and take you back to the city and commit you. Then all your plans, everything, will be for nothing. It's okay, feelings are hard to bear, but everyone has to do it. Calm down, calm down, calm down…* These words repeated themselves endlessly in my head as I felt myself beginning to calm down. My breathing slowed. The tears stopped. As he felt me relaxing, Beech took his knee out of the small of my back and loosened his grip on my hands. He reverted to sitting cross-legged beside me and stroked my hair. His face, when I finally turned to look at it, was a mixture of love and confusion and worry. We sat like that for a long time.

"I'm sorry," I finally said. I actually meant it. I actually wanted him to forgive me. I was actually ashamed at how I had just acted.

"Everyone has a meltdown from time to time," he said gently. "It's okay."

I laugh. I laugh long and hard. Then I realize I'm exhausted.

26.

So there it is. When I woke up this morning it was though I had never felt a thing before and never would again. The wall that had been torn down by Beech's declaration of love had rebuilt itself overnight. I have no urge to ever see what I had seen on the other side of it. It is time to go. It is time.

I go back to the doorway of the bedroom and look for a few moments at Beech's sleeping body. He is so still it looks like he might be dead. I find I feel nothing. A vague fondness, but nothing else. He will be better off without me.

Going back to the kitchen table I take out this memoir and write these last few words. I will leave it here where he will see it first upon getting up, likely before he even realizes I am gone. I will have at least a few hours head start while he continues to sleep and probably half a day or more before he is finished reading this, maybe even longer. As soon as I stop writing I will gather my things, get Gable and Stella and go out the sliding door. I will walk across the dew-covered field into the sunrise and disappear into the woods on the other side.

ABOUT THE AUTHOR

R.K. Finch is the former editor-in-chief of two popular online magazines and a prolific writer of fiction, non-fiction and poetry. Finch also has fifteen years of professional experience as a designer and manager in the Internet industry, has dabbled in federal politics and currently works and lives near Toronto, Canada.